Wall of Unknowing

By Susan F. Banks

Books by Susan F Banks

Red Souls of the Underworld Series

Red Souls

Wall of Unknowing

Wheel of Augustus

LEGAL

Third Edition 2025

ISBN for Kindle: 978-1-7328524-1-9
ISBN for Paperback: 978-1-7328524-3-3

For more information, email dgfisherpublishing@gmail.com

Banks, Susan F. Wall of Unknowing. DG Fisher Publishing. Kindle Edition, Paperback Edition

Cover Photo: Jeremy Thorpe

Cover Graphics: Clint Kruger, Protea Creations

DEDICATIONS

To Michael and the Usual Suspects

And to the wonderful writing group that helped me with constructive suggestions and honest feedback – Cherie, Anna, Bev, Marcia, Leslie – my great thanks for the help and the fun.

Main Characters

Gem – Guardian of the Gate to the Underworld

Circle of Augustus:

Willet Du Place

Audrey Du Place

Dean Simmons

Thomas Jefferson (TJ) Barlow

Jat the Deceiver – Lord of the Underworld

PROLOGUE

Four young adults living in Los Angeles were recruited into an ancient fighting force known as the Circle of Augustus, by a woman who claimed to be the Guardian of the Gate to the Underworld. The woman, named Gem, told them that Los Angeles was under attack by demon Souls. She needed their help to stop the demons from driving the people of the city to anger, violence and despair. Willet, Audrey, TJ, and Dean did not believe her. When Gem opened their eyes to the realities that exist beyond their senses, they saw the attacks for themselves. Everything in their lives changed.

CHAPTER 1

Audrey Du Place shuffled out the front door of Pine Siskin House in her blue chenille bathrobe and fuzzy blue slippers, her blonde hair twisted in a messy bun on top of her head. She drew a deep breath of early morning California desert air. Her obsessively organized thoughts calmed in the pre-dawn quiet. She held a limp hose over her succulent garden and watered the circular plot surrounded by smooth stones. Water dribbled on the bone-dry earth. She was trying to relax and enjoy the peace, but she could not ignore the aberration that had recently appeared, a massive cloud of static and lightning in the distance. The purple-black cloud looked like a giant ink blot. *What is that thing? How did it get there?* Small at first, the dark cloud had grown, doubling in size every day over the past week. Maybe it was a storm cloud. She thought it would blow away after a while, but the thing persisted and grew until it turned into a dense wall obscuring the Western horizon. She hadn't seen a good sunset in days. It really made her mad.

The cloud first appeared after the Circle of Augustus returned home to Pine Siskin House from a bruising battle in Los Angeles County against Jat the Deceiver, Lord of the Underworld and his Red Souls. The Circle was battle sore and mentally weary after the psychic attacks thrown at them by Jat. Even Gem, their intrepid leader, seemed to need a rest. And then that wall appeared. The timing was suspicious. They all thought they had achieved a measure of success against Jat, but they weren't feeling quite as victorious now. Somehow, they knew the Deceiver was warming up for another attack. The unsettling cloud signaled a new beginning. Jat was coming after the people of L.A. once again.

Audrey worried about her sister. Willet was the Circle's Listener, their early warning system. She heard things before anyone else in the Circle could, sounds from this world and beyond it. If Willet heard voices speaking about an attack, no one doubted her. She was the first to hear the cloud hissing. She said it sounded like butter hitting a hot griddle. As the sound got louder, Willet got a migraine. The Circle couldn't afford to have the Listener down for the count. They'd be deaf.

When things got really dicey, the Circle looked to Gem for guidance, but Gem hadn't given them much explanation of what was going on with the cloud. Audrey suspected the Guardian knew more than she told them. Gem could be aggravating that way. She called the cloud a 'Wall of Unknowing' but in typical fashion, didn't explain any further, leaving her Circle scratching their heads. Audrey wanted to bombard the cloudy aberration with energy rings and make it disappear. She was the Ring Thrower of the Circle. When they needed to mount an offensive, she harnessed the energy of the Circle into hot rings and threw them like hand grenades with force well beyond normal strength. They had achieved great results in L.A. when they were dealing with an underground incursion of Jat's crystal that erupted out of the ground and toppled buildings. The rings spread out over the city and exploded, reducing all the insidious crystal Jat had planted to charcoal.

Audrey had been practicing with the rings on her own to improve her accuracy. Even small rings were very effective if she could throw them hard and fast at a target. Any demon or cursed object they hit burned to a crisp. It wasn't difficult to hit the cloud. The enormous thing would be impossible to miss. She lined up small rings of light on all ten of her fingers, hot and getting hotter. She linked them in combinations of two and three to increase their size and then threw them towards the cloud like Frisbees with sharp flicks of her wrists. The rings flew west across the desert and hit. A shower of sparks flew off the cloud's surface, and the rings disappeared inside it. She followed up with a bigger barrage of large and small rings. The cloud absorbed them all without a burp or a hiccup. Nothing hurt it.

Her frustration grew. Along with everything else, she worried about her computer engineering business. Communications between the desert and greater Los Angeles had become choppy to non-existent. She hadn't been able to reach any of her clients in the city by phone, email or text. After missing multiple appointments and not hearing back from anyone, she suspected the cloud was to blame. She began to wonder if Enterprise Architects, the business she had built so carefully, still had any clients at all, but there was no time to worry about it. Circle business took precedence. Where was Gem when they needed her? The Guardian had gone missing again, off to who knew where or for how long. Audrey felt uneasy when Gem was away. Gem was Chief Explainer of every weird and dangerous thing that had happened in the last eight months. If she did choose to explain something, it was always crucial to dealing with the situation. They certainly had a situation on their hands now.

****

Gem was off doing the work that only a Guardian could do. She was perplexed by the behavior of her Circle. "They grumble like children," Gem confided to Dora, her faithful black Lab who happened to be the Hound of Hell. "This is no time for grumbling. The negative shift of consciousness in Los Angeles has put everyone in danger." Dora turned her baleful golden eyes to the Guardian in quiet reproach. Gem understood the message in those eyes. "Yes, I know, they have concerns in their own lives, personal worries. I must be patient with them."

It had been more than a century and a half since Gem herself had a personal life to worry about. Her parents and her brother died long ago. Everyone she knew as a girl back in Ohio was gone. She had committed herself, willingly and joyfully, to the path of Light and Sound and now protected the people of L.A. from Underworld attacks at the behest of Augustus, the Guardian of all Guardians. That was her choice. She could not impose it on others. "The Circle has grown stronger and acquitted themselves admirably. I will leave them on their own for a while. They need time to heal and regain perspective. You and I will go forth and gather our own intelligence." The Circle needed information about what was going on inside the city now that it was cut off by the Wall. Gem slipped out of the Du Place sister's house in the middle of the night with Dora at her side and called upon the services of her friend and ally, Sonrisa Degas, known as the Traveler, to get them into Los Angeles quickly. Maria Sonrisa Degas de Megaro was a nun in sixteenth century Spain who was buried alive by the King of Spain for talking about visions of the beyond. While interred in a coffin, she learned to leave her physical body at will and became a Master of Space-Time Travel. Sonrisa could get them in and out of L.A. quickly if Jat tried to trap them.

The Traveler appeared on the driveway in front of Pine Siskin House like a glowing apparition stepping out of a fold in space-time. Sonrisa was tall, statuesque, with long brown hair. She was wrapped in a sky blue robe. She beckoned to Gem and Dora to join her. They all stepped back into another space-time fold. The fold closed around them and opened again just as quickly, letting them out at Griffith Park, the huge park near downtown Los Angeles. They stood on the observation deck behind Griffith Observatory, home to a giant telescope trained on the stars. Below them, the wide swath of L.A. lay under a leaden night sky. Los Angeles was usually lit up at night and bubbling with life, but a pall lay over the city. The night life was gone. To the east, the towering Wall of Unknowing separated L.A from the desert. To the west, another Wall of static was gathering like a storm. At full size, the walls would cut the city off to the east and west. Everyone who lived between the Walls would slowly suffocate, their spirit drained. It would leave them easy targets for Jat. The Deceiver would drag them down into the despair of the Underworld with the rest of his wretched minions.

A sliver of a crescent moon shed feeble light on a winged creature flying in slow circles in the sky. Its enormous span of wings, pointed head, and long limbs suggested a prehistoric predator waiting and watching for prey with sharp claws and daggers for teeth. It was Jat the Deceiver. In the distance, the Pacific Ocean churned as the Wall of static grew over it. "Jat waits for the city to fall on its knees before him," Sonrisa murmured. "When the Western Wall rises over the ocean, there will be no escape."

"It is happening faster than I expected," Gem replied. She stroked Dora's smooth black head. The big dog snuffled happily but did not take her golden eyes off the Deceiver's flying form. The Hound, the Traveler and the Guardian were surrounded by a nimbus of light that attracted the attention of the raptor. The circling raptor shrieked and dove straight at them with long claws sprung. Dora leaped at the beast, aiming for a limb with a giant chomp of her teeth and narrowly missed it as the raptor reared back and dodged away.

Jat's leathery wings flapped sharply and his long throat rippled and exploded in an ululating scream. "I will eat this world!" Steam poured from the raptor's mouth. The malice in that scream made every living Soul that could hear it cringe. The raptor descended again, more cautiously this time, and peered into the light around the travelers. "Why are you here, Guardian?" Jat's peevish voice emerged from the mouth of the raptor. "A little late to save this pathetic place, is it not? And you, Traveler, why do you waste your time here when there are so many more interesting places to go in space and time?"

Sonrisa turned her back on him.

The raptor's lips peeled back to flash sharp fangs. Thick slime dripped from the corners of its mouth, and its jaws snapped. "I will not be ignored, woman," the raptor said in a low growl.

"As usual, you underestimate the living," Gem said. "They will move toward light if given a choice. That is why we are here. Your time is running out."

A smug chuckle came from the raptor. "I have all the time in the world. The weak will be mine for eons, and the strong will eventually succumb."

Gem blew a long, cold breath over the basin below, chilling the air like a winter wind. Her breath spread out over the city until it rustled with sudden energy under the cool refreshment. She blew a stronger breath to disperse the heavy gray atmosphere. The wind lifted a few people off the ground and carried them away to the east. They disappeared into the dense static of the Wall, and hopefully, through it.

"Do you really think you can defeat me again with your *Freezing Breath*?" the Deceiver sneered. "I hoped you would have found some new tricks by now, to make the game more interesting."

"I defeat you every time we meet, Deceiver," Gem said. "Why should I change anything?"

"You can blow a few misbegotten souls beyond my Wall, but there is no certainty they will survive the journey."

"If they find their way to the Circle, there is hope for them."

The raptor salivated. "Oh, yes, I look forward to having your little Circle inside my Walls. I will reduce them to wailing skeletons and watch them fall broken in the wasteland if I don't die of boredom first. Metaphorically speaking, of course."

"Your threats are pointless," Gem said. "The Circle will come, and you will be driven back to the place from which you came."

"You make bold claims, Guardian. We shall see."

The raptor circled up and then dove at them head-first with its claws extended. The Traveler opened a fold in space-time. Gem stepped in and pulled Dora close. They all disappeared, leaving Jat trying to grasp a shimmer of light.

****

The static from the Wall hissed louder, and Willet's migraine grew to major status. What was loud to Willet might be undetectable to others, but even faint noise could give her a debilitating headache. All she could do was lay on the living room couch like a rag doll, take prescription meds and rest until it went away. Pine Siskin House had been built to protect against desert heat. The sisters upgraded it to ensure that the interior would have the hushed silence of a church. Thick-walled stucco construction, triple-paned windows and heavy wooden doors kept the place cool. Custom soundproofing installed by Dean Simmons, acoustics engineer and a Circle Warrior, kept it quiet. Sounds from the outside were not heard, but the static hiss of the cloud vibrated beyond physical wavelengths. It made Willet's delicate ear drums vibrate until they burned and washed out other sounds, so much so that she struggled to hear what people were saying right next to her. That was totally unheard of. She was called 'the Listener' for a reason. She heard everything.

Pain throbbed in her left temple. The headache meds were so strong she felt sluggish. She had a cool compress over her eyes, noise-cancelling headphones on her ears, and icepacks pressed to her neck and temples. Audrey brought her frosty fruit drinks in tall glasses. TJ sat by her side, rubbed her feet and tucked blankets over her legs. His handsome face showed his worry and distress. His sandy blonde hair and green eyes always reminded Willet of the ocean where they took their first beach walk. She remembered that day as one of the happiest of her life. Willet didn't want to worry him or the people she loved, but all she could do was stay quiet and motionless until the headache went away.

The Circle waited like children for Gem to get back and explain what they were supposed to do about the big cloud. *Pathetic*, Willet thought again. They should be able to figure *something* out for themselves, but when she tried to concentrate, her head hurt. How had they gotten involved in all this Circle business? Before Gem, Willet and Audrey had both longed for a different life. Audrey wanted a love relationship without constant worry about her invalid sister. Willet wanted to be free from the limitations of her impossibly acute hearing. She had wasted so much time hiding from the outside world, thinking there was nothing she could do with herself beyond existing. After meeting Gem, her world expanded and then blew up in her face. Now it was all about the Circle and protecting L.A. from the Deceiver. Would there ever again be a chance for normalcy? She wasn't sure she knew what normal life was anymore.

****

Outside in the front yard, Audrey threw ring after ring at the static-spitting cloud and watched for reactions. Nothing. She threw several at once and hoped she could perturb it into revealing clues about itself. The cloud turned a bilious green at the spot where the rings hit and ejected a shape that flew into the air and landed on the ground a few yards from her feet. It was one of those shadow forms with a human skeleton inside, flickering like an x-ray, the third such shadow to hit the yard in as many days. Usually, the skeletons just stood up and took off running across the desert. This one wasn't moving.

She spun a ring of light on her finger and held it above her head to get a better look. The form flinched at the light, but rolled onto its knees and crawled toward her, keeping its skull low to the ground. She let her breath out sang a long 'HUUUU' as the skeleton came nearer. The ring cast a wide aurora of gold light. The skeleton dragged itself to the light and poked at it with a bony finger. The fingertip flashed where it touched the light. The skeleton crawled all the way into its golden circle. An aura of pink flushed over the form, leaving a man on the ground, barely breathing. The dark-haired man was sprawled face down. She touched his wrist and felt his pulse. He was alive, but barely. “Dean, need a hand here!” Audrey called out. “We have another refugee.”

****

Inside the house, Dean heard Audrey calling his name. He pictured her long blonde hair framing her face, her inquisitive blue eyes and impish smile that suggested intriguing possibilities The honey-lemon scent of her filled Pine Siskin House. *When will we get our chance to just focus on each other?* He had fallen for her the first time she came into his shop to ask him about acoustic upgrades their house. Her sunlit beauty and sharp intelligence grabbed his attention and didn’t let go. He would go forth and do battle to protect the damsel from anything that threatened her. He hustled out the front door and found Audrey kneeling next to the supine body of a man. “How did he get here?” he asked, bending over the man.

“Like the others,” Audrey said and flipped her mane of hair behind her shoulder. She looked the man over. “He flew out of the cloud and landed on the ground. He was a skeleton. He was attracted to my ring light and wanted to touch it, so I obliged him. Red smoke poured out of his mouth. Then he passed out.”

“So, Red Souls are still in the city. Great. What do we do with him?”

“Let’s bring him inside before the red smoke returns. When he comes to, we can ask questions. If he came from the other side of the wall, maybe he can tell us what’s going on over there.”

“Some intel would be helpful,” Dean said, “before we wander into the thing like blind idiots.”

They hoisted the man to his feet and folded his arms over their shoulders, dragged him through the front door, and laid him down on the Persian rug in the entry hall. Audrey gingerly removed his shoes. "Phew, he stinks!" she said, covering her nose and mouth.

"That's probably the least of his problems. He's still breathing, right?" Dean asked and held his finger up to the man's nose.

Audrey knelt beside him again. "Sir," she said, patting his cheeks. "Can you hear me? Wake up."

The man's eyelids fluttered. He mumbled something under his breath.

Audrey leaned in closer to hear him and then drew back, holding her nose again. "His clothes are disgusting, and his breath is rank. When he comes to, we should ask him to shower. I'll get him a glass of water."

She hurried away to the kitchen, and Dean tried speaking to the man again. "Sir, please wake up. I can't understand what you're saying."

By the time Audrey returned with the water glass, the man was flailing on the floor and ranting in a hoarse voice in Spanish. "Estrella! Estrella! No!" he said. "Mi amor!"

Dean slid his arms under the man's back, lifting him to a sitting position. Audrey held his head lightly by the hair and put the water glass to his lips. The man started sipping, slowly at first, and then in large gulps. When he emptied the glass, his eyes opened. He stared wide-eyed at Audrey.

"Estrella. Donde está Estrella?"

"Who is Estrella?" Audrey asked. "She isn't here."

"Estrella, mi esposa, my wife, I must find her." The man paused, and his body began to shake again. "No, it's too late."

"What happened to your wife?" Audrey asked.

Tears pooled in the man's eyes and rolled down his cheeks. His chin dropped to his chest, and he began to sob. "She jumped from the roof of our house. Her neck was broken como una muñeca, like a doll's. It must be a dream, please, God, it must be a dream."

"Where is your house, sir?" Dean asked.

The man swallowed with difficulty. "Jurupa Valley."

Audrey ran to the kitchen and returned with another glass of water. He gulped it down. "What is your name?" Audrey asked.

"Ignacio. I am Ignacio Silvas."

"I'm Audrey, and this is Dean. We can help you, but we need to know how you got here and what happened to you."

"I was working my field, turning soil for my tomatoes, pulling weeds. I hear my wife scream, and I run to the house. Estrella, she was afraid. She climbed on the roof and jumped off. I think she is dead."

"What was your wife afraid of?" Dean asked.

"She say voices scream at her, but I hear nothing."

"Jurupa Valley is a long way from here, Ignacio. How did you get here?"

"No sé. I tried to go to my wife, but my legs no move. The wind lifted me, threw me far. I hit a wall of fire, and my skin burned. The pain muy malo. I fell to the ground and prayed to die."

"Ignacio," Audrey said. "You don't have any burns on your skin or your clothes. Maybe it was a dream."

Ignacio looked down at himself and shook his head as if to clear the fog. "Maybe the angel light healed me."

"Angel light?" Audrey asked cautiously. "When did you see that?"

"So beautiful, que maravilla, I crawl to it. The burning stopped. It felt cool, like heaven. I wanted to drown."

Audrey was glad he didn't remember the specifics of her ring light. There would be less to explain. She sniffed, and the pungent odors of Ignacio's person assaulted her nose. "You are welcome to take a shower here," she suggested gently. "I mean no disrespect. I know you were doing hard work in your field. You can wash clothes too if you like. That will help you relax, and then we can talk about what we can do for you. Okay?"

Ignacio stared blankly ahead, but in a low voice he said, "Si."

Audrey and Dean locked eyes. What would Gem have to say about this? And where in the world *was* Gem anyway?

****

Thomas Jefferson (TJ) Barlow sat at Willet's side, watching her labored breaths. His heart ached every time she moaned. She had once described her headaches to him, the spikes of pain in her skull, the dizziness and the pressure behind her eyes. He'd do anything to take the pain away, take it upon himself if he could. He tucked a strand of her spun-gold hair behind her ear and looked at her pale face, so pinched with pain. She seemed fragile, like a child, though she was twenty-four, only four years younger than himself. He had witnessed her strength in the face of many challenges. She never ceased to amaze him with her ability to rise above everything.

He used to think he had a handle on what was real in the world. That was before getting roped into the Circle of Augustus. After the last few months of running after phantoms, he had seen too much unexplainable weirdness to be sure of anything. His cabin in Big Bear was thrown off its foundation by a giant slab of crystal that inexplicably erupted from the ground underneath it. He and Willet had been asleep inside at the time. Pieces of weird crystal had landed on the roof of his music club in West Hollywood and sparked a fire. The club burned down completely. He had to leave his Mercedes on the road to Mount Wilson when they went searching for Gem in the mountains. Someone probably stole it by this time. Despite the good they tried to do, the cost of involvement in the ancient fighting force was high. He had lost a lot of property. Bad time to be a real estate investor in L.A., which he was. So many buildings had tipped over in the city. He had no idea if any of his rental properties still stood. He and his partner, Matt Gregg, might have to rebuild their small empire from scratch. If not for Willet, Audrey, and his best friend, Dean, being in the Circle with him, TJ would already have headed off to check on his house in the Hollywood Hills. Did he still have a place to call home? Now they had that big ugly cloud to deal with. Even he, the least convinced member of the Circle, could feel its menace. Gem would tell them to destroy it, but she wouldn't tell them how, exactly. They'd have to figure something out. That's how the Circle worked.

Willet stirred, her eyes opened, and she tried to sit up, but couldn't. She held her head between hands. "It's screaming," she whispered. "Make it stop."

"Who's screaming, sweetheart?" TJ said gently, helping to ease her back onto the pillows and helped her to take some sips of water.

She licked her lips. "He, he's screaming, and laughing. He's waiting for us, Thomas."

"Who?"

"Jat. It's a trap."

TJ didn't want to stress her with too much conversation, but he needed to know. The Circle needed to know. "Is it the cloud? Is that the trap?"

"He won't let us out. We'll die in there." Her voice was weak, piteous.

He knelt beside her and wrapped his arms around her. "We won't let that happen, babe. Trust me. We'll protect each other."

She shuddered. A teardrop rolled down her cheek.

****

Dean poked at the burning wood in the big stone fireplace in the living room, walked to the windows and looked out, and then back to the fireplace to poke some more. He couldn't stop fidgeting, and the others noticed. He told them he was watching for those skeletons trying to attack the house, but really, his energy was so amped, he could barely sit still. He just felt anxious, ready to jump out of his skin. After the battle in L.A., lights sparkled in the corners of his eyes and shapes moved just beyond his vision. When he turned his head to look at them, nothing was there. A rhythmic current ran through him that connected his heartbeat to every other sound around him, and his hands wanted to drum on any hard, flat surface. He was a drummer as well as an engineer. Maybe it was all the HU chanting the Circle had been doing. If only he could go home, climb behind his drums, and pound them until he dripped sweat. That would settle him down.

There was also a tune playing constantly in his head, a long flowing melody, sometimes sung, sometimes played on violins. There was no beginning or end to it. As a musician, he would usually welcome such an inflow of inspired music. He'd be at his piano, trying to capture the notes on the keys and record them into his computer. Now, he was suspicious of anything out of the ordinary that might suggest he was possessed by demons. He had experienced Red Souls invading his mind. They played with his thoughts and dreams as if he was a puppet and drove him to the point of considering suicide. He never, ever wanted to go through that again. He pictured his home in Manhattan Beach, the recording studio he had designed himself, and longed for them like lost loved ones. He missed his band, Shock Value. They had gigs lined up, but with a Wall to deal with, those would not be happening. He thought about his mother, and it drove him crazy. Was she safe? Was his younger brother with her? The not knowing ate at him. He wanted to check on them, but the Circle was getting ready to fight its way through that mutant cloud on the horizon. He couldn't abandon Audrey, Willet and TJ. Not now. There was a city to protect. Everything else would have to wait.

CHAPTER 2

Two sharp knocks at the front door of Pine Siskin House echoed through the hall. Audrey jumped up from the desk in the office, ran to the door and swept it open. Outside, the desert sun was high and blazing. Gem stood on the porch wearing her usual white peasant blouse and knee-length skirt in a reddish purple print. Macramé butterflies were swinging from her ear lobes. Her warm brown skin and blonde-streaked brown curls shimmered gold, and her brown eyes glowed. Dora sat attentively at her side.

"Thank God! Where have you been?" Audrey demanded. "We thought maybe something bad happened." She peered closely at Gem. "Are you wearing makeup? You're all sparkly."

Willet sat up from the couch and craned her neck, wincing slightly. "You've got that radioactive look again. Did you visit Augustus?"

"Nothing so pleasant as a trip to the High World, no," Gem said as Audrey waved Guardian and Hound into the entryway. "We have been to the other side of the Wall to assess conditions in the city. It stands on a precipice. Jat nudges it and waits for it to fall." Ignacio, who was sitting on the floor in the living room, caught Gem's eye. "Who is this?" she asked.

Dora trotted over and sniffed him thoroughly. A shower and clean shirt and pants had taken care of his body odor. To his credit, Ignacio didn't flinch from Dora or try to evade inspection. When the big dog was satisfied, she padded back to Gem.

"This is Ignacio Silvas," Audrey said. "He flew through the Wall like someone had kicked a football. He dropped near the house and crawled into my ring light. Then he passed out, so we brought him inside. He says his wife jumped off the roof of their house and killed herself."

Ignacio stood up to the side of the couch, his hair still wet from the shower. He shuffled from foot to foot without looking up.

Gem studied him. "I am sorry for your loss," she said gently. "Suicide is a great tragedy."

Ignacio met her eyes. "I was lifted from my house by a great wind. It brought me here," he said. "I wish to return and bury my wife's body. It is the last thing I can do for her."

"It is not safe on the other side of the Wall, Ignacio," Gem told him. "Your wife would not want you to risk yourself or your sanity."

The little man stood straighter and gave Gem an unflinching look. "I must go, Senora. I will not be able to rest in my own grave if I do not."

Gem nodded. "It is your choice, of course. As it happens, this group will make a trip through the Wall very soon. You can accompany us, but it will be a dangerous journey."

TJ and Dean frowned at each other when they heard Gem's words. "What is the danger, exactly?" TJ asked.

"The Wall of Unknowing is a barrier of psychic and physical static raised by Jat to isolate the people of Los Angeles from the rest of the world. The Deceiver does not want the Listener to hear what is happening in the city. Movement through the barrier will be difficult."

"What *is* happening on the other side of the Wall?" Dean asked.

"People forget the lessons they have learned – skills, relationships, how to care for themselves and each other. Threads of memory that bind people to each other and the outside world are breaking down. When those connections finally fail, the consciousness of the people will drop to the level of the Underworld. The city will become part of that world, and no one will remember Los Angeles ever existed."

"That can't happen," Dean protested. "People have relatives and friends outside the city. They'll realize an entire city is gone!"

"I am sorry to tell you they will not."

"Are *we* supposed to do something about it?" Audrey asked. "The Circle, I mean. What is the Circle supposed to do?"

"The Deceiver will create a stronghold in the city if he has not already done so. It will be the seat of his physical power. From there, he will try to drag the hearts and minds of the people down into darkness. It will be difficult to dislodge him while his stronghold exists. We must find his powerbase and destroy it before the city succumbs completely to the Unknowing and falls into the Underworld."

"My mother and brother live in Manhattan Beach," Dean said. "My grandparents live in Pasadena. What will happen to them?"

"You saw the Underworld. It is a desolate place and difficult to escape. Souls there forget everything unless they fight for the light. Most cannot until someone lifts them up."

"I don't believe it. My mother wouldn't forget me."

"Unfortunately, she *will* forget you, and you will forget her, unless something is done to prevent it."

"What will happen to us if we go through the Wall?" Audrey asked. "Will we forget who *we* are?"

"Unless we are vigilant and focused, we will begin to 'unknow' in the same way as everyone else," Gem replied. "It is more than loss of memories. It is a loss of understanding."

Gem turned her attention back to Ignacio. "We will not survive the negativity inside the city unless we keep the Light in our consciousness. You will need that protection too, Ignacio. You are welcome to chant with us if you wish when we sing 'HU'."

He dipped his head in a short bow. "I will do as you suggest, of course, Senora."

Gem settled on the couch and took a deep breath. "Then, let us begin."

****

Willet roused herself from the couch and began her chant. Her body relaxed. Thoughts drifted through her mind like leaves on the surface of a river. She had learned from Gem to let them go and focus attention lightly on the inner screen between her eyebrows. Gem sometimes said provocative things and didn't always bother to explain them. Willet hoped the Guardian had exaggerated the dangers they were going to face on the other side of the Wall, but something twisted painfully inside her. The dread of going back into LA after the battle they fought with the Deceiver churned her stomach. Memories of destruction and chaos – the ground crumbling beneath their feet, fires out of control and clouds of Red Souls chasing screaming people through the streets – had haunted her dreams ever since. Would there ever be an end to them?

She took a deep breath and let those concerns go for the moment. From somewhere deep in the recesses of her consciousness, a voice said, "Embrace adversity". It wasn't the answer she wanted. "Why do I have to embrace adversity?" she thought. "How much more adversity do I have to embrace before I'm done with it?"

****

Ignacio quietly watched the chanting Circle and didn't know what to think. *Dios Mio! What do these people do?* Everyone was sitting around the square coffee table. The girl on the couch dragged herself up and sat propped against a large pillow. Even the big black dog that sniffed him sat at attention. Lights were low, a small candle burned on the fireplace mantel. He sat in a deep stuffed chair trying to be unobtrusive, but no one seemed to remember he was there.

The Senora breathed slowly and made a long exhale that sounded like '*HUUUUUUU'*. The others did likewise, repeating the word over and over. Their soft voices hung in the air. The room vibrated. He could feel it in his bones, and it felt – nice. He decided to try the song himself, feeling foolish at first, but then he just let his breath do the singing. '*HUUU, HUUU'*. He closed his eyes, relaxed, and sang. A swirl of lights splayed across the dark inner screen between his eyes. Then a dream began like a movie in his head. He was standing on the porch in front of his house, looking out over his front yard. A sparkling light covered the lawn, so bright it made his eyes blink. He walked out to see what it was, knelt and put a hand into the light. His arm tingled up to the shoulder. Out of the corner of his eye, he saw his wife and turned toward her, but he began to recede from the scene. He held out his arms to reach for Estrella, hold on to her. He wanted so much to speak to her, but he fell backward through a long tunnel and ended up back on his chair. When he tried to chant and recapture the dream, it evaded him.

He took a peek out of one eye to see what everyone else was doing. They sat with eyes closed, hands in lap, absorbed by something inside themselves. Their lips moved silently. He wondered if they were dreaming too. After twenty minutes, everyone opened their eyes and shifted in their seats. *Now what?*

****

"I heard bells, like a wind chime," Dean said.

Gem shook herself from reverie. "Hmmm," she said. "Third Plane."

"I heard ocean waves," Audrey said.

"Second plane, of course."

"I heard bees," Willet said. "Why would I hear bees?"

"It is the sound of the fourth plane. A rare experience. You are fortunate."

"What does that mean? I didn't hear anything," TJ said.

"The inner worlds are vast," she said." Each level has its own vibrational sound. It helps us to recognize where we are when we are there. Ignacio, do you have questions?"

Ignacio squirmed a bit at the sudden attention. "Senora, I heard HU, as if it came from out of my heart. It brought visions. I never heard anything like it before."

Gem's eyelids lowered, and she took a deep breath, seeming to draw on inner resources. "HU is the most ancient of sounds. The fabric of creation is woven with it. Human beings have heard and sung HU from earliest times and used it as a word for 'God'." She waited for further questions, but everyone just stared. She rose to her feet. "We must go now. Keep the light within you, no matter what you see. Remember the sound of 'HU' no matter what happens."

The journey into unforeseeable circumstances required serviceable clothing and sturdy boots with rubber soles. No one knew what they might have to walk through. Fabrics were cotton blend, colors were neutral grays and greens, nothing to attract attention, loose fit for fast movement, arms, legs and torso fully covered. The static of the Wall looked nasty. It might scratch the skin or burn it. Who knew? Willet and Audrey pulled their long blond hair up and out of the way into tails. Dean strapped on a waist bag with first aid supplies.

TJ stuffed a small flashlight into his pocket. "Shouldn't we bring protection, like a gun or something?" he asked.

"The forces we fight cannot be stopped by guns," Gem said. "Only innocents would be harmed by them."

OK then. Willet grabbed her headphones, and Audrey fetched the car keys. Ready to roll.

CHAPTER 3

They all piled into the sisters' sedan parked in the driveway. It was a cozy fit even in such a roomy car. Gem took the passenger seat with Dora tucked under her feet on the floorboard. Ignacio sat in the back seat next to Willet and TJ. Dean drove, and Audrey perched between him and Gem. It could have been mistaken for a happy family outing if it were not for their ominous destination. The Wall was farther away than it appeared from Pine Siskin House. The drive took an hour. Judging from Willet's panicked breathing and her desperate attempts to press the headphones harder to her ears, the static hiss had increased to uncomfortable levels. The sedan lurched forward at over ninety miles per hour. Everyone held their breath.

"Dean, slow down, you're going too fast," Audrey exclaimed, clutching her shoulder belt.

"My foot isn't even on the gas!" Dean said pounding his foot on the brake as the car picked up speed. "It's like a magnet pulling on us. I can't stop it."

"We will hit the Wall with force," Gem said calmly. "Secure your seat belts."

The sedan was almost flying, tires barely touching the ground. The scenery outside blurred and the Wall loomed large ahead. When they hit, the sedan vaulted off the ground into an atmosphere thick as Jell-O and were sucked in. The sedan spun and somersaulted like a slow-motion bowling ball. Sparks flew off the grille and across the hood. One of the back doors swung open and banged back and forth. Someone would fall out if the door wasn't closed. TJ leaned over and reached for it. At that moment, the sedan was hit by a blast of energy and rocked awkwardly. TJ tipped forward and fell head first out the door, disappearing into the cloud.

Willet screamed. “No, No! Stop the car! Thomas fell out!”

Ignacio whispered a Spanish prayer. Dora raised her head and howled. The rest of the Circle shouted and argued about what to do next. The sedan made slow circles in the air and turned into a barrel roll before popping out the other side of the Wall. It righted itself before hitting the ground and bounced on its tires, rattling the windows. The sedan shuddered and rolled to a stop. They landed in the middle of a small town that looked like so many others in southern California. Strip malls lined the street, built of stucco and red tile with dusty windows and faded signage. The atmosphere of the place was dull, with meager light and no visible sun. People walked by without a glance at the sedan. If they noticed it falling from the sky and landing with a bang on the street, they gave no indication.

Ignacio threw his door open and bolted out. Ten feet away, he dropped to his hands and knees and vomited off the curb. Dean found a nearby trash can and leaned over it. Audrey stood and swayed with hands pressed to her temples, groaning softly. Willet sat on the ground near her, head hanging between her knees, and heaved deep breaths. Gem waited, composed and patient, while her Circle relieved their spinning heads and lurching stomachs. Despite physical discomforts, their bodies glowed with golden pink light and stood out like beacons in the drab atmosphere.

Dean straightened and wiped his mouth with the back of his hand. “We gotta go back and find TJ.”

A fight broke out across the street. Two men stood in front of a drug store and snarled insults at each other. An angry curse rang out, and a shoe flew out the doorway of the store, hitting one of the fighters in the head. Incensed, the fighter bashed the other man's face with both fists. A rising tide of anger swept up and down the street. Everyone within earshot joined in a loud rant, and the fight kicked into high gear. A crowd of people gathered, yelling and shoving. Red smoke swirled through the crowd, and the fight turned nasty. One guy kicked the other guy in the mouth as he lay on the ground. Blood spattered the sidewalk. Full-scale battle was incited.

Gem walked into the middle of the street, surveyed the length of it in both directions, and then leaned forward, releasing a long exhale. Cold, heavy fog poured from her mouth, blanketing everything and everyone in the street under dense mist and muffled silence. Then she stepped back onto the sidewalk and surveyed her handiwork. "When the fog clears, they will go about their business and wonder how they received their injuries."

"So, you can stop fights," Audrey said. "You can fix what's wrong with this place and we can go home."

"I cannot do it all with a freezing breath. It will take a more profound solution to cure what ails this city. That is why we are here together."

Willet jiggled with impatience. Her eyes darted in every direction. "Didn't you hear Dean? We need to go back *now*. Thomas fell out of the car!."

"The Wall is a difficult place to search," Gem observed. "Do you still hear the static?"

"Of course, I hear it! It's deafening. I also hear every vehicle for miles, every voice, people arguing and crying. One of them might be Thomas. He's probably hurt!"

"Mr. Barlow could have floated if he visualized properly."

Willet looked ready to explode. "You know he doesn't think that way. We have to find him. He might be seriously injured!"

Something scuffled nearby. Dora growled low, dropped to a crouch, ready to spring. Skeletal x-ray forms emerged from the fog and edged closer. "These Souls are attracted to our light," said Gem. "Throw a ring please, Ring Thrower. Let them see more of it."

Audrey spun a ring on the index finger of each hand and threw them above her head. The rings hung in the air, spreading a wide halo of light. The skeletons fell back with arms wrapped over their heads, murmuring words that were difficult to hear.

"What are they saying, Listener?" asked Gem.

Willet sniffled, wiped her eyes and listened. "They're saying, 'It hurts."

"Ah," Gem said. She took a deep breath, holding the air in her mouth and lungs for a long moment, and then exhaled an icy wind at the skeletons. They flickered and sagged to their knees, heads drooping and arms limp. Gem coated them with ice until they looked like ice sculptures.

The ice melted quickly, leaving dull pink bodies wrinkled as newborns. People of different ages, a man and two women, a couple of teenagers, one child, slowly rose to their feet. Ignacio trembled, mumbling prayers into his clasped hands.

"Can you hear me, people?" Gem called to them in a loud voice. The people looked at her with dull stares and mouths hanging open.

"Help each other. Remember this Light. Otherwise, the darkness will overcome you again. Do you understand?

Some of them nodded.

"Can we leave them as they are?" Audrey asked. "They don't look very strong."

"There are many who need our help," Gem said. "We have done what we can for these Souls." She turned to Ignacio and put a hand on his shoulder.

The little man breathed faster. Blood drained from his face, and he wobbled on his feet. "You are a bruja, senora." His voice quivered. "How do you make this magic?"

"It is not magic, Ignacio," she said quietly. "It is the power of Spirit that sheds both Light and Sound. That is all."

"El Espiritu. Si," he whispered.

"If you come with us, you will learn the ways of the Circle."

Ignacio looked like he was going to faint but gave a solemn nod. Gem walked to the sedan without looking back to see who was following. Ignacio was the only one who followed her.

Willet dug in her heels. "We have to find Thomas!" she shouted. "You said the Wall is dangerous!"

"We have to go back," Dean agreed. "If he's in there, he might get lost."

"He won't know where to find us," Audrey added.

"He will find us," Gem said firmly.

Willet would not be reassured. She sat down on the ground, hugged her knees and rocked, refusing to move.

Gem gave her a stern stare. "What is this childishness?"

"He fell from high in the air! He could have broken bones," Willet protested. "You don't seem to care he's missing!"

"Members of the Circle are always in my heart. And there are no accidents with Spirit, baby girl. Surely you know that by now."

"That's not what I meant, and you know it," Willet said through gritted teeth. "He might be too injured to walk out of the Wall."

"What I see at this moment are shadows gathering around us," Gem said quietly. "We are in perilous territory. Audrey, rings please. Throw them up."

Audrey spun rings on both hands and let them fly. Shadows sliding rapidly along the ground spread like black veils, approaching from every direction. The rings fell on the gathering shadows. They retreated, melting back into walls and side streets. "What are those things?" she asked.

"They are creations of the Deceiver. They do his bidding. Avoid them. To the car now before they return," Gem said. Everyone backed up and ran to the sedan, climbed in and slammed doors shut behind them. Dean started the engine.

“Wait, where’s my sister?” Audrey said. “We can’t leave without her!”

“Where’d she go?” Dean said, looking in all directions. “I can’t believe she bolted.”

Audrey bounced up and down in the back seat and shook Dean’s shoulders. “Drive around the block, she can’t have gone far!”

Dean drove down the side street as far as he could go, up to the main street, and then doubled back. He followed each intersecting street. Peering left and right, everyone looked for a head of blonde hair running away. At the far end of the small downtown, he turned the car around again. “Maybe she’s hiding,” he said.

“She cannot hide from the Deceiver’s shadows,” Gem said. “They will find her before we do.”

Dean took the car around again. This time, everyone looked for black shadows sweeping over the ground. No shadows and no Willet.

“I don’t understand,” Audrey lamented. “How could she have disappeared so fast?”

“Maybe she took a ride with someone,” Gem said.

“Willet would never get in a car with someone she doesn’t know,” Audrey said. “That’s crazy. And she wouldn’t steal one. I don’t think.”

“We know where she *wants* to go,” Dean said. “She’s desperate to find TJ, so she’ll go back to the Wall. If we want to find either one of them, we’ll have to follow her.”

Gem sighed. “Very well, we should stop her before she enters the Wall and loses her way. The Deceiver would be delighted to have the Listener trapped in that morass.”

****

When TJ reached for the handle when the sedan door opened, the door swung beyond his reach. He made a grab for it and lost his balance. He rolled, flailed and cursed his own stupidity all the way down through the Wall of Unknowing. The thick atmosphere seemed to cushion his fall otherwise he’d drop like a rock. Instead, he tumbled, almost in slow motion, and then fell on his butt with a soft thud. He closed his eyes, lying flat on the ground to assess injuries and regain his wits. *Arms and legs are moving. Tailbone feels bruised.* When he opened his eyes, he couldn’t make out where he was or what anything was around him. Narrow bands of fuzzy light streaked left and right like bad reception on an old black and white TV. Visually, everything looked fractured. The hairs stood up on his arms. He rolled to his feet and took a minute to balance. Unsure how close anything was, he held out his arms, walked unsteadily toward one shape and laid hands on it. It felt hard and rough - stucco. He stamped his feet - standing on pavement. *If I can’t see, how can I get out of here?*

“Hello! Hello!” he called out, turning in a circle. “Is anybody there?” It was like shouting in an empty room. He was inside the Wall Gem warned them about, and he was alone. Could it get any worse? Well, he could think of a few ways…

Where were Dean and the rest of the Circle? He got angry with himself. *Should have followed my instincts and gone home.* Now he was lost, and who did he have to thank? It always came back to

Gem. *Damn that woman*. He wished she were here right now. After she rescued him, he'd tell her off in no uncertain terms. He squinted and tried to find something identifiable nearby. The blur gave him eye strain when he tried to see through it. He thought of Willet with a twinge of pain. She'd be distraught, and insist they look for him. Could they find him in all this fuzz? The Wall they saw from the house had covered the western border of Riverside County. That was a big area to search.

He shuffled forward with both arms extended in front of him, trying not to bump into anything. After several steps, he felt the edge of a curb beneath his left foot just before his ankle collapsed. He fell, landing hard on his right elbow and hip. *Great. That hurts.* He felt for the curb behind him and sat back on it rubbing his bruised elbow and flexing his leg to make sure other bones weren't broken. He was usually so sure-footed. Not here.

He closed his eyes again and lay back on the pavement, oblivious to the filth that probably coated it. He had to do something, but what? The incessant static grated on his nerves. He remembered what Gem had said about the despair that takes over a person in a place like this. *Fight it, Tom. Fight it.*

He thought of Willet again. It helped to think of her, so he held her image on the screen of his inner vision. She smiled at him and puckered her lips in a kiss. He could almost feel the softness of her lips on his. She began to sing. He couldn't hear her at first, but then he could. She was chanting the word Gem had taught them. Her voice chimed. He repeated the words with her over and over until his breath slowed and his jangled thoughts calmed. Whatever would be would be. *Wasn't there a song like that?* The knot in his stomach eased. It felt good to let it go. He lay there for a while, drifting and dreaming, not feeling the need to do anything. There were stories in the news about people lost in some wilderness with no ability to navigate, how they got more and more lost until they gave up and died. He could relate. He might die here. It seemed like an actual possibility the more he thought about it.

A warm hand suddenly touched his knee. Startled, he gulped and sat up.

****

The Circle drove back to the Wall and followed it north and south, as far as the next town and then back again. No sign of Willet or TJ. Dean slowed the car and parked across the street from the churning, sizzling mass. It dared them to approach.

Dean sat back in the driver's seat and stared straight ahead. "What are we doing?"

"Our mission is to find Jat's seat of power. This must be done, no matter what else we do." Gem switched on the radio and let it scan for broadcasts. There was nothing but dead air. Then a voice rasped from the speakers, rough as sandpaper.

"This may be the end times. Now more than ever, our future and our families' future are at stake. The damned will fall, and witches will burn in hell. Be vigilant, my friends, and wait for my signal. We will act against those that try to subvert us."

"Ah," said Gem. "There he is, still babbling. He pushes the city closer to the Underworld. Does nothing faze him?"

"Theese," Dean said through his teeth. "That colossal ass is still alive?"

“I thought we left him for dead in the mountains,” Audrey said. “What’s wrong with his voice? He sounds like a snake.”

“A stray bullet hit him in the throat, from his own gun, I suspect,” Gem replied. “He blames me.”

“He shot you!” Audrey exclaimed. “Killed you, and he kidnapped Will.”

“Facts do not enter into his thinking.”

“His compound at Mount Wilson was trashed by the crystal,” Dean said. “How is he still broadcasting?”

“I suspect he has help. I must find out who is helping him. So, I will leave you for now. Ignacio, come with me.” Gem got out of the sedan and motioned to Dora to follow.

Dean and Audrey jumped out and hurried after her. “You’re leaving?” Audrey exclaimed. “You can’t just walk away! We’re here because of you!”

“I will reunite Ignacio with his wife, and then I must deal with Mr. Theese.”

“What about Will and TJ? How do we get them out?”

“It is now your task to find them and extract them from the static,” Gem said, pointing to Dean and Audrey in turn. “I will continue the search for Jat’s stronghold.”

“What about the car?” Dean asked. “Don’t you need it?”

"The car is yours. Do what you can, what you must, to reunite our Circle. I advise you not to take the car into the Wall, however."

"What about my mother and brother?" Dean demanded. "Are you going to save them? You promised you would."

Gem was already walking away. "I am Guardian of the Gate, not your fairy godmother," she said over her shoulder. "I have many souls to assist, many tasks to perform. You must trust me." She walked on with Dora and Ignacio beside her.

"We've trusted you quite a bit so far," Audrey said, a hint of acid leaking into her voice. "Why are we even here? When do we get an explanation?"

Gem halted and turned on them with cold blue light pulsing in the depths of her eyes. She had never looked at them like that before. Dean and Audrey took a step back from that icy stare. The radiant blue light focused on Dean. He shuffled his feet but didn't look away. "If we do not address the real problem before us," Gem said with quiet steel, "no one in Los Angeles will be saved."

Dean's shoulders remained stiff, but a note of pleading entered his voice. "My mom lives in Manhattan Beach. That's right on the ocean. I'll do whatever you want about the Wall, but I need to make sure she's okay. That's important too, isn't it?"

"A second Wall of Unknowing is rising at the shore of the Pacific Ocean," Gem said. "The Walls will spread inward until they meet over Los Angeles and become one solid mass. Confusion and Unknowing will take over the city, within days if not hours. *We* can prevent that if we destroy the Deceiver's stronghold. If not, the city will be lost in the Walls of Unknowing. Is this a clear enough explanation?"

“But you promised…”

“When I finish my tasks and you have finished yours, we will look for your mother.”

Dean took a deep breath. “Okay,” he said, not happy about it.

“Trust me, as I trust you,” she said, and then looked at each one of them in turn. “Are we ready to proceed?” Everyone nodded mutely, even Dora. “Sonny, a doorway, if you please,” Gem called out to the Traveler in a loud voice.

Light shimmered in front of Gem, and the air popped as a door into space-time opened courtesy of the Traveler. Gem took Ignacio’s hand and stepped forward with Dora into the doorway. They disappeared in a moment, leaving the air clear and unruffled.

Dean and Audrey stared into the empty space left behind and then looked at each other. “She actually left us. I can’t believe it,” Dean said, shaking his head. “Now what?”

“We go in there,” Audrey said, pointing at the Wall. “After that, no clue.”

Dean pulled out his phone and checked it. The phone smelled burnt, its electronics fried, probably by their trip through the static. “Yep, we’re on our own now.”

CHAPTER 4

Willet ran down one dingy side street and then another in the small town, changing course erratically while looking over her shoulder for the sedan. She emerged onto the main street where Gem's blanket of cold fog still lay thick. Two blocks farther down, a cab was parked at the corner. *Great!* She ran toward the cab. *Please, please don't be off duty.* In the driver's seat of the cab, a black-haired man in a red and blue plaid shirt sat with eyes closed, chewing placidly on a wooden toothpick. His swarthy skin looked oily. Pock marks dappled his lower cheeks. She didn't see any off-duty signs, so she walked to the driver-side window and gave it two light raps with her knuckle. Dark eyes snapped open with a glare.

She cleared her throat. "Excuse me, sir" she said in a low voice. "Are you taking fares?"

The window rolled down a crack. A strong odor of fried onions wafted through the opening, sending her back a step. The man's lips peeled back from irregular stained teeth clamped around the toothpick. "Where do you want to go?" He spoke with an accent, vaguely Middle Eastern.

"I'm going that way." She pointed in the direction of the Wall.

He gave her a cool appraisal. "That is the way of the lost," he said, chewing his toothpick. "Why go there?"

"I'm meeting someone."

"Oh?" He looked her up and down. "What do you offer?"

"I've got money," she said defensively. "Isn't that customary?"

He rolled the window down another inch and laughed in her face. "It will cost you more than money, lady."

"I don't know what that means, but I need to go there now." Willet peered back over her shoulder, expecting to see the sedan careening around a corner. "I'm in a hurry."

"So is everyone," he said and nodded toward the back seat. "Get in. It's your funeral."

****

A thin woman and a young boy stared down at TJ on the ground, close enough for him to see them despite the shredded lights. The woman wore a loose blue house dress and flip-flops. Wispy red curls floated around her head. The child, a boy of nine or ten, had a round belly peeking out from beneath his gray tee shirt. He wore faded jeans and scuffed sneakers and scratched his curly brown hair.

"Who are you?" TJ huffed, climbing to his feet. "Where'd you come from?"

"We saw your light," the boy replied. "So, we came to see what it was."

"What light?" TJ asked. He looked down at himself and saw what they meant. A halo of pink-gold light surrounded his body. It streamed from his hands and face and glowed in his chest. When he raised his hands above his head, they illuminated the street. What had looked like impenetrable distortion before became clear. *Why didn't I see this before?* He looked back at the woman and boy. "What are your names?" he asked.

The woman looked down at the boy and squinted. "I call him Diggie."

"And what about you, ma'am?"

The woman hesitated. A furrow creased the skin between her eyes. "What about me?"

"What's your name?"

Looking uncomfortable, "It's … uh…" She seemed unable to answer the question.

"Do you know the way out of this Wall?" TJ asked.

She looked around and twisted the skirt of her thin dress into a knot between her hands. "What wall?"

"The one we're standing in. The reason why everything looks so bent."

"I don't know what you mean."

"How long have you been here?"

The woman’s eyes pinched tighter together, and then she shrugged. “Where else would I be?”

He had to get out of the Wall before the place started to affect his mind the same way it had affected this woman. He had to find the Circle, but what to do about these two? “Well,” he said, “I have to get going now. There are people I need to find…”

The woman had no reaction, but the boy’s head perked up. “Take us with you,” he said.

“I gotta travel fast, kid.”

The boy stepped up to TJ and looked at him with big brown eyes. The top of his head barely reached TJ’s waist. “Please, mister. Things are attacking us, trying to do stuff to us.”

TJ’s eyes narrowed. “What things?”

“Red smoke flies around and tries to go up my nose.”

“Yeah,” TJ had to admit. “I know about that.”

“And the Bone Dabs try to stab us.”

“What are ‘Bone Dabs’?”

The boy gave a nervous glance left and right. “Bone Dabs is what I call ‘em. They have long needles for fingers like, and they try to poke ‘em into ya. If they sink ‘em into your bones, it hurts like hell. Then they pull ya under the ground. I saw it happen to a guy. He screamed a lot before he disappeared. It was bad." The boy's lower lip trembled at the gruesome memory.

"That's a new one," TJ said. "How did you two last this long?"

"We look for light."

"Where do you find light around here?" he said, looking around at the shadowed streets.

"You have a lot of it. That's how we found you. Other people had it too, but they lose it after a while. If you leave, we'll be in the dark."

The woman stood in the middle of the street, staring vacantly. He wracked his brain for a solution that didn't entail dragging her and Diggie along with him. Then he thought of Gem's chant.

"I can tell you a secret word that will keep your lights on. How about that?"

Diggie looked skeptical. "What secret word?"

"Here it is: *Huuuuu. Huuuuu.* You sing it just like that. Can you do it?"

The boy repeated the syllables in a low voice and looked at TJ expectantly. Light flared briefly from his eyes and out of his thin chest.

"See, that's easy, right? Do it again."

The boy tried to form the word but stopped. "What was that word again?"

TJ repeated the chant. Diggie sang the words, and then promptly forgot them. After several futile iterations, TJ gave up. The Wall had affected the boy's short-term memory almost as much the woman. He would not remember anything after TJ left him, so the decision was made.

"Let's see if we can find our way out of this static. After that, you're on your own. Okay?"

Diggie nodded. He looked back at the woman who was standing as if frozen. "We're leaving, Mom," he said.

"This is your mother?" TJ wondered who was taking care of whom.

"Yeah," Diggie said. "She's different now. I don't want to forget the way she was."

TJ sighed. "No, you wouldn't want to forget that. So, let's get moving."

"Where to?" Diggie asked hopefully.

"Out of the Wall, like I said. Do you have any idea which way is west?" TJ asked. "Which way to the ocean from here?"

Diggie scratched at his scalp and then pointed up a dark street. He didn't seem too sure, but TJ had nothing else to go on.

"Okay, follow me, and do what I tell you to do."

Diggie took his mother by the hand. TJ walked off in long strides, and they hurried after him, staying within the halo of his light. The light spread just wide enough to keep them from bumping into walls or falling off curbs. TJ looked for any kind of sign that might help him get his bearings. The farther they walked, the more things looked the same, the same maze of streets wherever they went. Everything beyond their light looked fuzzy. Arrowed bands of black and white static shot out and bent at sharp angles. Sometimes the arrows looked like the corners of buildings, so he tried to avoid them. Other times, he walked right through them. The loss of perspective made him unsure of his footing.

They walked for almost half an hour, and nothing looked any different. They might be going in circles. What was worse, his light was beginning to fade, and Diggie noticed. "Hey Dude," he asked nervously, "what's happenin' to your light? Are you runnin' out a juice?"

"My juice is fine," TJ retorted, but he wasn't sure. He struggled to remember the chant word, and started to sing it to himself, hoping he had it right. He felt better, but his thoughts drifted. A woman with blonde hair and blue eyes kept appearing in his third eye. He knew who it was and tried to say her name. *W-w-w-w… Willet, of course it's Willet, how could I forget that?* He returned to the chant and struggled again to recall it. That was bad. He needed backup.

"Diggie, sing these syllables with me. Get your mother to do it too. Take turns. Don't stop. We can't forget, so keep repeating them. One of us has to be saying them at all times. If we forget, we'll lose the rest of the light." *Huuuuu. Huuuuu*. He repeated the sounds to Diggie who repeated it slowly to his mother until she could say it with him. They mumbled at first, but their voices firmed. The circle of light around them brightened and spread.

TJ strained to see farther down the side streets as they walked. He couldn't tell if they had passed these streets before. When he looked back at his two followers, he was surprised to see four people walking in his wake. He stopped short. "What's going on?" he asked an elderly couple huddling in the light behind Diggie. "Where are you going?"

"Please," the white-haired man's voice shook. "We saw your light. My wife and I are lost. Can you help us? The shadows are attacking us, and my wife is terrified. The fear alone will give her a heart attack."

"Bone dabs," Diggie nodded. "Told ya."

It was pointless to argue. TJ couldn't turn away people who looked like his grandparents. "I'm trying to find the way out of this Wall and head west. As long as that's okay with you, fine. Just stay close." With that, TJ walked on, singing 'HU' out loud. He glanced back periodically to see if the group kept up. Every time he looked over his shoulder, he had gained another follower or two. A man carried a little black and white dog under his arms. A woman grasped two small girls by the hands. A teenager with face piercings and ripped-out jeans brought up the rear, his eyes darting nervously toward the shadows. It was getting crowded back there.

"Diggie," TJ commanded, "make sure everyone is singing the word. We won't have enough light to cover everyone if they don't say them with us."

Diggie eagerly took up his role as TJ's second lieutenant and repeated the words to everyone. As new voices joined the chant, the circle of light grew wider and attracted even more people. Before long, there were over thirty people trailing behind him in a large cone of illumination.

TJ came to another corner, stopped the parade, and looked back at the group. "Does anyone know which way to the ocean?" he called out. There were mumbles, finger pointing in conflicting directions, and a shuffling of feet. TJ prepared to press on, but the surrounding static rippled. Shadows swirled and slithered over the halo of light. The group pressed together to stay well within the halo. They sang 'HU' with renewed vigor.

Hooded heads appeared in the shadows. Needle-like fingers slid out from elongated limbs. The dark forms stabbed at the edges of the light. Cries of terror erupted from the group, but they kept singing. The needles didn't touch them. The hooded figures hissed and chattered, then slid back.

TJ thought of the blonde girl again and tried to picture her before he forgot her entirely. "Let's move, people," he yelled over his shoulder. "And keep singing our word."

The group lumbered along after him, chanting 'HU', low and steady. Their voices gained strength the farther they walked. The dark shadows slipped away and melted back into the static. TJ looked left and right down each side street. After another block, he looked left again. A car drove by in the distance, followed by another. He felt a surge of hope. Traffic. A woman stood on the side street with her back to him. Her curly hair, long skirt and white peasant blouse looked familiar. It was Gem.

That irritating, impossible woman - he was overjoyed to see her. He led the group quickly down the side street until he stood a few feet away. "Gem, it's me," he called to her. "It's TJ."

The woman slowly turned and smiled broadly. "There you are. I've been waiting for you."

"Where's the rest of the Circle?"

"They couldn't be here," she smiled.

"Why not?"

"They went their own way."

"Oh. Where's your dog?"

"My dog?" Gem's eyes narrowed.

"You're going to get us out of here, right?"

"Of course," she said. "I'll take you to another place."

TJ felt a tug of discomfort in his solar plexus. "What place?"

"A better place for you and all your friends." She kept smiling that big smile.

TJ took a step back. He had never seen Gem smile that way, at least not at him. "Well, I promised these people I'd lead them out of the Wall, so I'd like to do that, and then we can talk about where you and I are going, okay?"

Gem's eyes narrowed. "That wasn't the plan. You don't trust me?"

TJ thought about it, and then a realization hit him. "You're speaking in contractions. You never use contractions when you talk."

Her eyes flushed blood red. "Don't question me," she snarled. Black arrows shot out of her pupils and flew through the air. The arrows hit him in the chest. His vision blurred, and his knees buckled. His chest burned as if he had been hit by poisoned darts. "You're not Gem," he rasped. He could hear her laughing. The circle of light receded from him, leaving him unprotected on the ground. Dark shadows slid down from surrounding buildings and slithered across the ground, extending long needled fingers toward him. The needles clicked together like eager locusts. The first needles pierced his neck and then his legs, driving deep into muscle and bone. Hot pain burst from his mouth in a roar of agony.

****

Gem and the Traveler stepped out of space-time into a rural area of the Jurupa Valley with Dora at Gem's side. Between them, they held Ignacio up by his armpits. His knees kept buckling.

"Thank you, Sonny," Gem said. "I must make a few stops after this one, if you would be so kind as to assist."

"Of course, Guardian," Sonrisa replied. "I am at your service." She pulled up on Ignacio's arm. "What about this man? Will he accompany you?"

"That is his choice. Ignacio, we will release you now. Can you stand?"

Ignacio cautiously planted his feet. His ankles wobbled. He tested the firmness of the earth and satisfied himself that he was indeed on solid ground. "Si, Senora, forgive me. One minute I am on a street, and now I am at my home. It is impossible, yet true. The speed of it makes my head loco as if I am drunk."

"You are not drunk. This is Sonrisa," Gem said. "She is a Master space-time Traveler. Now that we are without a car, she will help us to move about. It takes some getting used to, I know, but it is quick. Let us see to your wife."

They stood in front of a small, gray clapboard house on a large lot with two separate sheds, a car port shading a dusty pickup truck, and a woman's body lying in the front yard. Dora gave a low growl, but Gem held her back.

"Estrella!" Ignacio cried. He ran into the yard to the body.

Estrella Silvas was indeed dead. Her neck was twisted at an unnatural angle, and her eyes were rolled up in her head. Ignacio fell to his knees and cradled her in his arms, tears falling in fat drops onto her hair. "No, no, no," he murmured through his tears.

Gem cleared her throat. "Forgive me for intruding, Ignacio, but your wife is still here in Soul form, and she is in much distress."

The transparent form of a small woman with long salt-and-pepper hair and wild hazel eyes stood near the body, brandishing a carving knife in one hand and a steak knife in the other. Her astral skeleton flickered in and out of focus. Ignacio could not see her until Gem put a hand on his shoulder and pointed him toward the woman. Then Ignacio could see her too. He cried out at the apparition and jumped to his feet.

"Estrella, que es esto, mi amor? What are you doing with the knives?"

Estrella leaned forward from the waist and a torrent of red smoke gushed out of her nose and mouth, Red Souls shattering and cackling in it.

"Nacio, help me," she gasped. "I'm burning!"

The whites of her eyes were bloodshot, and her skin was gray as death. Ignacio tried to approach her, but she slashed at him with her knives. "No, husband, stay away," she said in a whisper. "I am not safe. I am cursed."

"Estrella," he replied gently, "por favor, put down the knives. Let me help you."

Estrella flipped the knives toward herself and stabbed them into her own throat. The blades passed right through her neck and out the back "The fire eats me inside. I am evil, Nacio, like the voices said."

"No, querida, why do you say this? You are not evil. You are good!"

"The voices tell me that I am nothing. Over and over, they say it. I jumped from our roof to silence them, and still they haunt me. Now I am damned. I have sinned against God."

Ignacio looked at Gem with desperate eyes. "Senora, I know you can help her. She is a good woman. You can turn these torments to ice as you did for the others. Please. Please ease her sorrow, I beg you."

Gem eyed the hysterical woman who was now repeatedly plunging both knives into her stomach. The fact that they had no effect didn't stop her. Estrella was standing on the edge of an emotional cliff. She would fall into the desolation of the Underworld if she did not step back. Gem blew a soft breath through pursed lips, turning the air to ice crystals. She swirled it on her finger and blew the swirl toward Estrella. The flurry of ice dusted the frantic woman's hair and eyelashes and covered her shoulders. Estrella howled like a wounded animal. Red smoke poured out of every orifice and steamed off her skin. The red of her eyes cooled, and her skin turned pale.

"Estrella, hear me," Gem said. "You are not damned. Soul is never damned. The voices lie."

Estrella's howls died away, and her wild eyes focused on Gem. She looked at the knives in her hands in confusion and let them roll off her fingers. They disappeared as they left her hands. Tears glistened in her eyes. "What have I done?" she asked softly. "I have forsaken a great love."

"That love never forsakes you," Gem said. "It is always yours." She melted the snow with a spattering of rain.

Estrella closed her eyes and turned her face to the cool drops. Then she looked at Ignacio. "Nacio, what can I do?" she whispered. "I cannot go back to…that." She pointed at her body lying on the ground with its broken neck.

"No, mi amor," he said sadly, "our life together is over for now." Ignacio cast a worried glance at Gem. "Who will guide her?"

Gem gave him a small nod. "Soul knows the way."

As she spoke, Estrella's ephemeral body turned pale pink and transparent until she was nothing but a watercolor shimmer in the air. Her light receded into the distance and winked out.

Ignacio watched the light until it disappeared and heaved a heavy sigh. "Where did she go?"

"Far from this gray world," Gem said. "The destination is decided between herself and Spirit. What will *you* do now?"

He rubbed tears from his cheeks with the backs of his hands and sniffled. “I must bury my wife and tend to our home. This is our place.”

“As you wish, Ignacio,” Gem said softly. “Remember the word I taught you. Sing it with an open heart. It will be a boon in times of trouble. Never lose hope.”

A doorway folded opened. Gem, Sonrisa and Dora stepped backwards through the opening. The door slapped shut, leaving Ignacio to wonder if it had all been a dream.

CHAPTER 5

TJ screamed until he had no scream left. The needles of the Bone Dabs burned like live wires in his muscles and bones. Every inch of his skin stung. He writhed on the ground in agony, the pain so intense that his Soul body peeled away from his ravaged physical form and stood apart, watching his own misery.

"The human shell, such a tedious vessel," the woman cooed behind him. "Time to leave it behind." The voice certainly sounded like Gem, but the appearance was glaringly different. Her nose was melting off her face.

"You're one of those wax figures," TJ said. "You're nothing but dinosaur puke." In the Underworld, the Circle had watched the Deceiver spit a sort of wax from his mouth that morphed into animated bodies. Each body resembled a person they knew, and each one melted back to a puddle of wax right in front of them.

"Surprise," fake Gem replied brightly. "Fooled you twice."

"What do you want anyway?"

"I want you to move on. No time to waste now. Run along."

"Run along where? Where am I supposed to go?"

His ravaged physical body shuddered on the ground. The people who had been following him huddled in what was left of the light, singing *Huuuuu* for all they were worth. Light covered them like a blanket. Diggie broke from the group and ran to TJ's body, wrapped his arms around TJ's shoulders and sang directly into his ear. The Bone Dabs retracted their needles and scattered to a safe distance.

"Wake up, Mr. Tom, we can't stay here," he whispered frantically. "You told me to remember the words, right? I remember them," he said. "Listen." Diggie repeated *Huuuuu. Huuuuu* over and over, his lips next to TJ's ear. Please don't leave us. We need you."

The Gem imposter laughed. Her fingers decomposed, dripping wax into puddles at her feet. "These people are lost. They belong to the Needle Men now. Your place is in the next world."

"I know how this works. If I abandon my physical body, I die" TJ said. "I'm not ready die. I have things to do."

"Do you really want to go back into *that* body?" she said, nodding at his writhing physical form. "Must I remind you of the pain?"

TJ didn't want to go back, but something tugged at his belly button and pulled him back into the physical form. As soon as his eyes opened, the burn of the needles flared and ripped another roar of pain from deep in his chest. Bone Dabs slid back around him and jammed their needles deeper, chittering with excitement.

"See," fake Gem cajoled. "These people are nothing to you but baggage. Wouldn't it be easier to leave them all behind? Tell me your answer."

Diggie rested his forehead on TJ's chest and kept whispering the sound of the chant. TJ mumbled the word with him, and a halo of pale gold light spread over them. He slid an aching arm around Diggie's shoulders. "I'm not leaving this kid, so fuck you. That's my answer."

"Foolish man."

The needles bit deeper into his muscles. He could hardly breathe. All the followers ran to TJ and Diggie and circled them, lifting their voices in the 'HU' song until he was able to take a deep breath. Light flared around the group, and the shadows flittered away. For a brief, blessed respite, he was free of the pain.

****

The short cab ride ended across the street from the Wall. Willet thrust a fist full of cash at the cabbie and jumped out of the cab, not waiting for change. She darted toward the Wall with little thought as to what she would do when she reached it. She just knew she was going in. With a few strong steps, she plunged into the mass of static. The hiss and crackle stung her eardrums, and she couldn't make out a single thing inside. Stopping short, she closed her eyes and took a few deep breaths. *Okay, it's loud here. You knew it would be, so just relax, get control of your ears and focus.* Steadying her breath, she closed her eyes and analyzed the noise. Distinct voices and snippets of conversation wove through the hiss like silver threads through a tapestry. She habituated to the background noise, tuned it out and listened, concentrating on one voice after another until her temples ached. None of them sounded like TJ. *Maybe I should just yell out his name, see if he hears me.* She opened her eyes and brought her hands up in front of her face. They came into focus about six inches from her eyes. Light filled the space between hands and face. It emanated from her own body. She stretched her hands out and took the few steps forward she could clearly see in front of her. She thought of Gem and chanted HU, which centered her quickly. The light around her flared like a cape, giving her a wider circumference of light. Then she heard a familiar woman's voice followed by a roar of pain. *TJ.* Orienting toward it, she picked up her pace and walked as fast as she could go. TJ was groaning. *What is happening to him?* She tried to run and immediately tripped, got up and tripped again. Tears of frustration blurred the little visibility she had. *How can I find him like this?*

Slowing down, she felt her way along with arms outstretched, chanting under her breath until she heard the soft sound in her left ear that always answered her chant. A cool certainty filled her. She moved steadily, carefully stepping on and off the curbs. The agonized moans turned into desperate cries that broke her heart. *Please, please, stop hurting him, whoever you are.* The cries came from the left. She picked up speed in that direction, almost trotting, closer and closer to the cries. At a cross street, a woman stood next to a group of people huddled in a pool of light. The woman looked like Gem. Did she come to help him after all? Willet ran toward the group and came to a skidding stop. She broke through to where TJ lay on the ground and fell to her knees, throwing herself on top of him.

He groaned in pain and opened his eyes, looked at her in horror and pushed her off. "Another wax figure," he spat at her. You're not Willet. Stay the hell away from me." The young boy helped TJ sit up and lent an arm to keep him from falling backwards. TJ looked toward the woman who looked like Gem. "Do you think I'll fall for this again?" he said with derision. "How long will it be before the arms fall off the Willet doll?"

Willet didn't understand it, but something was wrong. "Thomas," she said, "I'm not a doll! It's me, Willet. I came to find you, to help you!"

The other people gathered around TJ and the boy. A warm light enveloped them. TJ gave Willet a grim smile. "As you see, I already have help. The *real* Willet is with the *real* Gem, where she's safe."

Willet felt foolish now. She had chased after him without thinking. Gem, Audrey and Dean had searched for her, and she ran away from them. *Now he doesn't even want me here.* "Who are all these people?"

"These are my flock," he said with a wave of his hand. "They protect me, and I protect them."

His tone was biting. Willet couldn't help but bite back. "So, you're a pastor now? I guess I missed the ordination."

"If Gem can call herself a Guardian, I can lead a flock. This is all her fault. I wouldn't be here except for her."

There was no point alienating him any further. "Thomas, please, we can leave here together and find Gem. This place is evil. We need to protect each other."

"There's no 'we', wax girl. Me and mine will do fine. And don't call me 'Thomas'. Only Willet gets to call me that."

That jab stung her deeply. She wanted to shake him. "*I'm* Willet, you idiot! I'm not wax! I'm here to help you!"

Members of the group helped lift TJ to his feet. His ankles collapsed, so they supported him with their arms and shoulders and half-carried, half-dragged him to the street within the cone of light that surrounded them. The group turned the corner and disappeared. The woman who looked like Gem did nothing to stop them. She was melting into pieces.

Willet felt drained. She struggled to understand what just happened. *He left me in the Wall by myself.* A crushing weight settled on her shoulders. She sat back on her heels and tried to think. Despair clouded her mind, but she brushed the fog away. *I will walk out of this Wall on my own two feet. I don't need anyone's help.* The resolve gave her a boost of energy. She got up and stumbled toward the cross street, but her steps flagged slower and slower like she was pushing through a mountain of mud. Finally, all forward momentum ceased. She fell to her knees and pulled herself forward along the pavement on elbows and hands, inch by inch, willing herself to crawl to the end of the street. *I will get out of this Wall.*

The Gem-woman spoke behind her. "Where do you think you're going? This is not like you trying to get away from your Guardian. Come back this instant."

It sounded like Gem's voice, but Gem would never speak to her that way. Willet kept clawing her way toward the street. Dark shadows swept over her. A needle plunged into her calf, then another two into her back, and then too many to count, piercing her muscles, her scalp, and the skin on the back of her neck. Every point burned. She tried to move faster, inching forward despite excruciating pain in her body. A brighter light beyond the Wall beckoned. She had to get there and almost reached the cross street when a heavy foot stomped hard on her back, pinning her to the ground and driving needles deeper into her spine.

"I said, stop," the fake Gem said in a vicious voice. "Do not defy me, or the Needle Men will teach you better behavior."

The foot wedged under her stomach and flipped her onto her back. Willet blinked up and stifled a gasp. The familiar voice came out of a stark white face with no features other than two gouged eye sockets. Lank brown hair hung limp from the top of a misshapen head. The body was more liquid than solid. "Don't recognize your guardian, girlie?" the voice cackled. "I'll take care of you. Isn't that what you want? A mother?" The shape was melting down to an amorphous lump.

Fear and desperation flushed through her. "You're just a wax dummy," Willet whispered. "Just like Thomas said." Shadow forms swarmed over her as she lay on the ground. Eyes in the shadows peered into her face. Needles plunged into her eyes. She howled like a dying animal and lost her sense of self. A soul-deep weariness over-powered her. Any strength or resistance she still had drained away.

Gem's voice laughed out of the pile of wax. "You won't need eyes anymore. There's nothing to see where you're going." The voice became indistinguishable from static.

Willet's eyelids went into spasms. She pried them open, but all she saw was darkness. *I failed the Circle and ran away. Now I'm blind. I deserve this.* The excited chatter of Red Souls surrounded her head, and Gem's voice whispered in her ear. "The Underworld awaits you, Lissstener. There will be a celebration." There would be no peace for her in that place.

****

Dean and Audrey stood across the street from the Wall of Unknowing, considering their next move. The Wall shimmered like a mirage in front of them, daring them to enter.

Audrey swallowed hard. "Gem didn't say what to do once we get in there," she said, "Other than 'don't take the car'."

"A few pointers would have helped." Dean shrugged. "Are you ready to see what's inside?"

"Willet and TJ will owe us big time for this."

Shoulder to shoulder, they crossed the street and walked up to the Wall. Audrey put her hand against it and felt for a reaction. Dean did the same.

"It feels funny," Audrey said, scratching her palm. "Like fizzy water."

"Yeah, it tingles," replied Dean. "Now it's starting to burn." He yanked his hand out.

"Wait, if you leave it there, the burn goes away." Audrey extended her arm farther into the static. "See? You just have to adjust to it."

"Okay, we plunge in, like it's an ice-cold pool." He reached for her hand. "Are you ready for this?"

"Not really. We could troll around out here, waiting for them to pop out on the street."

"That may never happen. We might be too late already."

"Yeah, we have to go in."

In agreement, they faced the Wall and marched forward. The Wall made a slurping sound as it swallowed them. The rushing hiss of static hit them. Low, grumbling voices murmured in the static, and lights flashed from every direction.

Audrey twirled rings on her fingers and tossed them above her head, lighting up their surroundings. Dean gave her a 'woot' of encouragement. They could see each other now. They stood on a city street lined with buildings. No people walked or stood nearby. The street was shadowed, neither dark nor light, but it was *not* empty of life. Pairs of eyes glowed in dark corners of the static distortion. The eyes stared fixedly at them without blinking. Ring light illuminated their skeletal forms.

“Skeletons, great,” Dean said. “Now what do we do?”

“The lights will keep them back.” Audrey multiplied the rings and scattered them in a wider circle. The skeletons cringed and drew back into the darkness.

“Let’s walk, see if they follow.” Dean started walking up the street. Audrey walked behind him, guarding his back with more rings. The skeletons kept their distance, but they definitely followed.

“As long as they don’t touch us, I say we do what we came here to do,” Dean said. “We just keep moving until we find Willet and TJ.”

“Aye, captain,” Audrey said. “I’ll just keep protecting our asses.”

Dean gave her a curious stare. “You sound annoyed.”

“You’re bossy sometimes. It’s a pain.”

“And you’re touchy. That gets annoying too.”

They eyeballed each other and then noticed the skeletons drawing closer.

“They’re attracted to conflict,” Dean said softly. “Gem’s not here to freeze them, so let’s just chill and keep moving until we find TJ and Willet?”

"Sure," Audrey replied archly. "I can chill. Watch me." She turned and walked away.

Dean hurried after her. "What are you doing? We need to stay together. What is your problem?"

Agonized cries in the distance brought them up short.

"That's Will, I know it!" Audrey exclaimed.

They hurried down one colorless street after another, past darkened shops and offices that looked abandoned. They couldn't locate the source of the screams. Bands of visual distortion forked and angled at their heads. Static sizzled. Even with the light of the rings, they tripped more than once. It was difficult to judge distance or depth.

Dean pulled at her arm. "Slow down, will you? Are we working together or not?"

She pulled her arm back. "Don't grab me."

"I wasn't grabbing you. I just think we should talk about what we're doing."

"*I'm* going to find my sister. What are you doing?"

"I'm going with you if you'll slow down a minute. If that's really her screaming, she's in terrible trouble. We have to be prepared."

"I'm prepared."

"Neither one of us is prepared. We don't know what's in here. What could be causing her to scream like that?"

"You're such a wimp."

He stepped back and glared at her. "You're insulting me now? You dragged me into this drama in the first place."

"Sure. Blame me. It's so much easier for you that way." She stopped, shook her head, and took a deep breath. "This place is really messing with my head. I have to find Will before I lose my mind. Are you going to help me or not?"

"That's why I'm here, for god's sake. What direction are the screams coming from? Can you tell?"

Audrey closed her eyes. "I'm not sure about direction," she said in a dull voice "The moving lines make me dizzy."

"Well, keep those rings lit and let's move. The skeletons aren't going away."

Another scream cut through the static. Audrey stared at her hands and didn't move.

"Come on, Auddie, let's go!" Dean said and took her hand to pull her along with him. The air squelched and popped around them, and they found themselves standing outside the Wall on the street where they started.

****

Willet felt like a single point of view bobbing on the surface of a black sea, disconnected from all sensation. A jumble of thoughts in her head pushed her back into physical consciousness, and she became aware of fire-hot needles piercing every muscle. She moaned and stared into darkness. *Oh yes. I'm blind.* Then strong arms lifted her under the armpits and half-dragged her over pavement. "Who are you?" It didn't feel like TJ or smell like him. *Am I being dragged into the Underworld?* She prepared to struggle, but whoever it was, carried her out of the Wall of Unknowing. She felt the change as soon as she left the static, like a tight film peeled away from her nose and mouth. She gulped deep lungs full of air, and oxygen surged through her blood. *I'm free. It feels like heaven.*

She was stuffed unceremoniously into a car. A door slammed shut beside her. "What do you want?" she called out. The driver door opened and closed. "Where are you taking me?" The motor turned over and the vehicle began to move slowly at first, then picking up speed. Willet found a shoulder strap to hold on to as the vehicle accelerated into a series of sharp turns. The movement threw her side to side, pressing the needles deeper into her muscles. She groaned. "Slow down. It hurts!" There was no response from the driver.

CHAPTER 6

"What the hell happened?" Dean said. He and Audrey stood on the street facing the Wall. He spun around and ran at the huge mass of static, trying to jump back in. The Wall of Unknowing bounced him off like a rubber ball. He tried again and again with the same result, and then he tried kicking it. Frustration boiled in his blood. "This thing spit us out! What do we do now?"

Audrey blinked at him, her blue eyes limpid and lost. Her arms hung, lifeless, at her sides. "Do? What is there to do?"

"Audrey, listen to me. We have to have a plan. TJ and Willet are still in there."

Audrey stared. Her lips tried to form words, but she couldn't seem to say them.

Dean took her hands in his. "What's going on? We need to help Willet, remember?" he prompted her. "We need to find your sister."

Audrey nodded slowly. "Willet, yes, my sister," she said.

He gave her an encouraging nod. "Yes, and TJ, our friend. We need to find TJ too."

She frowned and searched his face for answers. She had no words.

“Oh no, no, babe, this can’t be happening.” He squeezed her hands. “Do you remember me? What’s my name?”

She opened her mouth and looked hopeful, like his name was on the tip of her tongue.

“I’m Dean, remember? Dean.”

She smiled and nodded happily. “Dean, yes. I remember. Where are we?”

The excursion into the Wall had taken a toll on Audrey. He couldn’t believe how quickly it happened. They were only in there for a few minutes. When the Wall expelled them, it kept pieces of Audrey for itself.

Car tires squealed several blocks from where they stood. A taxi stopped at the curb and the back door swung wide open. The driver ran into the Wall and then carried a woman’s limp body out of it in his arms, shoved her into the back seat of the cab and slammed the door shut. Dean was sure the woman was Willet. He broke into a run and shouted. “Hey! Stop!” Was she being kidnapped? If the man heard the shout, he did not acknowledge it. The cab pulled away from the curb with another squeal of tires. By the time Dean reached the spot, the cab had disappeared. He looked back at Audrey still standing where he’d left her. He sprinted back. “Willet’s gone,” he said. “Not sure what to do now. TJ’s probably still in there.”

Audrey gave him a blank look. “TJ,” she repeated.

Exasperation leaked into Dean’s voice. “Yeah, remember TJ, our *friend*? He fell into the Wall.”

Audrey's shoulders sagged. "I don't know…" she mumbled, looking at her feet.

He felt sorry for sounding so gruff. She was clearly struggling. He put an arm around her bowed shoulders and hugged her. "It's ok, babe. Not your fault. It's just this place and that mass of static across the street messing with our heads. If we get some distance from it, the effects will go away. I hope." Audrey couldn't afford to lose any more memory. Who knew how or when her memory would return. He couldn't leave her alone or risk taking her back into the Wall either. He put his arm around her waist and guided her gently back to the sedan. "We need answers," he said. "We'll try to follow the cab, but what we really need to do is find Gem."

****

Willet felt every jolt whenever the cab jumped a sidewalk, and it did that a lot. She tried to adjust her posture to minimize the pain, but the needles were jabbing and burning in her legs and butt. When the cab finally settled into a straightaway, she leaned her head back. No one had spoken to her from the driver's seat. The weathered leather under her hands smelled faintly of orange oil, and a whiff of cinnamon wafted from the front seat. It might have been almost pleasant, except for all the noise. Her awareness of the pain came and went. Just when she almost forgot about it, some jarring of the car would bring it back to full, stinging consciousness. She tried not to move, tried not to breathe, but the respites of comfort were brief. The roar and whine of road traffic thrashed her eardrums. Electric currents buzzed in the air and voices shouted, screamed and cried. Her temples pounded so hard her eyes watered. *I wish I had my headphones.* A volley of gun fire cracked in the distance, followed by another. The sound sent a sharp pain shooting through her head from the left temple to the right.

"Where are we?" she gulped, her stomach lurching. She pressed fingers into her forehead to relieve the pressure. "I hear guns."

“People shoot each other rather than speak,” a matter-of-fact male voice answered. “This is the city we live in.”

The voice was familiar. Willet detected the Middle Eastern accent. “You’re the cab driver who drove me to the Wall.”

“It is true.”

“Why are you helping me?”

“I saw a woman in pain in an alley, crawling on her belly,” he said. “What else was I to do?”

She pictured herself clawing her way across the pavement and blushed hot with embarrassment. “You could have left me, I guess.”

“I would not be a man if I did that,” he replied.

She regretted her testy tone and tried to shake off the pathetic image of herself. “Where are we?”

“We pass through Chino. The aberration spreads west. I stay ahead of it, keep to the side streets.”

The Wall is spreading? That thought made her shudder. “How does it grow?” she said, more to herself than to him. She remembered Gem telling them that it would spread, so it wasn’t a surprise, but she hadn’t said why it would.

“It feeds on what people give up,” the cab driver said in the same matter-of-fact way.

"I lost a lot in there," Willet said, "The love of my life."

The cabbie gave no reply.

Her body ached, and her own misery was so heavy it took effort to lift her head. "My boyfriend left me in the Wall to die," she said after a minute. "At least it seemed like he did. That Gem monster hurt him… Or maybe he never loved me. I deserted my sister and my friends to find him, and he didn't even believe it was me. I don't know what was going on… He wasn't himself. Maybe it wasn't even him."

More silence from the front seat.

"And now I'm blind." For some reason, it was important that he understand the magnitude of her suffering.

"That is unfortunate," he said. "Do you have other senses?"

"Yeah," she said with a quiet snort. "I hear very well."

"Then you are not completely blind."

"I have needles under my skin. Every time I move, they burn like hell. And all the noise will give me a migraine."

"That is unpleasant. We all have problems, lady. I offer my sympathies for yours."

Clearly, he didn't appreciate what she was going through. That irritated her. "You have an accent," she said. Needles pricked her throat, and her voice sounded hoarse. "Where are you from?"

“I have lived many places, called many my home. Now I live here.”

“This place is doomed.” She leaned forward to ease the sting in her back.

He chuckled. “Doomed cities rise again. People return. New life begins.”

“You’re pretty philosophical for a cab driver.”

“Does a cab driver not wonder about life?” he said with a small reproach in his voice.

She thought she might have offended him and really didn’t want to do that. “I’m sorry. I didn’t mean to imply that you couldn’t or wouldn’t... I’m not usually this dense. It’s been a *really* bad day. I should have said this earlier, but thank you, so much, for pulling me out of that Wall. I would not have survived in there.”

“You are welcome.”

She wondered where they were going. “Do you have a destination in mind?”

“I am a cabbie, and you are my passenger. Where do *you* want to go?”

She thought about where she should go and had few ideas. “I’d really like to go home, but home is in the desert. We’d have to drive back through the Wall.”

"The time for going backward has passed. You can only go forward now."

"Can we go to Manhattan Beach? I know people that might be there. Maybe they'll forgive me."

"As you wish."

With her destination settled, she felt too tired to think. Her eyelids drooped and her head nodded. She automatically tuned into sound waves laced through the air, voices, so many voices. People conversed, spoke into phones. They quarreled and cursed. A lucky few laughed. Bright strands of energy crisscrossed her inner vision, weaving a fabric of light. Gem had explained so much to her about the inner sight, but she couldn't recall it. She needed those explanations now, more than ever. The chant Gem had taught her had to be sung before it slipped away. She sang what she remembered under her breath, a soft and steady HU, until the sound of it chimed in every cell of her body. The sharp pains of the needles piercing her flesh dulled. Despite the heartache when she thought about TJ, she was able to smile just a little. Maybe she could survive another hour. Maybe there was an explanation for his behavior.

An unexpected happiness bloomed within her. "Thank you," she whispered to the source of the happiness. In that moment, she felt at peace. The needles started to melt away like tiny icicles, delightfully cool under her skin and deep in every part of her body. Soon she couldn't feel them at all. New strength surged through her. She stretched, pain free, and her heart swelled with hope. She sat up straighter. "I've been rude," she said. "I never asked your name."

The driver rustled in the front seat. "I am Arhat, lady," he said.

"I'm Willet," she replied. "Pleased to meet you."

If he acknowledged that, she couldn't see it. The blindness remained.

The cab had stopped, maybe for a stop light. Gun fire stuttered close by and startled her so much that she popped right out of her physical body and found herself standing on the roof of the cab in Soul form. She could see in every direction at once. People ran in the streets waving sticks, bats and bricks. Someone shot a gun at a glass storefront and shattered it. A mob pounded down the street, headed their way. She felt herself drop heavily back into her physical body. "We're about to be attacked," she said. "We need to get out of here." Even as she said it, a scrambling horde surrounded the cab, pounding on windows and doors and shouting at them. Willet heard the window crack next to her.

"I will remove us from this situation," Arhat said calmly as if proposing a drive through the park. The cab pushed forward through the crowd. People pounded the roof with fists and hard objects and pulled on the doors trying to rip them off. Gunfire cracked. Arhat veered left, stepped on the gas. The cab jolted ahead and pulled away. Angry shouts trailed behind them. The cab sped up, made a sharp right and roared on, then veered left. The voices behind them faded. After a block and a half, they felt the lug and bump of tire rims hitting the ground. The back tires had gone flat. and the cab rolled to a stop.

"We need to keep moving. They could follow us," Willet said nervously. "What are you doing?"

"We must find another vehicle," Arhat replied. "I hope this is not a problem for you."

"How do you mean 'find'? Do you mean steal a car?"

"Yes, unless someone offers one to us out of good will. Fortunately, I am skilled at the hot wire."

"So, you've stolen cars before."

"Survival makes its own laws, miss," he replied and jumped out of the cab. He came around to the passenger door, took her arm by the elbow and pulled her out. He guided her up the street as fast as they both could walk.

"How long does it take to hot wire a car, Arhat?"

"It takes some small amount of time, Miss Willet."

She could hear new voices fast approaching. "We don't have that."

"At the end of the next block an SUV is parked at the curb. It looks unattended. Can you run with me now?"

Willet prepared herself. "I can't see a thing, but I'll try."

"Hold on to my arm and do not let go. We will run together."

Willet wrapped her hand around his elbow and bent her knees. "Ready."

Voices grew louder behind them. Willet and Arhat dashed down the street until he pulled her to an abrupt halt. She heard a heavy door open. He lifted her into a high seat, and the door slammed. Arhat climbed in the driver seat, and the engine roared to life.

“That was a fast hotwire,” she said, regaining her breath.

“The keys were in the ignition. Sometimes fortune smiles. Seatbelts, please.”

Willet was in the back seat, bouncing side to side, trying to wrap shoulder and lap belts around herself as the SUV lurched around corners, crashing over potholes and curbs. The yelling voices faded behind them, only to be replaced by new shouts from other directions. A rock hit the roof of the SUV, and a series of gun blasts whizzed past them. One hit the back hatch. Willet ducked her head down. Arhat took a hard left turn and then a right. The SUV hit something in the road and rattled.

“We must use Freeway 10,” Arhat said. “The streets are full of berserkers,”

“Why didn’t we do that in the first place?”

“The freeway presents its own dangers and offers no place to hide. We will be, as they say, sitting ducks.”

Willet gulped. “Sitting ducks for what?”

“Freeway driving has become a blood sport,” Arhat said as he twisted and turned the wheel. “We must drive fast and very well to avoid the Chuckers. And there are many obstacles on the road.” They roared up a freeway onramp and bounced into the merge lane on two left tires before leveling out and surging ahead.

Willet held tight to the seat belts and raised her head, wishing she could see. “What’s happening? I hear a lot of cars roaring by.”

“Oh yes, miss, many cars driving fast, trying to reach their exits before a Chucker appears. Everyone races to escape them.” As if to punctuate that point, he floored the SUV, hit the brakes and floored it again, veered left and sped on. Only the seat harness kept Willet from hitting the ceiling.

“I’m gonna need traction…” Her words were lost in a sudden squeal of tires.

“A Chucker approaches from behind. We must take evasive action.” Arhat hit the break, veered right, and floored it. He made a tsking sound and jerked hard left.

“What *is* a ‘Chucker’?”

“It is a vehicle customized to ram other cars for sport. Very nasty. Chucker drivers compete for prizes for the most cars destroyed. We are ten miles from the Mountain Avenue exit. I will do what I can to reach it in time.”

For the next few minutes, Willet was glad she couldn’t see what was happening. The noise was frightening enough. Glass shattered and metal crunched close by. Explosions and screams told her human beings were in harm’s way. Arhat drove like a madman. She could barely hold on, and finally just surrendered to the constraints of her shoulder and lap belts, letting her body go limp. Her teeth knocked together painfully. She locked her jaw. A headache spiked in her left temple. The least of her troubles… She breathed and chanted, breathed and chanted, trying to still her frantic heartbeat. A hideous crash exploded right behind them, and she popped out of her body again, with a 360-degree view of the scene. Smashed car parts, broken glass and bleeding bodies littered the freeway. Cars rolled over the bodies, unable to avoid them before speeding away.

The Chucker causing all the problems proved to be an oversized truck on huge tires with battering rams mounted front and back and large shovels on moveable arms attached to the sides. Sharply pointed spikes studded the front edges of the shovels. The Chucker side-swiped a passenger sedan and jammed it against the concrete wall next to the far-left lane. Spikes on the shovel ripped into the door and lifted the sedan off the ground. The Chucker raised and lowered the shovel, slamming the sedan on the ground once, twice, three times. The doors flew off and passengers fell out. The car exploded. The Chucker retracted the shovel and pulled away. Other cars swerved to avoid the flaming wreck and crashed into each other. The mangled bodies of fallen passengers spattered blood and body tissue all over the road. 'Very nasty' didn't begin to describe it.

Willet dropped back into her body, shaking with terror and tried not to heave. "Arhat, can you go any faster?" she gasped. "We do *not* want that thing near us!"

Arhat leaned on the horn, swerved and then shot ahead, making a drastic cut to the left and then the right. Car horns blared in angry protest. She cringed at the noise and immediately popped out of her body again, hovering above the SUV. Cars vied on each side, trying to get ahead of the traffic to escape the Chucker coming up from behind. The lumbering vehicle weaved between lanes and knocked other cars out of its way until it came up beside them. The driver jerked the steering wheel to the right, trying to ram their SUV. *Who is driving that truck?*

As soon as she processed the thought, she found herself kneeling on the front hood of the Chucker looking in through the windshield at the driver, who turned out to be a young guy in a black tee shirt with shaved head and a demented grin. Death Metal blasted at high volume from speakers mounted in front of the driver seat The 'music' sounded like two chain saws trying to kill each other. The driver's head bobbed spastically to the pounding beat. *No wonder he's insane.* Red smoke circled his head and flew in and out of his mouth. Red Souls in the smoke recognized the Listener and screamed her name. The spike in psychic energy seemed to affect the driver. His eyes glittered with bloodlust. Somehow, he could see her or sense her presence. He shrieked like a maniac and lost control of the steering wheel. The Chucker swerved left across two lanes of traffic sending other cars spinning, veered into the concrete wall, bounced off and hit it again. Sparks flew. It accelerated, slamming against the wall again and again. It seemed like he might be trying to bump her off the hood. The maneuver had no effect on her.

This guy must be stopped. She put her palms against the windshield and pressed. The grit of the glass scraped over her hands as she pushed through it up to her forearms and waved her hands in front of his face. *Can he really see me?* The driver looked confused. He struggled with the wheel, weaved out of control. A ramp on the left headed up to join another freeway. The Chucker roared up the ramp and hit a concrete barrier at high speed, then flipped over the side of the ramp into a ravine below.

She floated over the spot where the Chucker vaulted off the ramp, looking down at the pile of smoking wreckage in the ravine. The massive truck lay upside down on its roof in the middle of bushes and trash, huge wheels spinning in the air. The weight of the truck crushed the cab flat, leaving an arc of shattered glass around it. No way the driver survived that. Glittering red smoke streamed around the wreckage. Deprived of their host, the Red Souls flew off, looking for another vulnerable mind to possess.

She returned to her physical body the next moment, shocked and not sure what to say.

Arhat was in the middle of a conversation. "…do not know what happened to it. It was behind us a few minutes ago, now I do not see it."

“If you mean the Chucker, he, uh, took the last off ramp,” she said, her hands and voice trembling. “I’m sure we lost him.”

“Hmm, that is unexpected. They usually do not give up until their target is destroyed.”

As the SUV sped on, Willet’s mind raced, considering all the ramifications. *I actually caused a person’s death. The Chucker would have killed us, so it had to be done, right?* Arhat’s life and her own had depended on stopping the Chucker. She saved them both, along with countless other unfortunate drivers. She fervently hoped the end justified the means, but she couldn’t fully convince herself.

Arhat interrupted her thoughts. “Shall I take the next exit?”

“Does that go to Manhattan Beach?” she said, although at the moment she couldn’t remember why she wanted to go there. She tried to picture Gem’s face and couldn’t do that either. *Oh no.* Her memories were definitely slipping away.

“A Chucker approaches from the rear,” he said. “Now there are two.”

With monster-trucks trying to demolish them, she had a decision to make. As Arhat said, survival makes its own laws. She would disable a few more Chuckers on the way to wherever they were going. The city would be safer for it. Maybe she could do it without killing anyone.

****

TJ’s ‘flock’ accompanied him for an hour after they all walked out of the Wall. They supported his weight with their shoulders and elbows as he hobbled through the streets on painful feet stinging with needles. Signs and landmarks triggered memories in his followers. One by one, they began to leave him with a word or a look of thanks, before drifting away to pursue their own paths. TJ reminded them of the 'HU' in case they needed it later. Finally, only Diggie and his mother were with him. Needles stabbed into every muscle fiber of his body in parts he had never felt before. Diggie propped him up under one arm, and his mother supported the other. Diggie's mother had regained a small measure of her lucidity. She said her name was Evelyn.

"Where are we going, Mr. Tom?" Diggie asked, looking up at him with wide, trusting eyes.

TJ knew he didn't deserve that trust. "I don't know, boy. I'm not sure where we are now." He didn't want to lean so heavily on Diggie's small frame but draping his arm over the boy's shoulder kept him from falling sideways. Evelyn held the other arm and wrapped her arm around his waist to hold him up. TJ found it difficult to breathe. Every time he closed his eyes, he saw the face of a beautiful blonde woman, and his chest ached.

So many towns in Southern California looked just like this one. Unless they saw a familiar sign, they could be anywhere. People walked by silently, without a glance. Others just stood, staring with blank eyes, as if they had forgotten where they were going. A woman with a large purse on her arm collided with Evelyn and kept walking, as if she didn't notice the contact. Glass smashed a few blocks down the street. Footsteps pounded on cement, heading in their direction.

Diggie and Evelyn helped TJ cross the street against sparse traffic. His knees were weak. He stumbled to a storefront and sunk down against the wall to catch his breath. A man came out of the store and told him to move along. When TJ didn't move quickly enough, the guy kicked at him. Evelyn yelled at the man and kicked back. Another window shattered, closer this time. Men were running toward them with rocks in their hands. They needed to put distance between themselves and the rock throwers.

“I can’t walk much longer,” TJ said, rubbing at the painful needles in his calves. “We need some kind of transportation.”

At that moment, a city bus rolled to a stop right in front of them and the doors folded open. It seemed too good to be true, but given the lack of alternatives, it took only a moment to decide. “Let’s go,” he said. Diggie and Evelyn pushed him up the stairs into the bus and then climbed aboard behind him. The doors closed. A barrage of rocks hit the bus as it rumbled away. TJ collapsed onto a bench seat and Diggie sat next to him. Evelyn sat in the seat behind them. There was no one else on the bus.

“Where does this bus go?” Diggie asked.

TJ had no idea. He reached in his pocket and pulled out a ten-dollar bill. “Here, take this to the driver. Ask him where we’re going and it if it will cover three fares.” Diggie ambled away down the center aisle, swaying as he went. TJ glanced to the right and was startled to see a guy sitting there who wasn’t there before. He looked just like Dean. *No way.* “Dean? Is that you?”

The guy turned his head and smiled at TJ. His upper canine teeth grew out two inches until they touched his chin, and a low, flinty voice came out of his mouth. “Where ya goin’ wonder boy?” It was not Dean’s voice. “Do ya think you’re getting’ away? Yer in my territory now.” The guy popped out of existence like a soap bubble. A shiver of dread ran down TJ’s spine. The Deceiver was already taking over. They were in dangerous territory.

Diggie walked back up the aisle. “There’s no one up there,” he announced as he handed the money back to TJ.

TJ tried to compose himself and focus on the boy. "What do you mean?"

"I mean there's no driver." Diggie plopped down in the seat next to him.

Are city buses driverless now? TJ hadn't heard of that innovation in L.A. Transit. "So, the bus is driving itself…"

Diggie shrugged his thin shoulders. "Yeah, I guess."

"A demon is driving," a hushed voice said behind them. "Or maybe it's an angel."

TJ and Diggie turned to Evelyn, surprised to hear her voice. Those were the most words she had uttered since they met in the Wall. Evelyn stared at them with unflinching eyes and then turned back to the window, ignoring them.

TJ felt the skin on the back of his neck crawl. "We need to get off this bus," he said, trying to stand. The bus lurched, pitched him forward, and then threw him back before rolling on. He was too tired and sore to do anything except sit. The bouncing of the bus jammed the needles deeper into him in every part that touched the seat. He cringed. Who knew where the bus would end up.

****

Dean drove away from the Wall as fast as he could. The cab was long gone. He had no idea where it went and didn't want to drive aimlessly, so he headed west, determined to reach Manhattan Beach as soon as possible. The thought of what could be happening to his mother and brother made him crazy. Gem said she'd meet them there, though she didn't say when. He grasped at that hope. If anyone could rescue Willet and TJ, it was Gem. He began to sing Gem's word under his breath. *Huuuuu. Huuuuu.* A stream of coolness ran through the dark space behind his eyes. His breath evened out, and his shoulders relaxed. The air wasn't great, but he felt better. At least he could think.

Audrey was still in a fog, playing with the radio like a two-year-old. It got on his nerves, but he let it go. "There's nothing on," she pouted "I want some music." She pushed buttons and let it scan for stations. Nothing but static, but then they heard a familiar voice. Richard These, that horse's ass, hissing and crackling through the speakers. "This half hour is brought to you by Johnson Crystal Works, your first choice in crystal solutions for electric power, pollution control, and perimeter security."

"Not this guy again. Is he the only one left on the radio?" Dean said, peeved, and then he processed the words he just heard. "Wait, what crystal? Johnson Crystal?"

"With us today is Bart Johnson, scientist, inventor and owner of Johnson Crystal Works," Theese said in his gravelly voice. 'Bart, tell our audience about the Crystal Works."

"Well, Richard, when I first saw the crystal, I thought it could be important, so I studied it under laboratory conditions to determine its properties. What I found was exciting. The crystal can produce nearly unlimited amounts of electrical energy. It regenerates itself by absorbing pollutants from the air. So, it literally cleans the air and creates power out of pollution at the same time."

Theese gave a wheezy cough. "Amazing. I *knew* that crystal was valuable."

“I also designed a security system using the crystal to protect the perimeters of my property. It’s a patent pending design.”

“Where do people go if they want to see your operation or buy a security system?”

“Just take the West Temple Avenue exit off the 57 north of Diamond Bar and follow the signs for Johnson Crystal Works. You can’t miss it.”

Dean turned down the volume and waved his hand at the radio. “Bart’s growing crystal, Audrey. The idiot is actually growing it. Did you not explain to him what Jat used the crystal for? It’s a highway out of the Underworld for his crazed minions. We have to stop him before Red Souls start flying out of the ground and attacking everyone in L.A. again.”

Audrey looked bemused. “Stop what?”

“The crystal! He’s growing it! I thought we destroyed it all. Listen to me, we’ll need rings! We’ll need them to nuke Bart’s crystal.”

No response from Audrey.

“Do you still have rings in your fingers?”

Audrey looked down at her hands. “I’m not wearing rings.”

“I mean the light rings!” Dean felt himself getting agitated, took a deep breath and composed himself. “Can you spin a ring, Audrey? We need you to do that.”

Audrey shook her head. Confusion washed over her face. “That doesn’t make sense.”

“C’mon babe,” he coaxed. “Remember what we did when me, TJ and Willet helped you make really big rings, and then we threw them. The rings hit the crystal coming out of the ground and turned it into charcoal.” Dean made spinning motions with his fingers. Flickers of light flared briefly from his fingertips and then died just as quickly.

A glint of recognition lit in Audrey’s eyes. “Rings,” she said.

“Yes! Rings! We’re going to see Bart Johnson, remember him? He’s growing the crystal. We have to help him get rid of it.”

Audrey’s brow furrowed. “Bart,” she said.

“We’re going to talk to Bart. You like him and he likes you, right? If we nuke his merchandise without his permission, he might be angry. He won’t appreciate us putting him out of business, but you can explain things to him.”

“Talk to Bart,” she said uncertainly.

“Yes! Bart. You’ll remember him when you see him.” Dean wasn’t sure if that was true.

Audrey looked down at her hands and wriggled her fingers. Little half rings flared on her fingers and then blinked out. She looked startled.

“That’s good, babe,” he encouraged her. “That’s a start.” The expression on her face became distressed and then frightened.

CHAPTER 7

Willet dispatched three more Chuckers in quick succession as Arhat drove west. She pushed one driver out his door and sent him rolling onto the shoulder while his truck smashed into the wall. She put her hands over another driver's eyes. His Chucker swerved, hit another vehicle and stalled, after which a semi-truck side-swiped it and tipped it over. The third driver jumped out of his Chucker when it hit the left wall. He ran away down the freeway, looking back over his shoulder. She watched him go with a certain satisfaction. *I think I'm making an impression.* She had warmed to the idea of superphysical sight compensating for her physical blindness. With her viewpoint floating above her own head, she saw everything in every direction, and of course she heard everything as she always did. Best of all, no one saw her coming. She felt strong. She was a force.

Arhat, meanwhile, didn't ask questions when a Chucker crashed. If he suspected Willet had something to do with it, he never said. His immediate task was to evade other traffic, which he did by driving like a maniac. "Chucker at seven o'clock, miss," he said. "Coming in fast. Sharp change of lane here."

Willet slipped out of her body and rose above the SUV, scanning for the approaching Chucker. Within minutes, she sent the big truck crashing into the right-side wall of the freeway. The driver scrambled out the door just before it burst into flames. She heard shouts and cheers. Above the freeway, people looked over the wall, watching the destruction. They waved arms and raised fists when the Chucker blew up.

The driver ran down the freeway and was intercepted by six men. They picked him up by the arms and legs and carried him, kicking and yelling, to the exit ramp. When they got to the top, they wrapped a chain around his neck, attached it to the metal railing, and then threw him over the side into mid-air. The chain pulled taut, and his chin snapped up. He squirmed and pulled at the noose around his neck. His brown work boots flailed as he swung at the end of the chain and then fell still. She noticed another limp body hanging near him, both drivers she had ejected from their trucks. The violence of the execution was so perfunctory, the offhand way they threw the man over like a bag of trash and left him to hang. She froze, dropped into her physical body and rolled onto the floor of the cab struggling for breath. A headache pounded so hard in her temples that it turned her stomach. Dry heaves shook her shoulders and left her throat raw. Her whole body trembled. "I never wanted this," she whispered. She pressed her knuckles hard against her eyes to obliterate the image of the dangling body burned onto her retinas. The image wouldn't fade.

"They are human beings, after all," Arhat said, "misguided, vengeful, but human."

"I don't know what you mean," she said. But she knew. It was bad enough she had caused a fatal car accident. The idea she had also played a role in the lynching of two people horrified her. Arhat must suspect she was involved. At this point, what did it matter? "Those Chucker crashes – did you see how they happened?"

"The hand of Spirit is often disguised, miss."

A light flashed in the space between her eyebrows. A pair of familiar brown eyes looked back into her and then disappeared. "Are you the hand of Spirit, Arhat?" she said.

"I am your cabbie," he replied patiently. "And I regret to tell you a fleet of Chuckers approaches very fast from behind us. We must escape before we are surrounded."

****

TJ woke when the bus came to a sudden stop. Diggie and Evelyn helped him down the stairs and onto the street. His knees started to buckle, so they lowered him to the ground.

"It's the end of the line, Mr. Tom," Diggie said. "Now what do we do?"

TJ's body temperature had risen, and he sweated profusely. He probably had a fever. Voices argued and cursed inside his head. The rancor was so raw it made him physically sick. He couldn't think, couldn't even answer Diggie's question. He just closed his eyes and let his head hang between his knees.

He heard Diggie talking to someone. A man's voice replied, a hand slipped into his pocket, and then strong arms lifted him into a car. Doors slammed shut around him, and they began to move. TJ passed out. He didn't open his eyes again until someone pulled him out of a vehicle onto the street and slammed the door. Whoever it was drove away. He was left standing with Diggie and Evelyn in a place that smelled like coastal sage and sounded like the wind off the ocean. His bleary eyes focused on what was in front of him and then popped open. "We're in the Hollywood Hills! This is my house!"

Diggie looked up to TJ for confirmation. "That's good, right? Your house is safe, right?"

"Yeah! I thought it might be damaged by crystal. How did we get here?"

"We told the guy to take us to the address on your driver's license," Diggie said. "Pretty smart, huh?"

"What guy?"

Diggie gave him a sheepish look. "The Ride Hailer guy – he was parked near the bus stop waiting for a job. I asked how much it would cost to get to your place. It was pretty expensive. I had to use your credit card, sorry."

TJ checked his pocket and pulled out his wallet. The driver's license and credit card were missing. "Where are the cards?"

Diggie flinched. "Oh gee, dude, I forgot to ask for those back. The guy said he'd give them back at the end of the ride. I forgot about 'em."

A few choice words flew out of TJ's mouth and peppered the air. Then he straightened his shoulders and shuffled up the front walkway to his house. Diggie and Evelyn trailed behind him. A sigh of relief escaped his lips at the sight of his own front door framed by the birds of paradise he had planted with his own hands. As he approached the door, his steps gained strength. He unlocked the door with his key and pushed, but the door was already unlocked. Inside, he heard water running in the shower. *Did I leave the shower running last time I was home? I never leave the shower on. The water bill will be astronomical.*

Diggie and Evelyn went to the kitchen for water and looked for something edible in the refrigerator, while TJ walked quietly down the hallway to his bedroom door and listened. Someone was using his shower. He walked into the bedroom and then pushed open the bathroom door. A cloud of steam hit him in the face. He could make out a man's body through the steamy shower door, washing himself and humming.

"Hey," he called out. "Who are you?"

The water shut off abruptly, and the glass door slid back a couple of inches. An eye peeked through the gap.

"Barlow?" a voice said. "No way!"

"Matt?" TJ answered. "What are you doing in my shower?"

It was Matt Gregg, TJ's attorney, law school friend and real estate investment partner. The man fumbled for a towel and wrapped himself up before he slid the shower door open and stepped out.

"I could ask you the same thing. We thought you were dead!"

TJ was dumbstruck. "Why would you think that? And who's 'we'?"

The whites of Matt's eyes were red. He gave a nervous grin, and words spilled out. "Things happened so fast, with all that's going on, people dying in the upheavals and all the other people wandering around who are, you know, out of their fucking minds."

"I've only been gone a few weeks."

"You've got to be kidding. It was more like two years. When I couldn't reach you, I had to take some steps."

That sounded ominous. TJ frowned. "What steps?"

Matt's smile turned guilty. "Well, your properties were forfeit so I stepped in and bought a few... I always liked this house."

"Why would my properties be forfeit, counsellor? Property taxes were paid for the year, and I've been gone a matter of weeks!"

"Yeah, well the court declared you dead, like I said, because I told them you were…"

"You had me declared dead so you could take over my real estate?" TJ spluttered. "You back-stabbing crook!"

Matt stepped back with hands up, and his voice rose to a near-squeak. "The balance of probabilities argued in favor of your demise."

"That's bullshit!"

"I didn't want the properties auctioned off to strangers," Matt said, "so I saved the best ones. You should be thanking me!"

"I'll thank you in court when I sue you."

Matt's mouth curled into a sneer. "Sorry to tell you, buddy. Things have changed in L.A. The rule of law doesn't work quite the way it used to.You need to know the right people to win in court these days. You need clout."

The two men stared at each other, anger heating the air.

"You're crazy," TJ said. "What 'clout' do you think *you* have?"

"I have power on my side. Friends in very high places, you could say." Matt's eyes glittered. Red smoke rode on his breath.

Matt used to be a good-natured, honest friend. TJ hardly recognized him now. He was totally infected by Red Souls. "This is a bad day for you to turn into an ass," he growled. "I am *not* in a good mood." Needles dug in under his skin, making his eyes water. He had never felt so much rage. Brute strength surged through his arms, and his hands curled into fists. He stalked toward the wet and mostly naked man with grim determination. A wisp of the smoke darted out of Matt's mouth and flew at TJ's head. Matt put up his fists, but the first blow from TJ hit him in the jaw like a sledgehammer. The second blow hit him on the right side of the head, over the ear. Matt's knees buckled, and he lost his grip on the towel. TJ moved over Matt and slammed punches onto his head and shoulders. The needles were killing him, but they didn't slow him down. He needed to expend all that rage.

"I'm sorry!" Matt shrieked. "You can have the house back. I'll deed everything back to you." He raised his arms to protect his head and face, abandoning any attempt to cover his manhood. TJ was relentless as a battering ram. Matt's arms began to tire and droop. "Please stop," he said, gasping for breath after a punch to the stomach. "Don't kill me."

A woman's voice shouted, "Tom, stop it! Stop this instant."

TJ stopped in mid-punch and whirled around. Evelyn stood in the doorway with Diggie clutched to her side. The woman stared daggers at TJ. Diggie's eyes were big as saucers in his pale face.

TJ dropped his fists and looked back at Matt. "Get out of my house." he said quietly, "before I do kill you."

Matt grabbed a towel to cover up and slid on the tile all the way back to the shower. Blood oozed from multiple cuts on his face. "You think I'm gonna let this go?" he said, breathing hard as he tried to stand. "You could've given me brain damage! I'll have you arrested for assault." TJ extended a hand to steady him. Matt swatted it away and stood on his own, grabbing his shirt and pants from the towel bar. "Get away from me, you son of a bitch," Matt said. "If I ever see you again, you'll find out what kind of punch *I* can throw." Matt stumbled past TJ to the doorway.

The woman and boy stood aside for him, and he disappeared down the hall. They heard the front door open and then slam shut. Evelyn gave TJ a hard look. That vague confusion she carried with her out of the Wall was gone. "You will not expose my son to such violence, do you hear me? I won't allow it. I appreciate the help you have given us, but your light has gone out." Evelyn's eyes were clear and unwavering. She spoke like an adult instead of the addled child she had seemed before.

The contrast startled TJ. His mindless fury ebbed. "I'm sorry, he said. "I thought Matt was a friend, but he sold me out. And pain is driving me crazy."

"Is that so?" she said. "You seemed pretty healthy when you were beating the man. Pain didn't stop you then."

Remorse began to grip him. "It's not an excuse, Evelyn. There's red smoke in this room. Red Souls - do you know what those are?"

Evelyn's look was shrewd. "I know what flies in the smoke. What will you do to drive them away?"

"I'll chant. I'll contemplate. Does that satisfy you?"

"It's not me you have to satisfy."

"Gaah, you sound like – that woman," he said, trying to remember the Guardian's name.

TJ noticed Diggie almost hiding behind his mother. "Digg," he said," I'm sorry. I shouldn't lose my temper or hit anyone. It wasn't right, and it won't happen again, I promise."

"Okay," Diggie said, but the boy didn't meet his eyes. That cut into TJ's heart.

TJ felt suffocated in the steamy bathroom. He pushed past Evelyn and Diggie and headed to the living room, slid the patio door open and stepped out to the porch, drawing a deep breath of fresher air into his lungs. He felt embarrassed and agitated, and ready to jump out of his skin. He went to the railing and looked out. The ocean view always calmed him, but today he couldn't see through the heavy layer of gray mist that rose at the shore. Was that fog? It looked strange, and then he recognized it for what it was - a Wall of churning static hovering along the Pacific coast, obscuring the ocean behind it. It seemed close, too close for comfort.

"Evelyn," he roared. "Come here. We've got a problem."

Evelyn ran out to the porch and looked west. "Oh no," she whispered. She started shaking. "Not again. I can't go through that again."

"No one is going in there," TJ said in a low voice. "Throw some food in a bag and grab Diggie. We're leaving."

****

Radio host and provocateur Richard Theese was broadcasting from a new studio in East Hollywood these days, modest by his previous standards, small and dingy with outdated equipment, but he had a chair, a desk and a microphone, so the Richard Theese Show was on the air.

Gem, Dora and Sonrisa watched him from outside the soundproof glass of the broadcast booth. Theese was doing his usual rant and rave about what he called 'intruders'. He waved his arms and challenged people to rally against the supposed invasions of their country, but there were dangers right around him of which he was unaware. His chair and desk floated over an open pit of fire and smoke. The flames licked higher and higher at his feet. That was the reality of his existence, danger so near and yet so far from his physical senses.

"The Deceiver has withdrawn patronage and left him to turn in the wind," Sonrisa said softly. "Mr. Theese is oblivious."

Gem nodded agreement. "Someone else must serve as Jat's sponsor in the physical world now. The question is who?"

A red light over the door of the studio flashed as Theese spoke. "No one tells you the truth like I do, friends," he rasped into the microphone. His voice sounded like he was gargling rocks. "The truth is we have to protect ourselves from those who would take advantage of us.We have righteousness on our side, and you have yours truly, Richard Theese, on *your* side. Stay tuned for more after a message from our sponsor, Matthew Gregg and Associates."

"The name 'Matthew Gregg' is familiar," Gem said. "I met him before, an associate of Thomas Barlow. Could that be his new sponsor?"

Theese went to commercial, clicked off the mic and pushed his chair back. He picked up a bucket from under his desk and coughed into it, releasing the phlegm clogging his throat. It was a fact of his life ever since he took that gunshot to the neck. He put the bucket back down and leaned back in his chair, folding his arms behind his head with a grunt of satisfaction. When Gem opened the studio door and walked in with Dora and Sonrisa behind her, Theese glanced toward her, and the blood drained from his face.

"Not you," he whispered. He stood unsteadily from his chair and shooed them away with his hands. "Be gone, foul spirits."

"Foul spirits?" Sonrisa looked at Gem. "Is he addressing us?"

Dora arched her back and gave a low, curdling growl. Her sleek black fur stood on end. The Hound of Hell had not forgotten how Richard Theese had shot Gem in the head.

The growl sent Theese back a step. "If you're here to destroy the mining business, you're too late. It was liquidated."

"Your business does not concern me. What is your relationship with Matthew Gregg?"

Confusion flickered in his eyes. "Mr. Gregg? What do you want with him? Are you going to tell lies about me, make him stop his support for my program?"

"Your program does not concern me either. I want to talk to him. Do you have an address?"

"How did you even get in here?" he said, looking over their shoulders to the room outside. "This office is locked."

“Do you know Matthew Gregg’s location? It is a simple question.”

“I never met the guy,” he replied, exasperated. “His secretary calls me when he wants something. He has an office in the Dragon Head Building downtown.”

Gem frowned. “What Dragon Head Building?”

“It’s the building with the dragon-headed man on top, you know, sitting in a big chair, wearing a suit. It’s the tallest building in L.A, been there forever.”

“Really,” Gem said. “I have guarded Los Angeles for over one hundred forty years and I never saw a Dragon in a suit on top of any building.”

Theese swallowed hard. “Well, you’re a friggin’ lunatic,” he growled. “I knew that from the git go.”

Gem and Sonrisa put their heads together, ignoring his mutterings about ‘crazy woman’ and ‘makes no damn sense’. “A dragon’s head is the Deceiver’s image,” Gem whispered. “It cannot be a coincidence. What would make Theese think the building has been there forever when it was never there before?”

“The Wall has altered the perception of time for people in the city,” Sonrisa said. “Jat creates a new building and puts it in plain sight. People are made to think it has always been there, so they do not question its sudden appearance.”

Theese watched them impatiently. “Mr. Gregg’s a busy man,” he said. “I wouldn’t try to bug him. He doesn’t have time for the likes of you two and your rabid dog. And stop wasting *my* time while you're at it. I have a radio show to do."

"What does Mr. Gregg ask you to do for him?" Gem asked.

"I don't have to do anything! Well, he gets free advertising, of course, because he's paying for the show and some public service announcements. He's a patriot like me, doesn't want to see the country taken over by hooligans and infiltrators. We see eye to eye on that."

"Do the public service announcements encourage so-called patriots to attack people they view as hooligans or infiltrators?"

Theese raised his fists and shook them. "I don't know what you're talking about. Get out of my office before I call the police, you crazy witch! I'll have that mongrel put down too."

"I will be in touch, Mr. Theese," Gem said. "Then we will talk about your precarious situation." Gem, Dora and Sonrisa took a step backward into a space-time doorway that opened behind them. It folded shut and they disappeared before Theese could blink.

He stared at the empty place where the women had stood and could not wrap his mind around anything that just happened. A woman he was sure was dead had appeared in his studio, threatened him and then disappeared into thin air. He took his pulse and felt his forehead with an unsteady hand. He went back to his desk and swallowed two heart pills before collapsing into his seat. He spit into the bucket again and took a deep breath. With microphone clicked on, he leaned forward and licked his lips. "Folks, it's yours truly and what can I say, those complainers demonstrating on Whittier tomorrow will get an earful from our side. Counter-demo starts at eleven. Bring your sharp elbows. This is Richard Theese."

He sat back and felt better, as if he had exacted a small measure of retribution from the woman for upsetting him. The thought of his followers butting heads with the wimps on Whittier made him smile. Yes, he felt in control again, but his face felt flushed. *Am I getting a fever?* Sweat began to bead and run down his forehead. The soles of his shoes were getting hot too. He looked down and in a momentary flash of clarity, his sight opened on the pit of fire beneath him. Flames rose to his knees. He yelped in panic and climbed up on his chair, fell backward and hit his head hard on the floor. He scooted back to the wall, slapping at sparks on his pants.

"Jesuzz! Where did the fire come from?" he exclaimed as he rubbed the back of his head. "The witch is trying to kill me."

The specter of the fire pit faded. He got up and went to his desk, picked up his phone, and called Matt Gregg's secretary. "Hello Georgina," he said when a woman's voice answered. "This is Richard Theese. I have a message for Mr. Gregg. Tell him trouble is heading his way. A crazy woman is looking for him. I don't know what she wants, but she'll cause a ruckus, I'm sure of it. She just left my studio, along with a vicious dog and another female lunatic. They are heading to the Dragon Head building now. And Georgina? Let him know these women are dangerous."

He sat down again and wiped the sweat from his forehead with each sleeve of both arms. Any type of physical exertion taxed him these days. He was working too hard. That's all it was. He slowly caught his breath and took a moment to think. The phone call to Matt Gregg was a good move. It couldn't hurt to warn his sponsor about possible danger, but he still felt uneasy, like he was overlooking something important. The back of his head hurt. He felt dizzy and closed his eyes. A confusion of images and sensations swirled in his head: driving up a mountain; the sound of gunshot; that crazy woman with a bloom of blood on her temple, falling to the ground; the black dog jumping at him, bumping his arm. And it all came back. He had fired the gun, shot the woman in the head. She died on Mount Wilson and that wasn't even the most horrifying part. Her body had disintegrated before his eyes in a blaze of light. He saw it, and other people saw it too, yet she had just been in his studio, solidly alive and speaking to him.

He got dizzier, gasped and slumped to the floor. The pain in his head spiked. Stars exploded in front of his eyes. He heard a pop, felt movement, and then he was floating, looking down at his own physical body on the floor. A familiar voice spoke. "Dad, what are you doing?" the voice said. It was his son, Jimmy, standing nearby wearing the army fatigues he wore in the Mid-East wars before he was killed. Jimmy held a young child under each arm, one girl and one boy, their faces soot-covered and streaked with tears.

Joy surged through Theese in a way it hadn't for years. "Jimmy, my boy," Theese said. "I've missed you so much! How can you be here? Am I dying, son?"

"We all die sometime, Dad. I don't know when," Jimmy said.

"Who are those children?"

"These are children I tried to protect in the war I fought to help them."

"You're a hero, son, and a patriot. I couldn't be prouder."

"This is not about me, Dad. It's about you. Let the Guardian help you."

"You don't mean that demented woman, do you? She's a witch. How would she help *me*?"

"She just opened your sight and gave you a view of another world that is very close to you. She can show you how to avoid going into the fires. That's what she does."

The image of Jimmy holding the children began to fade. Theese thrust his arms out, desperate to hold on to his son, but another image formed in its place. That woman, Gem, her brown skin and tight brown curls tinged with gold, the penetrating brown eyes looking at him. Her diaphanous form drifted closer, shedding light through the studio.

"I am here to help you," Gem said in a voice he had come to loathe.

"Didn't you just leave?" he growled. "You ruined my life. Haven't you done enough?"

"You must understand how you have ruined your own life, or you cannot move forward."

"I despise you, woman," Theese hissed through his teeth.

"That is unfortunate for you, but it does not change anything. You must make choices now."

"What choices do I have?"

"The choices you have earned."

"What do you mean? Can I go where my son is?"

"Your son died protecting others. You cannot follow him into the place *he* earned, not now."

"Then what, where? What do I do?"

"Look at your mortal body. It is in distress, but you still have time to save it. You looked unwell before I left your office, so I called the paramedics. They will break through the outer door at any moment and try to revive you. If you choose to return to your physical life, they will prevent damage to your brain, but your body will be disabled. If you choose *not* to return to your physical body, you will fall into the Underworld, the place of fires you have just seen."

"That's it? Those are my choices – disability or hell?"

"The Underworld is a place of correction, not eternal damnation. Nevertheless, your time there would be unpleasant. You have hurt people, Richard. These debts must be paid."

"If you mean that I shot you, well, I'm sorry. I shouldn't have done that."

"I forgive you."

"I wanted to protect my country. That can't be wrong, can it?"

"Were you protecting country, or making judgements about people you did not know from a high horse you had no right to ride?"

Theese heard noise in the outer office, the cracking of wood and the sound of something heavy hitting the floor. The paramedics had broken through the door. He looked down at his body lying below him on the floor. The skin was turning blue.

"There is little time before that body is no longer viable," she said gently. "You must choose to return to it, or not. If you do, you will have the opportunity to make changes in your life and one day, you might join your son."

"How do I do that?"

"Change your state of consciousness, all else will follow. I will help you."

"Is it too late to choose hell?" He dropped into his body and lost consciousness before he could hear her answer.

CHAPTER 8

TJ sat on his bed and tried to rub away the sting of the needles in his feet. It was difficult to walk, but there was no time for sitting around. He had to get Diggie and Evelyn out of the Hollywood Hills before the Wall moved in and covered them, and there was only one option for a quick getaway. He got up and walked gingerly to his garage, raised the door and beheld his one remaining vehicle, a VW Van he used to travel back and forth between his parents' house and law school. He had held on to the van mostly out of nostalgia, hadn't driven it hardly at all in the last two years. Was there gas in it? He unlocked the driver door and slid into the seat. The smell of leather and a certain aroma of grassy smoke brought back memories of consequence-free fun and an abundance of confidence. He could barely relate to it now. The gas gauge indicated about half a tank. It would have to do. Hopefully, they'd find an open gas station before they ran out, if such an ordinary thing still existed in this messed-up city. There was also the issue of his driver's license, which he no longer had. He wasn't sure it would matter if the rule of law had truly gone out the window like Matt said. He walked around the van, checking the tires, which were low on air. He found his electric air pump and filled them. He planned to drive fast. They didn't want a blow-out on the way.

Diggie and Evelyn stood on the driveway watching him work. Evelyn had a shopping bag over her arm, and Diggie held a gallon of water in each hand. "We're leaving?" Diggie asked. "With you?"

"Yes, Digg, we have to get out of here. Many reasons. This is the only vehicle I have left, so when we reach a safe place, you and your Mom can go your own way if you want."

"I thought *this* was a safe place." Worry clouded the boy's eyes.

"I thought so too, but things have changed. Let's talk about our options on the way."

"On the way to where?" Evelyn asked.

"Right now, I'm thinking about getting out of L.A. altogether, going to my parents' place in Santa Cruz. We just have to get north of the mountains."

Evelyn nodded.

****

The turnoff to the Johnson Crystal Works was easy for Dean to find. There were signs everywhere. He wondered how Bart's enterprise had grown so fast. The last time they saw him, he was living in a motor home in the driveway at Pine Siskin House. Things had really turned around for him.

Dean stopped the car at the entrance road to the Crystal Works, stared at the big red arrow pointing toward the sales office, and took a long breath. Convincing Bart of the crystal's danger would be a tough sell. Bart hardly knew Dean, but he did know Audrey. Her present state of memory loss did not inspire confidence. Dean imagined Bart would get offended, at the least, and more likely angry at the suggestion he was creating dangerous material. Things could get ugly if Audrey threw a ring of energy that destroyed his product, assuming she still could. Audrey sat demurely in the passenger seat with hands in her lap, staring straight ahead.

“Audrey,” he said. “Spin a ring for me.”

Audrey giggled at him. “You’re so funny.”

Not a good sign. Dean continued up the long asphalt road to the sales office. Several cars parked in a dirt parking area, and people were heading to an area behind the office building. Dean and Audrey parked and followed them. Visitors strolled through open fields where long veins of crystal ran in neat rows through tilled dirt. The crystal sparkled in the sun, clear as glass. No red smoke flowed in any of the veins. What was even more surprising - the air over the field was fresh and light, unlike the stale gray atmosphere in the rest of the city. It was a pleasure to breathe. Dean filled his lungs with several deep breaths of the wonderful air before he shook himself and refocused.

“Let’s find Bart,” he said. He took Audrey’s elbow and led her to the office.

Inside, a small crowd gathered in front of the counter. It was easy to spot Bart behind the counter, head and shoulders taller than everyone else. Dean edged closer, got in what looked like a line and motioned to Audrey to join him. He cleared his throat, and Bart looked up. His eyebrows jumped up to his scalp when he recognized them.

“Audrey! And Dean, what are you guys doing here?” It’s great to see you!” Bart rounded the counter and came out to shake hands. He gave Audrey a big hug.

“Hey, Johnson,” Dean began, “we heard about your operation. Very impressive. You’ve accomplished so much in such a short time.”

"I've been working on it for over a year."

"A year? Really? Before you met Audrey? It couldn't have been a year. I thought you got the crystals from her."

The Wall had stretched time in Bart's memory. He looked confused for a moment but shrugged it off. "Anyway, I was lucky to score some startup money from Matthew Gregg and Associates. They really got me going. Things just took off from there."

"Matt Gregg? I know him, TJ's friend. I didn't know he was into investing in minerals."

"He seems to have money to burn, but this was an easy decision for him. The crystal sells itself. It can do so many things."

"Yeah, about that," Dean said. "We'd like to talk when you have a few minutes – privately if possible."

"Sure," Bart replied. "I think there's enough counter help. Let's go to my office. Audrey, you look great by the way, how've you been?"

Audrey squinted at him and pointed a finger. "You…you," she stuttered, trying to say the name on the tip of her tongue.

"Audrey is a bit under the weather," Dean said. "Nothing to worry about, we hope. We can talk about that too."

Bart led the way to a separate building with windows facing the crystal fields. Inside, a desk and several stuffed chairs dominated the space. Bookcases overflowed with textbooks and papers. When they were all seated, Bart looked across the desk at Audrey, who was staring out the window. "Okay, what's up?"

Dean rustled in his chair. "There's no easy way to say this, Bart. First, let me ask - after all the chaos and destruction in L.A. caused by crystal, why would you want to grow more? People died because of it. Your house slid into a ravine as I recall."

Something flickered in Bart's eyes. "Are you questioning my right to run a business?'

"Absolutely not, no, I'd just like to understand why *this* particular business."

Bart folded his hands in front of him. "Well, for one thing, all the electrical power required to run this operation, including my lab, is generated by the crystal. It's a virtually infinite power source. For another thing, take a look out the window." Bart gestured toward the glass. "The air over this land is the cleanest air in California, possibly in the world. The crystal consumes any pollutants in the air – gas fumes, dust particles, smoke - and turns it into power. Isn't that worth pursuing?"

That was news. "Yeah, sure, but there are things about the crystal you might not be aware of. The pieces Audrey gave you caused spontaneous fires, burned down my friend's club. You were there."

Bart's face hardened. "It was an anomaly in the original sample. I haven't been able to replicate it in the lab."

Dean took a long breath and braced himself for the next speech. "The crystal connects the physical plane with other planes beyond. Usually there's an energy barrier between them, but anything in the crystal gets through it. Destructive energies from the Underworld come into our world through the crystal. Very destructive energies, Bart. All the crystal in Los Angeles had to be incinerated to protect the city. Do you know how the crystal was destroyed? Audrey hit it with energy rings she created on her fingers and burned it down to charcoal." There. He said it. He could tell Bart's reaction from the incredulous look on his face.

Bart looked back and forth between Dean and Audrey and laughed. He leaned back in his chair, laughed some more, and then stared at Dean. "You're out of your mind, Simmons. Audrey isn't safe around you. I'm about to call the paramedics and have you restrained."

"I realize this sounds incredible," Dean said, "but we can show you. Audrey can show you."

"Show me what?"

"Can we walk outside for a minute?"

Bart laughed again. "Sure, let's go. I've wasted enough time here. Show me whatever it is and then get off my property. Audrey is welcome to stay, of course."

They walked outside to the edge of the fields. Rows of crystal glistened in the sun. The effect was almost blinding. People took pictures. At the far end of the field, Bart's mobile home was parked with an awning up, a grill and lawn chairs underneath it.

"You live here?" Dean asked.

"Yeah, it was quicker than trying to rebuild my house after it got demolished. That'll take a while, if ever."

Dean nodded. "You've grown a lot of crystal. How did you get it to grow so fast?"

Bart forgot his pique for the moment and warmed to the subject of his enterprise. “I cultured seed crystals in my lab, and they grew. Fast. Then I tried planting the seeds in the ground. They took off like a shot. Within two weeks, I had what you see here, and the air was clear.” His chest swelled with satisfaction.

“I *am* impressed, believe me,” Dean said. “This could be really valuable, but Audrey and I have something to show you too.”

“So, do it, already,” Bart growled. “I’ve got customers.”

Dean wasn’t sure if this would work. “Audrey, how do you feel?” he asked. “Can you spin a ring?”

Audrey stood apart from Dean and Bart with her arms spread wide and her face raised to the sun, eyes closed, drinking in the warm light and fresh air. When she looked at him, she seemed clearer. “I feel fine, Dean,” she said with a smile.

“Great,” Dean said. “Bart would like to see you make a ring. Can you do that?”

A flicker of doubt crossed her face, but she held a hand up in front of her. Two small rings appeared on her index finger and began to spin. She looked startled.

“Can you toss the rings onto this crystal here?” Dean asked, pointing to the row at their feet. “We need to see what they do.”

“The crystal is so beautiful,” she told Bart. “I don’t want to hurt it."

Bart watched in bemusement. He couldn’t see the rings. “Do it already.”

Audrey let the rings slip off her finger onto the row of pure, clear crystal. The crystal smoked and caught fire. Within seconds, fire raced down the entire length of the row like a lit fuse. The crystal burned brightly. A minute later, it was nothing but a line of charcoal. Anxious murmurs rose from other people around the field.

Bart's mouth opened and then snapped shut. "What did you do?" he demanded. "Did you light a match?"

"No," Dean said. "We're using a different kind of energy."

Bart flushed red all the way down his neck. Anger and disbelief battled fascination for control of his face. "What are you talking about?" he sputtered. "What kind of energy?"

"I'm talking about superphysical energy."

"You're truly insane, you know that? You're a danger to yourself and others."

"Bart, what you have here is amazing. It could truly benefit the world, but it must be protected from forces that would use it for evil purposes. Have you ever seen anything of a reddish color inside it?"

"No, it's white, pure white!" Bart himself looked free of the red smoke, no red eyes or smoky breath. That was a good sign. He wasn't infected by Red Souls, but he looked about to explode in anger.

"If the crystal ever turns red," Dean said carefully, "it *has* to be destroyed."

"If you threaten my business, I'll have you arrested!"

"Believe me we don't *want* to destroy your business. I'm just letting you know the crystal is susceptible to a kind of infection. There's no way to get rid of it except to nuke it with strong energy and reduce it to charcoal."

"What does that even mean? How do I get that kind of energy?"

"Audrey has it in her fingers. She creates rings of energy that burn crystal on contact."

"I didn't see anything." Bart said to Audrey. "How did you burn the crystal?"

"There were rings on my finger," she said, studying her hands. "They got hot. I threw them at the crystal."

Bart stared at her. "Audrey, I took you for an intelligent woman, but you've lost your mind too. Dean's influence is bad for you."

"Dean is in the Circle," she said brightly.

"What Circle?" Bart asked.

She thought about it. "People we know. Where are they, Dean?"

"Audrey's memory got a bit jumbled coming through the Wall," Dean said, putting an arm around her shoulders.

"What Wall?" Bart looked back and forth between them, totally befuddled. "What in the world are you talking about?"

“Have you looked east lately?” Dean pointed to the eastern horizon, where the Wall stood long and tall, and closer than ever. “Do you mean to tell me you haven’t noticed?”

Bart looked where Dean pointed. “What is that? Fog?”

“Fog comes off the ocean, not the desert. That there is a nasty, mutant mass of static.” Dean raised his voice and shouted to the people strolling around the fields. “Folks look over there, to the east. Do you see a fog?”

Everyone around the fields turned to look. Their faces registered the same reaction as Bart’s – befuddlement, as if they had never noticed the Wall before. No one said a word. People pulled out their phones to take pictures. A couple lifted binoculars to get a closer look.

Bart shifted uncomfortably. “What are we supposed to do about it?

“Well, I’m having second thoughts about that,” Dean said. “I thought your crystal would contribute to the problem, but it actually might help. We should test that theory. You may need to plant more.”

“Now I have to plant more?” Bart shook his head. “I thought the crystal was dangerous.”

“It could become dangerous, but your crystal looks clean right now. Through events too complicated to explain, we, meaning TJ, Audrey, Willet and me, can see the higher energies. Audrey can also throw them in rings, and Willet can hear them. We’re working with Gem to expel them from Los Angeles.”

“I knew there was something wrong with that woman.”

Dean laid his hands softly on Audrey's shoulders and looked in her eyes. "We need to find her, Audrey. We need to find Gem, right?"

"Gem," Audrey nodded slowly. "Need to find her."

Bart waved his hand. "Yes, move along, feel free. I think Audrey should stay here, though. Your influence on her is unhealthy."

Dean had to admit Bart could be right about Audrey staying put. The clean air and sun over the crystal fields helped Audrey regain her wits. If she left the crystal, she might revert to her previous clueless state. On the other hand, her rings would be needed in any fight.

"Audrey, what do you want to do?"

Audrey's blue eyes narrowed. "I want to… Where's my… W-w-w…?"

"What is she talking about?" Bart's eyes narrowed. "What's wrong with her?"

"You have no idea what's been going on," Dean said. He was done coddling Bart. "The four of us fought for this city against a major attack from the Underworld and almost lost our lives, not to mention our Souls. The fact that you're still here is because of us."

"Oh, wait a minute," Bart sneered. "Is that why you were passed out in the Jeep? Because you were busy fighting for the city? I had to carry your sorry ass into the house. Almost broke my back."

"We were in another world."

Bart stared at him. “Wow, Deano, I didn’t realize how far gone you were.”

“You can laugh, but I’d worry more about the Wall of static out there. It’s moving this way, and you won’t like what happens when it gets here. Your crystal may be the only protection any of us have. I suggest you think about that and help me use it.”

****

The needles in TJ’s body stayed mostly quiet for the time being. Sometimes he could almost – almost - forget they were there, but then the sting or ache would return all of a sudden until they drove him just short of crazy. He needed to concentrate on getting Evelyn and Diggie out of L.A. Any brief respite from pain was very welcome.

The most direct road to Santa Cruz from L.A. was the Coast Highway. It was a winding scenic drive. TJ wasn’t interested in scenery. He wanted to go as fast as the VW Van could carry them, so they would have to take Freeway 5, despite possible traffic jams. With Evelyn and Diggie in their seats, he backed the van out of the garage, onto the street and punched the gas. The Van rattled in every metal joint. Evelyn grasped the passenger seat with white fingers and clung to her seat belt. Diggie cheered from the back seat. The boy was the only one enjoying himself. Fleeing for their lives, leaving behind everything they knew wasn’t a pleasure trip. Towns and cities flew by. Evelyn closed her eyes and tilted her head back against the headrest, her lips moving silently. Just north of Santa Clarita, a fog bank loomed in front of them. They were in it before they could stop or exit. TJ could barely see the road. The van slowed to a crawl. *The sun was out a little while ago. Is it going to rain?* The fog got thicker before it began to thin out and burn away completely. TJ stepped on the gas and checked the highway signs for upcoming exits. Diggie said he had to pee.

"Wait a minute," TJ said out loud. "Didn't we pass Sylmar earlier? We're passing it again."

The cities he expected to pass were coming in reverse order. They were traveling south, back to L.A., instead of north. He must have taken a wrong fork in the fog. He took the next exit, crossed over the freeway to the other side, and got back on the northbound. In a few miles they entered the fog bank again and slowed to 3 miles per hour. Past the fog, he checked the signs. They were once again traveling south. Something was blocking them from leaving the city. He quietly alerted Evelyn.

"What do we do?" she murmured.

"We could try the coast road," he said.

Evelyn checked the back of the van where Diggie dozed on a small mattress. "The Wall already touched the coast when we saw it from your balcony," she replied. "What chance it will be any better now?"

"Probably zero," TJ admitted. "What do you want to do?"

"I want my son to be safe. Where can we go so he is safe?"

He was at a loss. "I can't take you back to your apartment, can I?"

Evelyn's face blanched white up into the roots of her curly red hair. "That was in the Wall! No! We woke up in chaos! Our apartment was filled with blurring lines. We could barely see our own hands, and the phone didn't work. I took my son out to the street with me to find help, and we got lost. Things attacked us, things I can't bear to think about." She was shaking now, her face in her hands. "There has to be someplace else."

"Okay, okay. There aren't a lot of choices."

"What about you, Tom? Will you protect him if something happens to me?"

TJ squirmed. "Nothing is going to happen to you."

"I'd feel better if you promised. I know you care about him."

Her eyes were on him. He couldn't avoid them, so he nodded and made the promise. He did care about the boy and would try to protect him any way he could. It made the drive back to the city all the more tense because he wasn't sure he actually could. The needles sticking into his muscles started to sting again. Pictures drifted across his mind's eye like clouds across a blue sky. People. Places. He knew they were important but couldn't quite remember why. It was difficult to concentrate.

"I have a small warehouse and office in West Covina that I use for my businesses. Matt Gregg wasn't in on the purchase, so he won't know about it. We can go there and lay low until we decide on the next move. Sound good?"

Evelyn nodded once, and then looked away, out the window. What more was there to say?

TJ pushed pedal to metal back to the city. As they approached L.A. Downtown, he took the 10 Freeway East and stepped on it, fervently hoping there would be no unpleasant surprises along the way. The traffic moved fast, flying by the van on both sides at ridiculous speeds. The old van could only chug along at maximum 70 mph. Then traffic slowed to a stop as they approached West Covina. A possible reason for the slowdown came into view. Five bodies hung by their necks from the railing at the top of the freeway wall like bloated piñatas. TJ did not want Diggie to see this. He wasn't sure Evelyn could handle it either, so he didn't say anything. Besides, something else was happening on the other side of the freeway that also caused traffic to slow to a crawl. He was close enough to the left shoulder to get a good look. Two lines of enormous trucks faced each other in the west lanes, blocking them completely. The trucks gunned their engines as if they were about to enter into battle.

A silver SUV idled between the two lines of huge trucks, trapped in the gauntlet with no escape. A shimmer of light across the roof of the SUV made him blink. He rubbed his eyes and then looked again. In the shimmer, he detected the form of a woman. She turned slowly toward him. He shook his head to make sure he wasn't mistaken. A name danced on the tip of his tongue. The image of a cascade of blonde hair on a bed pillow came to him. *It's her, the woman I was trying to remember.* One thing was clear – she was in a precarious position.

TJ waved at Evelyn and raised a finger to his lips. "Can you drive this van?" he asked in a low voice. "It's a stick."

Evelyn's eyes got wide. She nodded tentatively.

"I have to stop and get out, and you need to get off this freeway. We're almost in West Covina, you can take the next exit. Here's the address of my warehouse." He pulled an old receipt out of the glove box and scribbled an address on the back, hoping he remembered it correctly. He stuffed the paper into her hand and then fished in his pocket and pulled out a key. "This is a key to the office. If you can find the place, go in and lock the doors. Otherwise, find a library or a grocery store or someplace public and go inside." He pressed the key into her other hand and jerked his thumb toward the back of the van. "Do *not* let him look out the windows until you're far away from the freeway. Hear me?"

She nodded and took a deep breath. Her face was so white that her red hair looked like it was on fire. TJ saw her hands were shaking.

He dropped a few dollars on her lap. “This is for gas. Be careful,” he said, and searched her eyes. Behind the obvious distress, a small, steady flame burned within them, a mother’s determination to protect her child. He would have to trust it. He opened the driver door and stepped out. Evelyn slid over into his seat. He ran to the freeway divider and climbed over to the other side. The trucks revved and snarled. If Evelyn managed to shift the van into gear and pull back onto the freeway, he didn’t hear it. The conflagration in front of him was deafening. He had to do something before the trucks charged and the SUV got crushed.

CHAPTER 9

Chucker engines roared like angry grizzlies. They made Willet's head throb. She had slipped out of her physical form and rose above the SUV in her Soul body. Now she could hear *and* see. The trucks were aimed at them like loaded guns. She would not be able to confuse and divert every Chucker driver before one of them rammed into Arhat and the SUV. She dropped back into the physical with a huff. "Arhat, what do you think?" she asked. "Is there anything we can do here?"

"They have trapped us, miss," he said, shaking his head. "Our chances of escape are not good."

They sat in silence, anticipating what would surely be a grisly death.

****

The element of surprise was in TJ's favor. He crept up to the nearest Chucker, climbed onto the running board of the massive truck, and pulled the door open. He wrestled the driver out the door and took his seat. That moment of surprise was now lost. The other drivers knew he was not one of them, and they would bash his truck to smithereens. He had never seen vehicles like these before, as big as tanks and hung with demolition equipment on all sides. He looked around quickly for exits There was one behind him. On reflex, he threw the truck into reverse and powered backwards, coming to a screeching halt just short of hitting a wall. The truck was too big to drive up the ramp, He'd have to get out and make a run for it.

Three of the big trucks ground gears into reverse and slammed his truck up against the freeway wall with their battering rams. The front and left sides of the truck crumpled. He threw himself across the passenger seat, flung the door open, jumped out and ran for the ramp like he had never run before. Another truck headed right for him. He reached the narrow ramp and kept running up as the truck tried to follow him but then rolled backward. People yelled from the street above him. He felt a small flicker of hope until he saw three more bodies dangling from the railing, hung by their necks. Men waited for him with bats in their hands. This would be an ambush, not a welcoming party. Then he noticed something else – his VW van, idling near the railing. *Damn it, Evelyn. I told you to go to the warehouse.* He accelerated into a sprint with the last of his strength, trying to get to the van before the lynch mob caught him.

****

Willet and Arhat watched in amazement as the Chucker right in front of them backed out of the line and veered sideways, leaving a large gap in the line of trucks.

"That truck just gave us an exit!" Arhat exclaimed. "It is our chance." He shifted and slammed on the gas. The SUV bolted through the opening before any of the other big trucks reacted. Once clear, he put distance between them and the truck lines and then skidded to a halt.

"Arhat, we have to help that man! He's running toward the ramp. Those men will hang him!"

Arhat spun the SUV around in a tight circle, drove through a gap in the center divider to the east bound lanes, and raced up the next off ramp. He took the overpass and sped back to where the man would emerge when he reached the top of the ramp. Willet popped out of body above the SUV again. Did that man intend to save their lives? She had to know who he was. In the next moment, she was floating, watching the man run for his life up the ramp. He seemed familiar. Something about his sandy blonde hair, long limbs and strong energy. Memories bubbled up of a morning at the beach and a smile so sexy it seared her skin. Memories would have to wait. She watched helplessly as the man ran straight towards the rabid mob. *What is he doing? I have to help him!*

Willet was suddenly floating among the bat-wielding men at the top of the ramp. The sandy-haired guy was still running for all he was worth. *He'll try to barrel through this mob. He won't make it.* In her out of body state, she could confuse people. She gave one bat-wielding maniac a psychic slap to the forehead and jabbed her fingers into the eyes of another man. The men lost their balance and stumbled into each other, knocking other men aside. In the confusion, the blonde guy broke through the mob and made a dash toward a van idling nearby. He swung a door open, jumped inside and slammed the door behind him. The mob swarmed the van with bats raised, ready to smash windows, but the van peeled away, knocking the mob back to the curb.

Arhat drove up, and she dropped into the SUV with a feeling of unbearable anxiety. "Please follow that van," she said. "Please. I have to find him."

****

"Are you crazy?" TJ yelled at Evelyn as she sped away, leaving a patch of smoking rubber. "Those guys would have killed you! I told you to go to the warehouse. It's too dangerous here!"

Diggie was wide awake now. He wrapped his thin arms around TJ's neck from the back seat and leaned his forehead against TJ's hair.

Evelyn didn't answer until they were some distance from the freeway. "You were in trouble, Tom," she said firmly. "I could see what was happening from the street. After all you've done for us, I couldn't just leave you."

"That was foolish, Evelyn," TJ grumbled. "Those men would not have hesitated to pull you out of the van, Diggie too. If anything had happened …" His voice trailed off and he shook his head.

"It's best we stay together," she said, seeming cheered by the prospect. "We can go to your warehouse now. I'm not good with directions. I never would have found it by myself."

CHAPTER 10

Arhat and Willet followed the VW van through the streets of West Covina. The van entered a light industrial area of offices, warehouses and truck rental lots, and came to a stop in front of a garage at one of the warehouses. TJ got out of the van and punched some numbers on a keypad beside the garage door. The door rolled up. He waved Evelyn into the garage and walked in after the van pulled in.

Arhat parked the SUV a short block away. “I have to talk to him, thank him for helping us,” Willet said, and climbed out of the SUV on her own. Her Soul body hovered above her head and road her shoulders like a double-decker bus. It took a few moments to get her balance using the two-level perspective, and then she walked on without a backward glance. She entered the open garage and found TJ standing with a woman and a boy. The woman was pale and thin in a blue cotton housedress which brought out her blue eyes and curly red hair. The boy had brown hair and wide hazel eyes with a gangly frame. He looked about ten. His scruffy t-shirt and jeans hung on him. They all turned and stared at her.

“You were on the hood of the SUV,” TJ said. “How did you get here?”

“I took a cab.”

The red-haired woman looked from TJ to Willet and back again. Her hands twisted the front of her blue dress into bunches. "Tom," she said finally. "Who is this woman? She was in the Wall, wasn't she? What is she doing here?"

The woman's questions irritated her. "Yeah, *Tom,*" Willet said sharply. "You left me in the Wall. Who am I? Who is she?"

"A woman who looked like her was in the Wall. I thought she wasn't who she appeared to be," TJ said. He squinted at Willet, walked to her and looked her up and down. "You're split in two. What's wrong with your eyes?"

"I'm blind, genius," she said. "I'm using nonphysical senses."

"No," he said, shaking his head. "No. That can't be it."

She glared at him with fists curled at her sides. "Don't tell me what it can't be. We were both in the Wall and you walked out, remember? The Needle Men stuck me like a pin cushion, including my eyes. I was blinded by needles, no help from you."

He glared back. "I'm full of needles too. You don't look so bad, other than the blindness thing."

"The body needles went away after a while, but I'm still blind, so excuse me."

His eyes narrowed. "How?"

"How what?"

"How did the needles go away?"

Willet had to think about it. "Don't know exactly. I sang my chant word and they melted. At least that's what it felt like."

His gaze on her was intense. "What word *exactly*?"

"The word…. The one she told us, that woman…" The woman's name and the exact word eluded her at that moment.

"Yeah, I remember that woman. She's evil." TJ slid the sleeve of his shirt up and held out his arm. "It's all because of her. These things stab me every time I move."

Willet could see the needles pulsing in his flesh. A swollen red aura covered his skin like a deep sunburn. "It looks painful," she admitted.

"Quite a bit," he said with a snort. "How did you escape that place?"

"Arhat, he's a cab driver, he pulled me out and drove me away in his cab. He brought me here. He's waiting outside, so I have to go tell him what I'm doing."

TJ continued his intent study of her face. "What *are* you doing?"

The woman behind TJ cleared her throat loudly and tapped her foot. "You two are beginning to annoy me. What's going on between you?"

TJ turned to the red-haired woman. "I'm sorry. I should introduce you. This is Evelyn and her son, Diggie," he said. "They helped me escape the Wall. I wouldn't have made it without them. Evelyn, Diggie, this is Willet."

"My name is Jonah," the boy informed them. "I remembered when I was sleeping in the van."

Evelyn stepped between Jonah and Willet with a stern expression. "What are your intentions? Why are you here?"

"I came to see him because he saved my life. Now I just want to punch him."

"Well thank him or punch him. Then you can get lost. We have things to do."

"Whoa there, Evelyn, calm down," TJ said. He stepped back from Willet and put a hand on Evelyn's shoulder. "What's with the hostility?"

"We need a safe place for my boy," Evelyn snapped. "You promised to protect him. We're wasting time."

"And I will protect him, to the best of my ability. What's the problem?"

Evelyn gave a derisive snort, stalked off to an open doorway into a separate room and slammed the door behind her.

"What are you doing here?" TJ said turning back to her. "You never said."

"I don't know." Willet tried to organize her thoughts enough to figure out what she was after in being there. "You left me in that horrible place. It hurt so much, I'm not sure I can ever forgive you. Then you risked your life to save me from the Chuckers. Why would you do that for someone you left for dead?"

TJ squeezed his eyes tight shut, opened them and gave her another searching look. "I didn't know it was you in the Wall, but now I do. I've thought of you, and I have memories of us, but pieces are missing, like someone rearranged the desk inside my head, and now I can't find anything. Please tell me your name."

"Willet," she said softly. "I'm Willet."

"Willet. Yes." He breathed as if inhaling the name into his lungs.

"How could you do that to me?"

"What happened in the Wall is a blur, except for a lot of pain. I wasn't sure what was real, and all I wanted to do was get out. I thought you were wax. I'm sorry. It would have been wrong to leave a living person in there. The needles drove me crazy, and I couldn't think straight."

He looked at her helplessly. She almost felt sorry for him. "Thomas," she said when the name came to her tongue. "You told me you didn't need me because you had a 'flock', like a parish priest. Are Evelyn and Jonah your flock?"

"I don't remember that at all. If I said it, I was delusional. But I can picture long blonde hair on my pillow and blue eyes smiling at me across a breakfast table. I know it's you." He moved closer and took her hand in his, pulled her closer and studied the ephemeral form riding on her shoulders. His gaze returned to her face. He leaned in and kissed her on the cheek.

"No," she said pulling back, pushing him away. "You betrayed me. You left me."

"I wasn't my true self. Let me make it up to you." Those sea-green eyes that she loved stared into hers. He pulled her to him again, kissed her forehead and then his lips lingered on hers. The softness of his kiss felt so tender, her heartbeat stuttered. Her Soul body merged into her physical body, and the darkness of her physical vision cleared.

He stroked the space between her eyebrows with his index finger. "Willet", he said. "Yes, that's it. It's you. I remember now."

She drank in the details of his face as if her memory were parched. Fragments of images overwhelmed her like so many shards of a broken mirror. "Thomas," she said. "What are we doing here? I don't remember why we came."

He hugged her closer. "I'm not sure, babe, but we'll figure it out. The memories will come back if we search for them." He glanced down at the boy who stood near them. "And you're Jonah, huh? It suits you. This is Willet, Jonah," he said. She'll be staying with us from now on."

Jonah shifted his feet back and forth. "Mom's pissed. I don't think she'll like it, no offense to Willet. She seems nice."

"We'll have to show your mother that I'll still protect you. Willet can help too."

Willet excused herself and went out the garage door to let Arhat know she planned to stay, but the SUV was gone.

****

Richard Theese had trouble sleeping after his stroke. Visions of his son carrying two children through a hail of bullets plagued him. Jimmy had fallen into a trench, bleeding from multiple wounds, still clutching the children to his chest when he died. Reports from the army tore his father's heart to shreds every time he thought of them. He suffered the loss of his son over and over. And then there was the so-called Guardian who haunted his dreams. Last night, she stood at the foot of his bed, challenging him, saying things he didn't want to hear. He woke up in a cold sweat, and remembered he'd never walk again. It was like waking from a nightmare of hell and realizing he now lived in hell.

"Graciela!" Theese shouted. *Where is that woman?*

Graciela Metucha, his nurse-assistant, rushed into his room. His memory was blurry on exactly how she came to be in his employ. She was at the hospital after his stroke, started fluffing his pillows and wheeling him around, telling him what to do. Most annoying, but he needed her for almost everything. When he was discharged, she brought him home and never left.

"Wha', Meester Teese? Is there a creesis?" Graciela was five-foot two-inches tall, Filipino, with thick brown hair in a ponytail and an air of bustling energy. She knew English well enough but spoke it with a strong accent. The faster she spoke, the thicker her accent became. Most importantly, she could lift him into and out of his wheelchair, which amazed him. He had lost a lot of weight after the stroke, but he was still a big guy. The strength in her arms was impressive.

“No, not a crisis. We’re going out,” he announced. “I want to go to the studio.” Theese hadn’t been to the radio studio since the stroke. For some reason, he felt a strong urge to go now. He depended on Graciela to transport him in the van. She also cooked his meals, nagged him about his medications and assisted him with bathing, which embarrassed him no end.

“My fans probably wonder where I am and why I’ve been off the air,” he said. “I need to correct certain misunderstandings in my previous broadcasts.”

“Radio can wait,” she said as she helped him slide off the bed into the wheelchair. “First, you eat something. You lose too much weight.”

“Don’t fuss, woman. You’re not my mother, lord help us.”

“Lord, help us, yes,” she replied as she wrapped a blanket around his legs. “Especially you.”

Graciela wheeled him into the bathroom to the sink, and then withdrew, closing the door. He peered at his face in the mirror and shook his head slightly. *When did I get jowls? I’m starting to look like a basset hound.* He had always prided himself on his intimidating height, broad shoulders and muscled arms. His face had been pleasing enough. Now he saw a pot-bellied old man with thinning hair, gray stubble chin and useless legs. The night before, he had prayed for death to take him, begged for release from the prison of his immobility. The only response he got was an ocean of silence, and then SHE appeared at the foot of his bed.

“What do you want to do?” the Guardian asked him. Her voice echoed, as if she were in a cave.

He pulled himself up to a sitting position. “What am I supposed to do? My legs are paralyzed!”

“You still have brains, hands, a beating heart, and a big mouth. How will you use them?”

“If you don’t have anything better to offer than a lame pep talk, then get lost.”

“You chose life, so I am here to help you,” she replied. “There are lessons to learn, such as cause and effect. We experience what we set in motion.”

Theese groaned. *Why me?* “You’re a moralizing pain in the ass, ya know that?”

“Your opinion of me is of no concern. It will not help you.”

“I realize some of my actions may not have turned out well, but I had good intentions.”

“You shot me in the head and threatened my friends. What were your intentions then?”

Theese fumbled with his sheets. “There was a voice… said it was my duty.”

“You shot yourself in the throat with your own gun. Did the voice tell you to do that?”

A galling memory of the moment blazed across his mind's eye. "The damned dog made me do it," he growled. "Hit my arm, deflected my gun hand."

"You raised the gun in anger and fired it to do harm. What you set in motion came back to you. That is cause and effect. Neither Dora nor anyone else is to blame."

"The voice told me I was the only one who could kill a dangerous witch! I had to do it!"

Gem sighed and shook her head. "I am not a witch, Mr. Theese, despite your insistence on it. I am a being of soul and body, just as you are. Murder carries a heavy karmic debt. You are paying it now."

"Ok, I made a mistake, though you don't look much the worse for wear. Can I donate to a charity or something?"

"Money will not settle your debts. You promote anger and violence on the radio. A girl of seventeen is still undergoing skin grafts from an explosive that hit her during one of your rallies. A man beaten with a flagpole by one of your followers had his arm broken in three places. A woman and her infant almost died from smoke inhalation. Was that your duty?"

"Bad decisions made by others," he mumbled. "Not my fault."

"The people who listen to you do these things under your influence. Until you understand that you will make no progress."

Gem's image faded away from the foot of his bed as if she was never there, leaving him a lot of time to think. He thought all through the early morning until Graciela came to help him wash and dress and then bundled him into the van and drove him to the studio in East Hollywood. Taking the elevator up to the third floor, he fervently hoped no one else would get on with them. He didn't want to see those pitying looks people give when they see someone in a wheelchair. The picture he had of himself was pathetic enough. At his desk in the studio, he recovered some sense of his former confidence, but what should he say? Woman and infants getting hurt – he couldn't be responsible for that. He sat for several minutes, clearing the loose gravel in his throat and spitting into the trusty bucket under the desk. He stared at the microphone for several minutes before turning it on.

"I'm back, folks, your old friend Richard Theese. I know we have a rally coming up tomorrow. We have every right to express our views in a free country, but let's keep it civil. No one should get hurt, no matter what side they're on. Obey the law, don't use explosives, and no fights."

Graciela gave him a smile and a nod. He had noticed lately how rosy her cheeks were. Warm brown eyes… He shook himself and continued. "Be especially careful around children. We don't want any children hurt. This is Richard Theese."

He sat back and switched off the mike, feeling very unsure of himself. Was that enough to make amends? Would the Guardian ask more of him? Graciela of the rosy cheeks and chocolate brown eyes approached him with a cup of water.

"I told you, don't fuss, woman," he said, taking the cup from her and chugging the water down. He didn't realize how thirsty he was.

"It is my job to fuss," she said, patting his shoulder. "You make a good speech."

“Hrmph,” he grunted. “My fans will think I’ve turned into a wimp.”

CHAPTER 11

Bart agreed to work with Dean on a mission to test the effects of the crystal on the static of the eastern Wall of Unknowing. Bart had twenty-five one-gallon burlap bags of crystal scraps in the shed behind his lab. They hoisted the bags into the flatbed of Bart’s dusty Ford truck, climbed into the cab, and headed east, planning to introduce the Wall to the crystal and observe the reaction. If the crystal had no effect, then there was no point counting on it as a deterrent in the future. Conditions on the streets had gotten worse since the last time Dean drove through them. Many stores were closed and boarded up. There was little car traffic, unusual for a workday. People on the sidewalks shuffled slowly, almost stooped over. The dull gray sky felt heavy and oppressive.

“It was sunny at my place,” Bart said. “What happened?”

“You don’t get out much, do you?” Dean replied. “This is the new L.A. Depressing and dangerous. Your property is an anomaly, I think because of all the crystal.”

“You think? Of course, it is.”

Dean turned on the radio, and the rough voice of Richard Theese came through the speakers. Dean was about to turn him off, but something was different. There was a distinct change in tone. Theese sounded less combative. He used words like ‘calm’ and ‘civil’. Instead of ‘losers’ and ‘foreigners’, he referred to people as ‘those of different backgrounds and opinions.’ He called for lawful conduct at demonstrations. It was a complete one-eighty.

“What happened to this guy?” Dean murmured. “He used to be a real ass.” He scanned for other stations, found none, and finally switched it off.

The subject of conversation inevitably turned to Audrey. She had remained safely behind at the crystal fields and was not happy about it. “So how long have you known Audrey, Deano?” Bart asked in an off-hand tone. “A long time?”

“I did some work on her house last summer. That’s how we met.”

Bart nodded. “Not that long, then.”

“What we lack in duration, we make up for in intensity.”

“Sure. So, are you two tight, like committed? Or is it a casual thing?”

“There’s nothing casual about me and Audrey. We’ve been through too much together.”

“Yeah, I’d like to understand that because, ya know, Audrey and I had a pretty intense beginning too. She must have told you how I pulled her out from TJ’s club before we were both asphyxiated by smoke and burned to a crisp.”

“Yes, Bart,” Dean said patiently. “She did tell me. What’s your point?”

"I don't want to step on any toes here, but I think Audrey is pretty special."

"She's certainly that."

"Right? I mean I'd like to see her, regularly that is, if she's not otherwise entangled."

Dean could barely suppress his exasperation. "Do we have to discuss this *now*? There are pressing issues to deal with, like saving this city! If we don't figure out how to stop the Wall, no one will be seeing anyone!"

Bart stared straight ahead with a far-away look in his eyes. "I've thought about Audrey a lot lately. A lot."

"Okay, let me clear this up for you," Dean said. "Audrey and I are definitely 'entangled'. Our relationship hasn't been typical, due to all the insanity we've had to deal with. If the world ever gets back to normal, Audrey and I have plans to take it to the next level."

"So, it's every man for himself," Bart said. "Fine, I can compete."

Bart refused to hear what Dean was telling him, and Dean couldn't blame him. There was no way Bart could imagine the things he and Audrey had been through together - their escape from the mountains, the battle with Jat, and the flight through space hanging on to light rings that *she* created. Those events would confound even the most open mind. Then there was the threat of the Wall. Bart still didn't take that seriously. He didn't appreciate what they were up against – an aberration from the Underworld of monster proportions – and he needed to understand it. So, Dean began to tell the story slowly, glossing over many details about the Circle of Augustus and its fight against the crystal. Dean skipped the part about his truck falling off a cliff and being saved from certain death by the Traveler. He also didn't mention Gem's return from the dead. How much could the guy be expected to accept?

Bart snorted and chuckled at first, stared at Dean, and then fell silent when Dean got to the part about TJ and Willet disappearing into the Wall, the screaming, and the skeletal forms lurking in the dark. "You're insane, you know that buddy?" he mumbled.

"You said that before," Dean said. "I wish it were that simple." He explained again about what the Wall could do if left unchecked. He wasn't sure Bart was really listening. The closer they got to the thing itself, the more Bart fidgeted. When they got as close as they safely could, Dean parked on a side street near a group of four small stucco houses sitting on squares of lawn. They both got out, grabbed bags of crystal chips and started walking toward the swirling mass of instability that was the Wall. When they got within three yards of it, sweat was rolling down Bart's forehead. He was paying attention now. The Wall extended north and south out of sight and rose into the sky until it disappeared from view. The static roiled like a storm cloud. Every tree, plant and shrub near it was dead.

"Holy Mother of…," Bart said under his breath. There was no more laughing.

The Wall looked different from the last time Dean saw it. Fuzzy tentacles of gray static floated off the surface, probing the air, making sparking noises like live wires. The air smelled of ozone. A tentacle darted out and wrapped around the trunk of a nearby tree with a flurry of white sparks. It spread over the tree like a fuzzy mold. The mass of the Wall followed the tentacle, spread out to the tree and swallowed it. So, that's how the Wall grew, taking ground foot by foot.

"What do we do?" Bart whispered as they stared at the spot where the tree had stood. "How do we stop it?"

"We'll throw a handful of chips at it and see what happens."

"Are you sure?" The anxiety in Bart's voice rose. "What if it gets mad and attacks us?"

"Then that would be good information to have. We'd run like hell."

A long tentacle shot out from the surface of the Wall at that moment, aimed straight at them. Dean pulled a handful of crystal from the bag and hurled the pieces at the tentacle, which recoiled into the Wall with a crackle of sparks. The Wall shrunk back from the pieces that landed on the ground next to it, ceding a few feet of ground. "That looks promising," he said. "If we spread it around, it might cause the thing to retreat. Oh no. Incoming… Get ready to throw some crystal."

A mangy yellow dog trotted down the sidewalk toward them, sniffing the ground, oblivious of any danger. A hungry tentacle sprang out of the Wall, heading for the animal. Dean shoved his bag of chips into Bart's chest. Without waiting for a reply, he took off down the sidewalk toward the dog, making soothing noises as he went. The dog stopped in his tracks, and the tentacle of static paused just a second. It struck at the dog just as Dean reached him. When Dean pulled the dog away, the tentacle wrapped around Dean's waist. Bart ran toward them and threw a fistful of crystal. The tentacle snapped back like a rubber band.

"Ya-ha!" Bart exclaimed, but the tentacle changed course and shot out at *him*, too quickly to avoid. It wrapped around his neck and sparked wildly. Bart dropped the bags, fell to his knees and shrieked, trying to rip free of it, but there was nothing in the static to hold on to. Dean let go of the dog, grabbed two fists full of crystal and threw them into the air over Bart. As the chips fell, they cut through the tentacle, leaving floating fragments of static that snuffed out.

Dean pulled Bart to his feet. “Run!” They grabbed the bags and peeled down the street, tossing chips over their shoulders as they went. The dog ran ahead of them. They turned a corner, around a hedge, and didn’t stop running until they got to the truck. The dog kept going and disappeared down the next street.

“That was close. Are you okay?” Dean asked as he leaned over to catch his heaving breath.

Bart wheezed and gasped. His body seemed close to convulsing. He rubbed his hands over his neck. “I felt an electrical burn,” he said. “It could have electrocuted me.”

“You have to remember,” Dean said. “A lot of what you experience in these situations is not of the physical world. It feels real as hell but doesn’t do actual physical damage.”

Bart slowly recovered his wind. “Well, thanks for the reassurance, but it was real enough for me. I don’t want to be in anymore ‘situations’. We got the info you wanted. Let’s go.”

Dean jumped in the passenger seat, and Bart climbed into the driver side. He tried to put the key in the ignition, but his hand shook so hard the key rattled. Dean laid a hand on his arm. “I know it’s unsettling. Once you’ve seen it, you can’t un-see it.”

Bart’s voice rose to a squeak. “Unsettling? That’s what you call it?” He shrugged his arm away but pulled the key away from the ignition and leaned back in his seat. “What are we supposed to do against a thing like that?” he said. “This is so screwed up.”

Dean nodded. "Well and truly screwed, but of all the people in L.A. you are the one person that can actually do something about it. You grow the crystal. Now we know the Wall is repelled by it. We need to grow it and spread it as much as possible in the path of the Wall."

Bart folded his arms across his chest and looked straight ahead. "I don't want to be involved. I'm going home before one of those things grabs me and doesn't let go."

"You're already involved. All you can do now is fight or go down with the ship. The Wall will cover all of Los Angeles eventually. It will reduce the city to a suburb of hell. Believe me, I just wanted to forget when I first started seeing stuff like this, but it's impossible. Besides, you owe me for saving you from that octopus arm thing."

"Gee thanks," Bart said with a grimace. "I saved you too, and that mutt didn't even wait around to thank us. So, what now?"

"We have twenty-three bags of crystal in the truck, and we've seen the effect it has. I say we spread it around where it could do some good. These houses are in the path of danger. Let's start by protecting them."

They carried bags of crystal over to the houses and got to work, kneeling in the dirt and spreading a perimeter of crystal chips around the square of each small house. Engrossed, they didn't notice a bald man in a gray T-shirt and jeans standing near them until they heard a gun cock. He was pointing a rifle at their heads. That would be disconcerting enough, but the man looked abnormal. His skin stretched tight over his head and across his face, showing the contours of his skull. His eyes bulged, and his body was emaciated. His arms shook holding the gun, as if it were too heavy for him.

"What you do there?" he demanded in a dry, cracked voice.

A young girl about eight years old stood a few feet behind him. Dressed in faded yellow shorts and shirt, she had the same stretched skin, protruding eyes, and skeletal limbs as the man. Tufts of blonde hair sprouted out of her scalp in uneven patches.

"Tess, get in the house," the man said. Tess just stood there and chewed her thumb.

"We're trying to help you and your family," Bart said, slowly raising his hand to show a couple of crystal chips in his palm. "This crystal will protect you from the Wall."

The man shifted his feet. "What wall you talkin' about?"

Bart pointed over the man's shoulder, but the man didn't turn. "We don' look there," he said sharply. "No point in it."

It didn't take a genius to figure out that proximity to the Wall had been unhealthy for this man and his daughter. Mentally and physically, they were deteriorating. Dean held out a few pieces as Bart did. "These are for you."

The man's eyes darted between Dean's face and his hand. Finally, he let go the rifle with his right hand, tucked it under his left arm, and snatched the crystal off Dean's palm. He peered at the pieces, sniffed them and licked them. Then he smiled a ghoulish smile, showing gums so receded that the roots of his teeth were completely exposed. "More," he said.

The man helped himself to the pieces Bart offered and squeezed them in his hand. He closed his eyes and took a long breath. After a minute, he opened his eyes and re-shouldered his rifle. "I want," he said, nodding at the bag on the ground. A flush of blood flow warmed the color of his face from gray to light pink.

"OK," Dean said. He put another handful of chips on the ground and gestured toward them. "They're all yours. They grow like seeds. You can plant them."

The man succumbed to the lure of the crystal and stooped to pick up the pieces. Dean and Bart rose to their feet and backed away. "We're leaving now." They turned tail and ran. In a few seconds, they heard a gunshot, then another. They zigzagged across the lawn and headed for the street. Fortunately, the man was a poor shot. They made it to the corner and turned out of the line of fire. For the second time that morning they fled to the safety of the truck and piled in.

"The Wall is draining those people, sucking the wits and life energy out of them," Dean said when he caught his breath again. "That's what will happen to everyone. The crystal can help."

Bart chewed his lower lip, eyes darting left and right. "You're making a lot of assumptions, Simmons. I can't ignore your point, but I saw how long the Wall is, how high it is. I don't have enough crystal to stop that thing."

"We have to figure out a way to grow more, spray it into the Wall on a large scale and really spread it around. Ignoring it is not an option."

A hiss came from behind them, so loud they both spun around to see what it was. The Wall had moved to within ten yards of the truck in the time it took to blink. Tentacles of static extended out, reaching for something to grab, and sparks flew.

"Drive," Dean yelled. "I'll try to hold it off."

Dean swung out the passenger door and jumped into the flatbed. There were five bags of crystal left. He ripped one open, grabbed a handful of chips and threw them as hard as he could at the Wall. He kept throwing until the bag was empty, and then he ripped into another one. The truck lurched forward, and he fell on his face.

****

Bart couldn't see Dean in the rearview mirror anymore but was afraid to slow down. He swerved onto side streets, taking evasive action, and gained a little distance, but the Wall was still in view. *I can't just leave him. Audrey would never forgive me.*

Cursing under his breath, he swung the truck around in a strip mall parking lot and headed back the way he came, keeping one eye on the Wall ahead and the other eye on the streets looking for Dean's body. Could he grab Dean and outrun the Wall if he drove fast enough? He heard a loud knocking noise, took another look through the back window, and then screeched to a halt.

Dean was lying in the truck bed with his fingers wrapped in a cargo net, stomping his feet on the metal floor. When the truck stopped, he scrambled back into the passenger seat and grabbed the seat belt. "What the hell are you doing?" Dean yelled. "You're driving right toward it!"

"I thought you fell out! Did you want me to just leave you?"

"Talk later! Go already!"

The Wall was five yards behind them. Bart jammed the gas pedal to the floor. The truck lurched forward and then stalled. "What the hell," Bart swore between his teeth and tried the ignition. The truck started up and stalled again.

Dean climbed up on the seat and looked through the back window. Tentacles of static brushed over the back of the truck like nervous fingers, looking for someone to grab. One long tentacle had latched onto the tow hitch. The truck wasn't going anywhere. "It's got us," he said. "Damn."

"Is there any crystal left?"

"Two bags in the cargo net. Can you handle things here?"

Bart eyed Dean with mixed apprehension and respect. "That thing could grab you, man."

"Got any other ideas?" Dean said as he opened the passenger door.

Bart shook his head. He couldn't think of a thing.

"If you feel it let loose, gun the engine and drive. Don't look back." Dean climbed out and swung himself into the truck bed to face the Wall.

CHAPTER 12

Sonrisa and Gem sat on a bench in Griffith Park with the ever-vigilant Dora, Hound of Hell, sitting at their feet. The newly forming Wall in the west swirled. It already obscured the view of the ocean. There would be no more golden sunsets in L.A. The air felt dead under the leaden gray sky, like a tarp had been thrown over the city. Starry nights were over too.

They looked out over the L.A. Basin toward the Dragon Head Building, watching for signs of Underworld disturbance. The dark structure towered over every other building on the L.A. skyline, ninety stories high and topped by a ten-story statue. A building like that could not simply materialize out of thin air without serious power behind it. They had no doubt about the source – Jat the Deceiver. Now it was a matter of confronting that power and finding out what his plans were.

Sonrisa folded the here and there of space-time until they touched and then moved Gem and Dora from the park to the top of the building. They stepped onto the flat roof at the foot of a massive black marble statue of a human figure with a dragon's head. The figure sat on an enormous gray granite chair. Big, blunt hands and claw-tipped fingers draped over the long armrests. The figure wore a black marble morning jacket and striped pants crafted in alternating shades of black and gray marble. Clawed feet extended out of the pants were planted flat on the roof. The Dragon Head Man stared impassively toward the ocean. Dora growled and showed her teeth.

Gem looked into the statue's slit eyes. No consciousness there, just a blank stare, but that didn't mean anything. Jat the Deceiver could animate any form. "I think we have found Jat's seat of power, but what will he do with it is the question. How did it come to exist in the physical world? We must find out what is inside this building."

Sonrisa brought them back to street level. They entered the building in the conventional way through glass double doors leading into a lobby of chrome and mirrors. The building directory had only one listing - Matthew Gregg and Associates, on the eighty-ninth floor. Guardian, Traveler and Hound entered an elevator and pressed the button, stopping at various levels to see what was on them. Every floor was under construction, just wooden framing with bare concrete floors. Drills whirled and hammers pounded somewhere out of sight. Sawdust floated in the air. At the eighty-ninth floor, they stepped out of the elevator into a large space with finished walls. A metal desk occupied the middle of the room, the only furniture. In the far wall, a long bank of windows looked out over the city. Wires hung from open panels in the ceiling. A ladder and saw-horse stood underneath. Torn plastic, nails, and cut wire littered the floor.

"The spaces inside this building are in flux, Guardian," Sonrisa murmured to Gem. "Neither fully physical nor fully nonphysical. It is in the process of becoming."

Matthew Gregg stood in front of the desk in an expensive-looking gray silk suit, black button-down shirt and shiny, gray silk tie. His brown hair, oiled and slicked back off his forehead, gave him the look of a mob boss. Behind the desk, seven large men in the same understated, expensive suits stood impassively in a half-circle with hands behind their backs.

"Here you are," he said, looking over the two women and dog standing before him. His smile was almost sweet, but his eyes glittered, and a forked tongue flickered between his lips. "The

Guardian, as expected. Who is this enchanting woman you have brought with you?"

Sonrisa's gaze remained steady. "I ensure the Guardian travels at will. She cannot be constrained or captured."

"Really." Matt Gregg looked at Dora. "And a dog," he said sourly. "How – nice."

"Mr. Gregg," Gem said. "You have changed since we first met."

"Oh? Why do you say that?"

She stepped closer and studied his features. "You resemble a snake."

A surprised grin spread across his face, and fangs peeked out below his upper lip. "I consider that a compliment," he said.

"Then you have spent too much time with the Deceiver. What did he promise you?"

He laughed lightly and straightened his tie. "I will have justice. Your little Circle-pet, Thomas J. Barlow, will be in my hands and at my mercy."

"But why? Thomas Barlow was your friend."

"He owes me for the injuries he inflicted, the embarrassments to which he subjected me, in my home, in front of a woman no less. He will pay."

"Do you really want to pay the karmic cost for revenge?"

A shudder ran through his body and twisted his face into a mask of rage. "I have already paid!" His voice echoed around the bare walls. "I'm the victim here!" The ugly look melted away. "*I* will be the new Guardian of the Gate, by the way," he continued sedately. "Your services are no longer required."

"That is not Jat's decision to make, or yours," Gem said. "The assignment comes from above the Fifth Plane."

"And how miserably you've failed in your duties," he snapped "The Gate has been breached, *again*, and your Circle is scattered to the winds. They barely remember their own names. This land belongs to the Dragon now, and I will be his right hand."

"Jat dangles power like raw meat in front of those who are hungry. He does not share it."

"If you think I'm the Dragon Lord's dog, you underestimate me." His lips stretched to show off his teeth, and his jaws snapped. "Your version of truth no longer applies in this city," he said with a dry hiss. "It is cliché. The people have forgotten."

"One person's cliché is revelation to another."

Matt Gregg raised his hands to the front of his chest and spread them apart, palms facing each other. A grid of sparking red light rays ran from palm to palm. He stretched and bent them like a child's game of cat's cradle. A high-pitched whine hummed between his hands. "How's this for revelation?" he said. "Do you hear it? The Scourge Wind, a magnetic wave that I control. I can sweep it across Los Angeles and pull every metal object for miles to my feet. Barlow's a human pin cushion these days, isn't he? I'll drag him through the streets." He turned his hands out toward the room. The ladder tipped over and skidded across the floor. Metal pieces swirled up off the floor, flew like bullets and hit his palms. He winced slightly as blood beaded on his skin. "Flying metal leaves nasty cuts," he hissed. "If you turn Barlow over to me now, I will beat *him* bloody, but I will spare this city the blood scourge of a metal storm."

The suggestion that the Guardian would ever hand over a member of her Circle to a puppet of the Deceiver got a reaction. The light in Gem's eyes froze diamond bright. Ice hovered on her breath and her nostrils steamed. Matt Gregg's smug expression faltered under her cold stare. He motioned to the men behind the desk. They moved quickly to the front to flank their boss on both sides clenching ham-sized fists, ready for action.

Dora leaped in front of Gem. Her body exploded to three times her normal size. A thundering growl rumbled in her massive chest, rattling the windows. Her teeth extended into four-inch daggers dripping saliva. The heavies stopped short and back-pedaled until they hit the desk.

Gem did not play power games. It was her duty to 'guide and guard', as Augustus always told her, not to punish anyone, but these men were in thrall to the negative power of the Deceiver. Dark passions riddled their lower bodies. They would cause harm without hesitation or remorse. Only a deep freeze of their emotions would stop them. It was one of the Guardian's most potent abilities. The air in her lungs grew frigid. She let it build until it exploded from her mouth with the force of a hurricane. Windows rattled and cracked. A blizzard of ice and snow followed the wind and swirled through the air. Matt Gregg's thugs went flying, crashed into the back wall of the room and disappeared into thick snow drifts that had accumulated there. No one got up.

Matt Gregg slid backward on his behind across the top of his desk into a pile of snow that collapsed on top of him. His muffled voice came from inside the pile. “You’re finished as Guardian.”

“I am a long way from finished, Mr. Gregg,” Gem said, wiping snow off her nose. She blew a stream of cold breath across the snow drifts and froze them solid. It would be a while, measured in years, before Matthew Gregg and his Associates escaped the ice. They’d have time to think about their life choices. When they emerged, they would have a chance to resume their lives with clearer heads.

Dora shrunk to normal size and licked delicately at the snowflakes on her paws.

Gem raised her eyes toward the roof where she knew the Deceiver sat on his chair, listening. “This building is an aberration in the physical world,” she called out. “It cannot be allowed to exist. The Circle of Augustus will see that it falls.”

Sonrisa swept her hands apart and opened a fold in space-time. Gem stepped backward into it, called Dora, and the fold slid shut in front of them. It was time to gather the Circle.

****

While Dean and Bart were off confronting the Wall like medieval knights challenging a dragon, Audrey paced at the edge of Bart’s crystal fields, fuming. She was left behind to twiddle her thumbs like the fragile damsel in a tower, and she didn’t like it. All the visitors had departed, and the office closed. The eerie quiet unsettled her, and she felt both attracted and repelled by the crystal. The mounded rows of it pulsed with energy at her feet. Light reflected from a billion facets and prismed into rainbow colors. There was a faint ringing sound she hadn’t noticed before. She was drawn to touch the sparkling stuff but was afraid to do so. The purity of the light proved too enticing to resist. She stepped into the field, crouched down and laid her palms over the crystal mounds to feel their energy. A warm current streamed up her arms. Her head swam. She pulled her palms away and stood swaying on her feet. Then she yanked off her shoes and socks and pressed her bare feet against the crystal. The soles of her feet tingled. Energy surged up her legs, causing every nerve and muscle fiber to vibrate. It felt like liquid sunshine flowing in her bones and blood. Energy rushed to her brain. It was so overwhelming, she had to hop out of the field onto the dirt path and catch her breath, but separation from the energy flow left her feeling deflated and sad. She brushed one hand lightly across a mound of crystal and then the other to regain that wonderful feeling. When she pressed both palms down, it was too much. Dizzy, she stumbled backward.

Her inner vision flooded with images, and her ears buzzed. Vivid memories assembled from fragments, of Bart guiding her through a smoke-filled room to an open doorway, of Dean pulling her away from a pile of rock and crystal that was about to tip over on top of her. She remembered a heated kiss from soft lips pressed urgently to hers and strong arms pulling her against a hard chest. She ached for that kiss, wanted to bury her fingers in dark brown hair and surrender to those muscles, but *which man was it*? An image of Dean flashed in her mind's eye. He kissed her and said he wanted more, just before they jumped out of that flying pod to escape from the Underworld.. She had wanted more too, so very much, but now? What did she really want?

And then another memory – of Bart leaning in to kiss her as they sat on the couch at Pine Siskin House. He had seemed like a good-hearted geek, but he wasn't shy. His kiss exuded a sexual heat that surprised her. At the time, she thought she'd like to explore those hidden depths, see where they led. Was the opportunity lost? Two handsome heroes had saved her life. They both said they wanted her intimately. In simpler times, she might have been ecstatic over the possibilities, but so much had changed. She had changed. She craved something deeper now.

A staccato of loud crackles to the east made her head spin. It sounded like gunshot. Geysers of white light spewed out of the blurry darkness on the eastern horizon. Dean and Bart were in a fight now. A moment of panic split her conscious viewpoint in two, and she stepped away from her physical body into nonphysical consciousness. From that perspective, the crystal fields looked like an island of dazzling light surrounded by darkness. Churning gray clouds crashed against the borders of the light, unable to break through it. In the distance, the Wall was deep purple and seething. Spikes of lightning shot out in every direction. If Dean and Bart didn't see what she saw, they might have no idea how much danger they were in.

Her fingers got hot, and she looked at her hands. Small gold rings were spinning on every one of her fingers. That was familiar. She knew what to do. When she tapped her palms together to ease the stinging heat, the small rings melted into one larger ring, a foot wide. She spun the large ring on her right index finger. Instinct and memory took over. *I throw this ring before my hand burns. I'll need a clear shot at that monstrosity out there.* With that thought, her viewpoint expanded into a wide view of the Wall. She hurled the ring east like a discus with all the force she could put behind it. It flew to the horizon and disappeared into the Wall's billowing static. Another set of rings appeared on her fingers. She merged them into an even bigger ring and sent them flying. The Wall swallowed that ring and burped out a puff of gray smoke. Soon she was throwing rings from both hands as quickly as they formed on her fingers. The Wall hurled barbs of lightning at her in response, but they fell short, unable to pierce the island of light on which she stood. Ring Thrower and Wall traded shot after shot, projectiles of light and energy cutting through the air and turning the sky white in a clash of the lightning gods for those with the vision to see it.

****

Bart's truck was stalling every time he turned the ignition. A tentacle from the Wall had hold of the trailer hitch and wouldn't let go.

Tentacles slithered underneath the truck, latched on to the tailpipe and muffler, and lifted the back end off the ground. If the truck tilted up any further, it would flip forward and land upside down on the roof. From the truck bed, Dean opened one of the last bags of crystal and hurled a handful into the static. One long tentacle snaked out fast and grabbed him by the foot, yanked him hard, and dangled him in the air. Only his grip on the cargo net held him back from being dragged out of the truck. The net was bolted into the metal body of the truck. Eventually it would tear loose. Something had to give, and he hoped it wouldn't be the tendons in his ankle. Finally, the net did rip away. The tentacle holding Dean by the ankle began to reel him in. He closed his eyes and prepared to be swallowed by the mass of raging static. Something flew past his head, so close he could hear it whistle. The tentacle holding his ankle dropped him abruptly and snapped back. He slid across the truck bed on his stomach, tried to scramble to his feet, but got tangled in the net and clawed frantically to get free. Out of the corner of his eye, he saw a large gold ring spinning past him through the air. The Wall sizzled when the ring hit. The tentacle holding the tailpipe recoiled, and the truck dropped hard onto its back tires.

After that, energy rings flew in like a squadron of bombers and disappeared into the Wall's swirling darkness. Dean knew where the rings came from. Audrey had somehow rediscovered her mojo, but she had also revealed her location. The Deceiver's forces could find her now. He hoped she stayed at the crystal fields like he asked her to do. It was the safest place for her. Dean extricated himself from the net, tied it around one of the net hooks and looped the other end around his waist. He picked up the bag of crystal and started throwing handfuls at the Wall, which backed further and further and retracted the rest of its flailing tentacles. This was their best chance to escape. He slapped the back window and shouted at Bart, "Move it!" The engine groaned and turned over. This time it didn't stall. Bart slammed on the gas, the truck spun its wheels and lurched forward. Burning sparks spewed out of the tailpipe, and the truck sped away.

****

Audrey threw bigger and bigger rings until no more formed on her fingers. Her viewpoint shrunk down to normal, and she dropped back into her physical body, sobbing. *They still need help! I'll lie down and close my eyes. Just a minute. That's all I need.* Knees buckling, she slumped over and passed out.

****

Bart drove a hundred miles an hour, hitting every bump. At least that's what it felt like to Dean who was still in the back, watching the Wall recede and hanging on to the net so tightly his hands cramped. After many minutes of spinal impact, he pounded again on the back window. "Slow down a minute! Let me in." Bart slowed and stopped long enough for Dean to climb back into the cab. "Damn, I'm gonna need traction," Dean said. Sparks had burned holes in his shirt and peppered his arms with scorch marks.

Bart's face was white and his breath was ragged. He was in no mood for humor. "Did we lose that thing?" He kept looking into the rearview and over his shoulder through the back window as he sped down the road.

"Yes, we did, and we have Audrey to thank for that. If she hadn't thrown her rings, we would have been pulled into the Wall, truck and all."

Bart hit the steering wheel with his fists. "Just shut up," he said through gritted teeth. "I don't want to hear any more about rings or walls or any other bull. I'm done." He jammed the gas pedal to the floor and tore down the road.

Dean's head bounced against the back window. "Whoa, hyper down there," he said. "We don't need an accident now after what we just went through. Forget what I said. We do need to get back to your place and make sure Audrey's okay."

That got Bart's attention. "Why wouldn't she be okay?"

"It gets into the whole ring thing you don't wanna hear about. Let's just say she's made her presence known, and it could put her in danger from powers that be."

"If anyone hurts Audrey, I'll kill 'em," Bart growled as he barreled down the street, white-knuckled fingers twisting on the steering wheel. "Seriously, ready to kill."

"You're wound pretty tight, dude." Dean glanced out at the right side-view mirror. "Oh no."

"What, oh no?" Bart looked in the rear view. "Oh no."

The Wall was trailing them. Its surface churned in shades of black, deep purple and putrid green. *Like a bruise. It looks pissed.* Dean decided not to mention that thought to Bart.

CHAPTER 13

TJ was trying to get rid of the needles as Willet had done. He wrote 'HU' on the back of a white paper plate in large letters, sat in the chair at the warehouse office with eyes closed and sang the word over and over in a low voice. After almost an hour of quiet chanting, his head nodded to his chest. Willet found him asleep. There was no place to lie down in the office, but the van had a mattress in back. She gently pulled him to a standing position and helped him to the garage. He got in the van, lay down on the mattress, and mumbled something about 'just closing my eyes for a few minutes' before he fell into exhausted sleep.

She sat down next to him and started a chant of her own. The syllables chimed in her head, and her consciousness rose above her physical body. Her viewpoint slowly turned 360 degrees, and her higher senses came alive in the world between worlds. The air looked red-tinged. Something crackled above her head, and she looked up. Thomas was strung up like a marionette in a web of light beams. The beams held him in a rigid grip, electrocuting him. The needles in his body glowed hot, and his skin smoked.. His eyes were wide and mouth open in a silent scream.

The horror choked her. "Thomas!" she pleaded. "Thomas! How can I help you?" If he heard, he gave no sign. She dropped back into her physical body and bolted upright. *Oh no!* She looked around quickly and found TJ still slumbering on the mattress. The breath she held escaped her chest in a shuddering gasp. Cold sweat covered her skin. She wanted to shake him awake to make sure he was okay, but he seemed peaceful and oblivious. She took a few calming breaths and assessed her own situation. She needed to pee, and she wanted to clear the vision from her head. Trying not to disturb TJ, she climbed out of the van through the driver door and headed to the office to use the restroom.

Evelyn blocked her path through the office with arms crossed. "So," she said. "Did you get what you came here for?"

Willet stopped short. "What do you mean?"

"You want to get your hooks into Tom again, don't you? That's why you followed him, even though he left you for dead in the Wall. Can't take a hint, can you."

"I have no idea what you're talking about, Evelyn. Get out of my way, please."

"Tom has commitments now. He's committed to me and to my son. He has no time for you."

"Hate to break it to you, but you're not married to him," Willet said calmly. "I can see he cares about Jonah, maybe about you, too. Beyond that, you're delusional. He loves me."

Evelyn snorted. "In your mind, maybe. I've been traveling with him a while. He never talked about you, not once. What do you think about that?"

"The Wall is messing with our minds, making us forget things. Surely you see that."

"Yeah, I see a lot of things. Tom deserves a family who loves him. My son is the good in his life."

"He's helping you out, that's all." Willet had to get to the bathroom so urgently, her leg began to shake.

Evelyn's hands clenched, and her eyes narrowed. "Get over yourself. I've known women like you all my life. You think it's about you all the time, but things are different now."

Any goodwill Willet held toward Evelyn evaporated, and something cold seeped into her blood. "You don't know anything about me," she said. "Nothing at all."

Evelyn smiled. "I know you can't get by on a pretty face anymore, princess."

Willet was not one to sneer, but she had no trouble doing it now. "And you're a clingy bitch, Evelyn. Guys despise clingy bitches, ya know that? Especially Thomas. Now move it."

Willet pushed past her. Evelyn looked ready to throw a punch but then shrugged and let her pass. They bumped shoulders hard as Willet went by. Once inside the restroom, Willet locked the door and took care of business. She heard a scuffing sound in the office, and then a bump against the bathroom door. When she tried to turn the doorknob to get out, it jammed. She was locked in. "This is childish," Willet called through the door. "Let me out. You won't win any points with him this way." Minutes later, she heard the garage door roll up, the van start, and the next moment, she heard it pull out of the garage, turn into the alley and zoom away. Evelyn had taken off with TJ in the van. Willet kicked herself. *I'm such an idiot.*

The bathroom was small, with a white porcelain sink and toilet and a wire waste basket. There was no window. Willet pushed her shoulder against the door as hard as she could but couldn't budge it. She banged on the walls. She closed the toilet lid and climbed up to look through a small vent, couldn't see a thing, so she sat down, thought of Arhat and wondered why he left. *I can't just sit here.* She got up and pounded the wall again, called for help over and over, and then listened - no one was around to hear her.

Maybe I can kick a hole in the door. She boosted herself up on the sink, wedged her behind into the basin for leverage and started kicking at the door handle with her heel. *Damn. This thing is sturdy.* She kicked and pushed until her whole leg ached. Then she heard a car drive up and park. A car door opened and shut. Someone walked through the garage, and then into the office.

"Help," she called out, hitting the door with both fists. "I'm locked in the restroom. Please let me out!"

That someone walked to the door, jiggled the handle and pushed it open. Arhat stood there, holding a metal chair in his right hand.

"Miss Willet," he said with wide eyes. "How did you get in this predicament?"

She rushed out and threw her arms around his neck. "Thank you, thank you, I'm so glad to see you!" She stood back and gave him a narrow-eyed look. "Where have you been?"

"I went in search of gas," he said. "It is not so easy to find these days."

"Evelyn kidnapped Thomas. I don't know where they're going, and I don't trust her. She's not in her right mind. I have to go after him."

"That is unfortunate. Do you know where they went?"

"I don't, but when Thomas wakes up, I'm sure he'll be angry enough for a serious confrontation. I hope Jonah doesn't get caught in the middle."

At that point, Willet took a good look at Arhat. It was the first time she'd seen him since her physical sight returned. He didn't appear the same as she remembered him from their first meeting. His eyes and skin were clear, his clothes clean. He smelled faintly of sage. His teeth were even and white when he smiled. Was this another case of her memory slipping? If so, she was really losing it.

"You're looking well," she said, hoping that was not too personal.

He studied her too. "Your vision has improved."

"Yeah, I don't know how or why, but it happened when I found Thomas."

"Then it was good for you to come."

"Yes, but Evelyn wants him, and she's desperate. We have to find him before she does something stupid and risks both their lives."

CHAPTER 14

"Mr. Theese. Richard. Hear me."

Theese buried his head under a pillow, but he could still hear Gem's voice. "Whadya want?" he said, clinging to sleep.

"You have a service to perform. It is part of your lessons."

"What service?" he mumbled with eyes closed. "What lesson?"

"You must broadcast a message on your radio station to the Circle of Augustus."

Sleep was slipping away. He reached an arm out to the lamp on the bedside table, switched it on, and groaned. "Can't you just pop in on them the way you do to me? Am *I* the only one plagued this way?"

"I do not know where they are. If they are in the Wall, the dense static will obscure my vision. A radio broadcast might work if they are listening. Yours is the only station on the air in this city."

"What are you talking about?"

"The Circle of Augustus. A radio message. Have you been listening?"

Theese gave in to the inevitable and dragged himself up to a sitting position. He pulled a porcelain bowl from the bedside table, coughed into it to clear the phlegm from his throat, and then put it back on the table. He looked around the room.

"Where are you?" he asked. "I don't see you."

"My location is of no importance. What I need is your immediate assistance."

"You need this done *now*?" He looked at his phone on the table. "It's almost midnight." He didn't want to disturb Graciela at this hour. A trip to the studio would require her to drive him.

"A crisis is imminent," Gem's disembodied voice said flatly.

"It would help if I understood what was going on. A crisis, you say?"

"Your employer, Mr. Gregg, will subject this city to a devastating metal storm if he frees himself from the deep freeze I put on him. The Deceiver will use him to complete the subjugation of Los Angeles after that."

Theese blinked rapidly to clear the sleep from his eyes. "Those words make no sense."

"He must be stopped. Use your access to the airwaves for good."

"Mr. Gregg pays for the station," Theese protested. "You know that, right?"

"He is unable to stop you at this moment. Besides, your association with him is temporary."

"We have a contract."

Gem's voice huffed. "Contracts mean nothing to the Deceiver. You must act quickly. The survival of many depends on it."

"You're putting me in a tough spot here, lady."

"Your spot will only grow tougher, Mr. Theese. If you choose to help, broadcast this message. Repeat it continually, until everyone in the Circle hears it." The Guardian's voice dropped to a low murmur and the message entered his ear directly. Then her voice faded.

He felt the absence of her as soon as she left him. "One line?" he groused out loud, reaching for pen and paper. "That's the whole message?" He didn't expect an answer, and there was no point arguing with her anyway. She'd be back to bug him if he didn't comply. He reluctantly sent a text message to summon his nurse from her bed and prepared for a ride into the night.

****

Arhat drove circles around the warehouse area, searching for the VW van with TJ and Evelyn in it, and then widened the search area to encompass more of West Covina. A strip mall sat on every other block, apartments, motels, and miles of pavement broken up by an occasional palm tree. It all looked the same. The van could hide on any side street or behind any building.

"If Thomas took over driving, he might go home to the Hills," Willet said. "No, wait, he'd come back to the warehouse for me, unless Evelyn made up some lies and told him I left."

"What do you want to do miss?" Arhat said. "We must choose a direction."

Willet's head swam. She didn't want to miss him if he came back, but Evelyn could have driven them into a ditch by now. "We'll go back to the warehouse, see if he's there. We'll give him some time to return. If not, we head for Hollywood Hills." Flimsy as it was, having a plan made her feel better. Arhat nodded and headed left down a street in the direction of the warehouse. Then he turned on the radio. Willet heard a crackle from the speaker. Buried in the distortion, a raspy voice spoke very softly but not soft enough for her to miss it. "Circle of Augustus, meet the Guardian at Griffith Observatory," the voice said, and then said it again.

She knew that voice. It triggered a flood of memories of a big man in rolled up shirtsleeves, his hairy forearm locked around her throat, stuffing her into the trunk of his car and then throwing her to the bottom of a mine infested with Red Souls, leaving her to die. She felt loathing mixed with a heavy dose of fear. Why would he talk about the Circle and the Guardian like he knew their business? Unless the Guardian made him do it. *Am I really supposed to go to Griffith Park?* The urge to return to the warehouse to look for TJ was so strong, she could barely think of anything else, but she couldn't ignore the message. What if it was a summons from Gem? She had started to wonder if her memories of the Guardian had come from a dream rather than real life. She studied Arhat's profile and wondered what he understood from the radio message. "I don't know what to do," she said quietly.

He glanced her way. If he thought she was referring to the man on the radio, he didn't show it. "Do you want to continue this drive?

What if your man is not at his business or at his home? We would have gone a long way for no good purpose."

True enough. No time to waste driving aimlessly around Los Angeles. A more solid plan was needed, so return to the warehouse to see if TJ is there. If not, go directly to Griffith Park and see if Gem was waiting for them at the Observatory. If she was, then there would be answers, or at least suggestions. If not, move on to the Hollywood Hills. She relayed the new plan to Arhat, and he nodded again.

They drove back to the warehouse, and Willet walked into the empty garage. Her echoing footsteps on the cement floor gave her a hollow feeling. She didn't want to be there. Memories of Evelyn's insults and the bathroom ambush really ticked her off, and she missed Thomas so much it hurt. She checked the office and the bathroom. No one was there. Somehow, she knew he wouldn't return. Perhaps the radio message was intended to lure them to a secluded place for an ambush. Willet wouldn't put it past Theese, so she planned defensive measures. She'd listen carefully for Red Soul chatter all the way to the park. If she heard anything suspicious before they entered, Arhat would have time to turn around and drive away. If not, they would continue up to the Observatory. If they saw Gem, Willet would examine her from every point of view before they got out of the SUV. If she saw weird light around her, a deranged smile, or drooping wax features, then they would leave fast. A lot of 'if-thens'. Willet refused to be caught by another fake Gem. The memory of needles still burned in her eyes.

She hurried back to the SUV. "No one here" she said. "On to Griffith Park."

CHAPTER 15

Willet had never been to Griffith Observatory, though she'd seen pictures of it. Griffith Park is an enormous area of natural forest and canyon land full of scrub oak, sage, barrel cactus and barberry right in the middle of urban Los Angeles. The white brick Observatory building with the dark blue dome sits on a large mesa overlooking the L.A. Basin. It was late afternoon when she and Arhat drove in. The pungent scent of sage hung on the air as the temperature dropped. She heard coyotes moving in the underbrush. Bird chatter was dying down to sporadic peeps. Arhat was lucky to find a narrow spot in the parking lot in which to wedge the SUV. To get up to the Observatory, they had to take a shuttle which was packed with visitors. The riders didn't look like tourists. People from all walks of life - executives in suits, nurses, a couple of nuns, restaurant workers in uniform, construction workers carrying tool belts around their waists – seemed like they'd just been teleported away from their jobs. What were they doing in the park on a weekday afternoon?

The shuttle arrived at the Observatory and stopped to let them out. A long expanse of manicured lawn with a fountain in the middle led up to the Observatory entrance. The mall was full of people wandering about looking up in the trees, staring out over the mesa and at each other, seeming to search for something. A small group of young people seated on the grass looked like they may be preparing to sleep outside for the evening. They layered in shirts and jackets. Sleeping bags were spread out underneath them, and their belongings were stuffed into plastic bags. They munched on apples and energy bars, watching other people walk by. Willet wondered why there was such a crowd. "Is there an event in the park tonight?" she said out loud to no one in particular. A woman with lank brown hair, wrapped in a fringed black shawl, stared at her.

A tall, bearded man in ratty sweatpants and a red flannel shirt full of holes approached them. "Where's the Guardian?" he asked sharply, peering sharply at Willet and then shifting his glance to Arhat. "You the Guardian? We heard the Guardian would be here." Willet recoiled from a particularly ripe odor. "No, we're not," she said, and backed up a couple of steps. The man spat on the ground and slapped his thigh before walking away. "Is that it?" she murmured to Arhat. "They must have heard the radio message. They're here to see a Guardian without knowing anything about her."

She listened carefully for threatening or chattering voices that would suggest a Red Soul invasion but didn't hear them. She did hear a rush of ocean waves coming from the other side of the Observatory building, though they were not near the ocean. It was a tell-tale sign. Gem was there. "I think I know where Gem is," she said to Arhat. "Could you please come with me? I'd like to introduce you to her." "Of course, miss," he nodded.

They headed toward the Observatory building. A man in green hospital scrubs came running at them across the grass and stopped short. "Where's the Guardian?" he said breathlessly when he reached the. "I have to find him. I'm in the Circle of Augustus." We're just going to the Observatory," Willet said, pointing at the building. The man walked off as quickly as he had approached, talking to himself.

If people think they're in the Circle, that might be a problem. They tried to walk casually like two park visitors out for a stroll and then slipped onto a path that led around to the side of the building, hoping no one noticed. At the back of the building, the Guardian herself stood at a waist-high white stone railing, wearing a calf-length sky-blue skirt and white peasant blouse. Beyond the barrier, the Los Angeles Basin spread to the horizon. Areas of the city were dark and silent. Tumbled buildings lay where they had fallen after the crystal churned up the streets. Across the Basin, downtown skyscrapers rose into the bleak gray sky, barely lit. One building stood taller than the rest. Gem was singing her chant word out loud on a long exhale. "Huuuuuuuuuu". The wind picked up, rustled her skirt and stirred the sage in the canyon. Dora stood at attention beside her and watched Willet and Arhat approach with unwavering golden eyes. When they reached the Guardian's side, Dora sniffed their hands. Their identity and intentions confirmed, she sat with a huff, looking up expectantly at Gem.

"Gem," Willet said at the sight of the Guardian. "You're here. I'm so happy to see you."

Gem turned to her and looked her up and down. "Ah. Good. You received my message. Arhat, I see you have taken good care of my Listener. Thank you for delivering her safely."

"Guardian," Arhat replied and made a small bow. "It was my pleasure."

Willet looked back and forth between Arhat and Gem. "You two know each other?" Their wide-eyed, innocent reaction was almost comical. She realized her mouth was hanging open and snapped it shut. *They know each other. Of course, they know each other. He works with her.* She felt like an idiot for the second time that day.

Arhat had been solicitous of her welfare to an unusual degree, drove her all over the city and hadn't asked for payment since the first few dollars she offered him. He had said things that were uncommonly wise. On some level she suspected he wasn't a regular cabbie, but she had needed help so badly she chose not to question it. "Why didn't you say something?" she demanded.

"It was your journey," he said. "You learned how to separate from the physical shell and take control of the Soul body. Extreme danger can be a catalyst for that transition. I provided a bit of cover and perhaps a nudge here and there. That was my role. The choices had to be yours."

Willet remembered her part in the deaths of the Chucker drivers. She felt deep regret at the thought. "You knew it was me crashing the Chuckers when we were on the freeway," she said, feeling the anguish all over again. "One guy fell off an overpass because of me, and others were hanged. I was complicit in their deaths, but I didn't know what else to do." She looked at her hands and realized she was wringing them. "I feel so terrible."

Arhat nodded solemnly. "You took action to save our lives and the lives of others. Difficult times call for difficult choices."

"Will I have to go to the Underworld? That's what happens, right? When someone does terrible things?"

His lips betrayed the shadow of a smile. "That is not for me to say, miss. All actions must balance in the fullness of time. Your intention to protect is part of the final equation."

"Arhat Faroud Anselmi of Persia is an Arahata," Gem said. "He has served the Circle of Augustus as a Teacher for centuries. He provides instruction, guidance and protection, as needed. I depend on him when I cannot be present to protect someone in my care."

Willet searched for words sufficient to express her gratitude but couldn't come up with anything. "Thank you, Arhat. Thank you," was all she could muster.

Arhat stood shoulder to shoulder with Gem. They both smiled at her. Light beamed from their faces and glowed around their bodies. They radiated love. Willet felt overwhelmed to be in their presence, realizing she had received a rare gift.

"Now Listener, attend to me, please," Gem said briskly, getting back to business. "I need you to listen well. Tell me what the city is saying."

****

Bart pushed the truck to its speed limits to put distance between it and the Wall behind them, flying through neighborhoods, detouring through strip malls, and dodging on and off the freeways to gain fractions of time. Dean hung on to the shoulder belt, not saying a word. When they reached the turnoff to the Crystal Works, he roared up the road, spun into the parking lot in a hail of gravel, and killed the engine. Both men jumped out and ran around the office building, calling Audrey's name. They found her lying in the crystal field, her body glowing as green as a 'go' light. She shook like she was having a fit. Dean dropped to his knees, pulled her out of the field and into his arms "Audrey. Audrey, talk to me."

Audrey opened a bleary eye. "Dean. You're back. So tired, I had to lie down." Her eyes closed again. "Just give me another minute."

"We need to go! The Wall's coming this way. This is not the time for a nap!" Dean pulled her by the arm into a sitting position. "You have to get up *now*." Dean and Bart each put a shoulder under her arm and lifted her to standing. She wobbled on unsteady ankles, trying to put one foot in front of the other. They half-dragged her to the sedan. Bart ran into the office, ran out and handed her a cold bottled water. She gulped it down.

“Where are we going?” Audrey said, slurring slightly. “Why are we going?”

“Gem sent a message to us on the radio. The Circle of Augustus needs to meet the Guardian at Griffith Observatory. She’s calling us. And you know who gave out that message? Richard Theese.”

Audrey roused herself. “He’s evil. Can’t trust him.”

“He’s the only one broadcasting right now. Somehow Gem used him to contact us. Even if it’s a hoax, we still need to go to find out. Did you hear me say the Wall is getting closer?”

Dean and Bart helped Audrey into the back seat of the sedan and closed the door.

“Follow us in the truck,” Dean said. “We’ll head to Griffith Park.”

Bart looked down at the ground, avoiding Dean’s eyes. “I’m staying here,” he said. “This is my land. My home is here. I’m not leaving it.”

Dean grasped Bart’s shoulders and shook him lightly. “Buddy. Don’t be stupid. There’s a lot of unstable distortion coming this way. You know what it does. The crystal may protect you for a while, but you can’t hide in your fields forever. Do you really want to take the chance of being overrun?”

Bart shrugged him off. “It’s the only thing I can do that makes sense at this point.”

They stood in silence for a few moments. “Your choice,” Dean said, “but you know where we’re going. If you have to evacuate, come find us. Until then, try to grow as much crystal as you can. Spread these fields out. I think we're going to need every inch if we have a prayer of defeating this thing."

Bart still didn't meet his eyes. "There are a few extra bags of crystal in the shed. You should take 'em with you, just in case."

"Thanks." Dean extended his hand, and Bart shook it. They studied each other in a wordless exchange that couldn't be explained to anyone who hadn't shared their experience at the Wall. They had survived, and it felt like a miracle.

Bart gave a short nod. "Take care of her," he said, turned on a heel and walked back to the office.

CHAPTER 16

"Mr. Tom! Wake up!" TJ felt someone pushing hard on his shoulder, trying to wake him up. He opened a bleary eye and saw Jonah's frantic young face. "Mom's drivin' crazy," Jonah whispered in his ear. "You have to stop her before we crash! She won't listen to me."

He shook himself out of a truly awful dream in which he was being electrocuted in a web of wires and felt the speed immediately. Why were they in the van? "Your mother is driving?" He sat up and tried to clear his head. "Why is she driving?"

"She said we had to get away before we lose you."

"Why would you lose me?"

"Don't know, man. She's whack." Jonah hung his head, looking embarrassed.

"Where are we going?"

"Don't know that either," the boy said. "That's why you have to go talk to her."

The van rocked side to side, careening into turns, and screeching into sudden slowdowns. TJ crawled into the passenger seat and took a look at Evelyn. Her face flushed as red as her hair as she struggled with the wheel. "Evelyn, talk to me." TJ tried for a calm, reassuring tone. "Where are you taking us?"

"Oh, Tom," she said. "You're awake. I got us out just in time."

“Stop the van. Please. Tell me what you’re doing.”

Her eyes were frantic. “There’s no time. We have an appointment with someone who wants to help us.”

“With whom? Help us with what?”

“She was going to take you away from us.”

“You don’t mean Willet, do you?” he said. “I told you, you’re wrong about her.”

“A voice spoke to me. He said I had to do what he said or something bad would happen. I think it was the voice of God.” Evelyn’s eyes were crazed and bloodshot red. Red Souls had taken her over.

TJ put his hands gently over hers on the steering wheel and slid closer to her on the bench seat. “Here, let me take over for a while, you must be tired.”

“No! No! He said I had to bring you, or I’ll lose Jonah!”

“You’re not going to lose Jonah. Trust me, Evelyn. Now slow down.”

They were entering the heart of downtown. Car horns honked as the van weaved. Evelyn fought him for control of the wheel. He swung his leg over her lap and jammed his foot down on the brake. She kept pushing the gas. The van veered sideways and rolled over the curb onto the sidewalk. He managed to avoid the corner of a stone building and ended up back in the street going the wrong way. He yanked the wheel and took the van down an alley, then out onto a side street. An SUV ran into the back bumper and pushed them against a cement trashcan with a jarring crunch. The other driver didn't wait around to exchange names. He burned rubber backing out of the alley and then disappeared down the cross street.

TJ checked on Jonah, who was hanging on to the mattress in the back. The boy looked scared but physically fine. Then he got out and surveyed the damage. The bumper was crumpled, and the trashcan had imbedded itself in the side door. A police siren squealed, and a squad car arrived on the scene in sixty seconds, an almost impossible response time. Two policemen got out, uniformed and armed.

"Well, well," one of them said, looking over the van. "Nasty accident."

"Somebody driving erratically," said the other. "Under the influence?"

It felt like a setup, like the cops were waiting for them. TJ told the police he was driving to keep the focus off of Evelyn. The cop asked to see his driver's license. He didn't have one, of course, because Jonah had given it to their ride share driver and never got it back. Officer Tripp, according to his name tag, immediately pulled out the handcuffs. "Handcuffs?" exclaimed TJ. This was overkill for a traffic accident, even in the absence of a license.

Evelyn and Jonah jumped out the driver door. "No, don't hurt him!" Evelyn said. "We have to see the City Manager. He's expecting us."

The other officer, named Barnes, grabbed Evelyn's arm. "Oh, you'll see the City Manager, alright. Mr. Gregg made a special request. You're going to the Dragon Head right now to see him."

Mr. Gregg? "You don't mean Matt Gregg, do you?" TJ asked.

"That's his honor, Matthew Gregg, City Manager of Los Angeles, to you," Officer Barnes said as he yanked on TJ's arms to slap on the cuffs.

"When did *Matt Gregg* become City Manager of L.A.?" Last time they met, TJ had found Matt in his shower and punched him in the face until he bled. Matt promised to kill him if he saw him again. Their reunion would not be fun.

"Since he was elected in 1963 and appointed Manager for life," said Office Tripp.

"He wasn't even born in 1963!" TJ squirmed as the hand cuffs clamped around his wrists. "You're arresting me for a traffic accident?"

"Driving without a license, reckless endangerment of a minor, public nuisance, resisting arrest – it's a long list," the officer said, smiling.

"This is ridiculous. I'm not resisting."

"Whatever, smart-ass, just get in the car. Watch your head now." Barnes stuffed TJ into the back of the squad car, none too gently. Evelyn and Jonah followed him in.

"This woman and her son have nothing to do with it," TJ said as Tripp climbed in behind the wheel. You can let them go."

"No one goes anywhere. Mr. Gregg wants you three brought in, so shut your yap. Let's go, Barnes," he called to the other officer. The squad car took off with a screech of the siren.

****

After leaving Bart at the crystal fields, Dean maneuvered the sedan through traffic and onto Highway 60 going west. His jaw clenched. Something was off with Audrey. “What’s with you?” he asked.

She squirmed and giggled like a teenager. “Did you see my rings? Pretty cool, huh?”

“The rings were awesome, yeah. How’d you do it?”

“The crystals looked so beautiful and refreshing. I put my hands and are feet on them so I could feel their energy. It charged me, Dean, and then I was slinging rings as fast as I could throw them. It felt great for a while, I have to say. Then I felt totally drained, like my battery had gone dead.” Her giggle became a laugh, and the laugh took on an edge of hysteria.

He heard a clicking sound and looked over at her. “Are you cold? What’s the matter with you?”

She didn’t answer him. Her eyes were wide. Her upper and lower teeth chattered and clacked together, and her head wobbled on her neck. A green aura glimmered off her skin. She shook like she was about to convulse.

Crystal overload. Damn. “Audrey, take a deep breath.”

She was soon glowing green like a neon bulb. The light spread from her, filled the inside of the car, and then leaked outside. The car sped up toward 100 mph, tires barely touching the ground. Dean slammed his foot on the brake, but the car just kept accelerating. All he could do was grip the wheel and try to steer. Cars swerved out of their way. Trucks honked wildly. Audrey must have absorbed an unhealthy dose of crystal energy while she lay passed out on the field. Now the energy was pouring out of her. It was pushing the car into high gear.

"She's a human battery," Dean muttered under his breath. He prayed all the head shaking didn't make her brain bleed and hoped he'd be able to control the car long enough to get them to Griffith Park without a major accident. Stopping didn't seem to be an option. He kept his hands on the wheel but exerted little control over it as they raced down the freeway. They were close to running out of gas. How far past empty could Audrey's energy take them? They went another fifteen miles after the gas needle hit 'E'. Audrey's shaking fit began to ease, and the sedan slowed down enough for Dean to steer it to an exit off the freeway. When they reached a surface street, they rolled to a stop on the shoulder. Audrey still glowed green, but the shaking subsided. Dean switched off the ignition and took a deep breath. Now what? The part of L.A. they were in was not an area he wanted to walk, but they couldn't just sit there and wait for someone to help. He got out of the car, took a look around, and spotted a gas station down the road. He could buy a gas can there and fill it.

"Audrey, listen to me. Stay in the car, please, and lock the doors. I'm going for gas." When he was satisfied that she had done as instructed, he set off on foot. The gas station attendant managed to scrounge up a dented red gas can. Dean filled it, paid an outrageous price per gallon, and returned to the sedan. He found two men staring inside the passenger window at Audrey.

"Excuse me, gentlemen, can I help you?" he asked as diplomatically as he could.

The guy with short-cropped brown hair, early thirties, wearing army fatigue pants and khaki long-sleeve shirt looked up. "What's with the lady? She's green and shiny. That's messed up." The name stenciled on his pocket said 'Hardman'. He looked like active military.

“She’s having some indigestion,” Dean said. “It’ll pass.”

The other guy, black, shaved bald and about the same age, wore jeans, white tee and battered bomber jacket. He lifted mirrored sunglasses up to his forehead and gave Dean a fish- eye stare. “What’d she eat? Radioactive waste?”

Dean unscrewed the gas cap on the sedan and lifted the gas can nozzle into the intake. “What do you guys want? I spent my last dollars on gas, so there’s no cash here.”

“We don’t want your money,” said the military guy. “We need a ride.”

Dean emptied the gas can and put it on the ground. “We’re going to Griffith Park in a hurry. Someone’s expecting us.”

“Do you know what the hell is going on?” bomber jacket guy asked. “People are walkin’ around like zombies. Stores are closed. My apartment building collapsed while I was at work, can you believe that? And where is the sun? Haven’t seen it in forever.”

“Oh,” Dean said. “That.”

“Yeah, that,” he replied. He and military guy exchanged glances. “See dude, it’s not just us.”

“Nope,” Dean said. “Not just you.”

“Well, that’s a relief, sort of,” said military guy. “I’m Nick. This here is Boulevard.”

Dean looked them over. “Why is your name ‘Boulevard’?”

“Cuz I know every street in the city,” bomber jacket said, preening a bit. “I’m a street expert. You can call me Jain if you want. That’s J-A-I-N, not the girl’s name.”

“So now you want a ride from me, is that it?” Dean said.

“Yeah,” Nick said. “I want out of L.A. This town is creepin’ me out.”

“And I’d like someone to explain what’s happening,” added Jain. “My Ducati was parked in the garage underneath my apartment. Got crushed like a beer can when the place collapsed. I’ll never see the Dream Machine again.”

Dean had to cut the conversation short and be on his way, but these guys moved in closer and closer. They expected a ride, and they apparently thought he had an explanation for the weird things happening to the city. He wasn’t sure what to tell them. “What kind of explanation do you think I could give you?” he asked.

“Why don’t we start with why your lady there is green,” Jain said, pointing at Audrey. “She don’t look well. Did you drug her or something?”

“Absolutely not,” Dean said. He decided the truth was easier to explain. “She got too close to some strong crystal, like the kind that came out of the ground everywhere and probably knocked down your apartment. Her energy is amp’ed at the moment, but she’ll recover.”

“If it’s not indigestion,” Nick said, “I’d like to hear that from her.”

"Who are you, the police?"

Jain pulled a small shiny gun from one pocket and a wallet from the other with an ID in it, which Dean didn't bother to look at. He pointed both at Dean. "I'm James Jain, licensed private detective, and I notice things, like when someone turns a color that ain't human."

"Let the lady speak for herself," Nick said.

Dean couldn't believe the luck of having to deal with these two, but he unlocked the sedan and stuck his head inside. "Audrey, can you step out a minute? They'd like a word with you."

Audrey gave him a dazed look and got out. Currents of green light swirled around her, and her lips trembled. She was definitely not free of the crystal's influence.

"Well now, darlin', I'm Nick. How're ya feelin'? You don't look well if I may say so. We could take you to a hospital if you want." Nick took her hand in his.

Audrey looked down at their hands and then at his face. "I'm fine," she said in a dull voice.

"You don't look fine," Jain said. "Is this guy hurting you?"

Audrey looked up sharply, and a flash of green current ran down her arm. Nick dropped her hand as if stung. "Ow!" he cried, rubbing his hand and arm. "She shocked me, J! She friggin' shocked me. How'd she do that? I'm numb to the elbow."

"Dean wouldn't hurt me," Audrey said irritably. "I told you I'm fine."

"Okay, okay, whatever," Nick said, backing away. "You're green. It's not normal."

Audrey looked to Dean for confirmation of that fact, and he nodded. "Listen, we got places to be," he said, "so if you don't mind, we'll be on our way." He edged toward the driver's side door. "Audrey, let's go."

Jain stepped up to the car. "Sorry, but we need the wheels," he said, waving the gun. "I must insist, all due respect to the lady. My friend here suffers from post-war trauma and flashbacks. We gotta split before he loses it again. We can drop you someplace. The lady can come with us if she wants. We'll see she reaches a hospital."

Dean thought fast "Look, guys, I can offer you this. We're going to see someone who can give you a real explanation of what's happening in L.A. She's at Griffith Park Observatory. You can come with us, meet her and talk to her. Then we'll give you the car."

"What's she doin' at the Observatory?" Jain snorted. "Lookin' for aliens through the telescope?" Nick's face expressed similar skepticism.

"She knows what's going on," Dean shrugged. "To an amazing degree. I guarantee you that."

Nick and Jain looked at each other. Silent signals passed between them in a language they both understood. They finally agreed to the arrangement Dean proposed. Jain got in the front passenger seat, Nick got in the back, and Audrey got in next to Nick. Not ideal. Dean wanted Audrey in front with him. He opened the trunk, put the gas can in, and removed one of the five-pound bags of crystal that Bart gave him. He went to the back seat and handed it to Audrey. Maybe it would give her some protection. She settled the bag on her lap. Dean climbed into the driver's seat.

Nick eyed the bag. "What's this?"

"It's rock salt," Dean said. "I needed room in the trunk."

"You're ready for ice." Nick shrugged. "Good to know."

Dean pulled slowly off the shoulder onto the freeway with great misgiving. There was a gun in the car, two carjackers, and a bag of crystal in Audrey's lap. What could go wrong?

CHAPTER 17

The squad car sped through L.A. streets with sirens blaring, screamed to a halt at the Dragon Head Building and parked in front. Officers Tripp and Barnes got out and opened the back doors, pulled TJ, Evelyn and Jonah out and led them into the lobby in a perp walk, and then shoved them into a waiting elevator. At floor number five, the doors slid open on a room full of bright lights and mirrors. Women's voices screamed somewhere inside. Officer Tripp pushed Evelyn into the room, and the doors closed behind her. Jonah cried 'Mom!' and beat on the doors with his fists, but Tripp pulled him back. "Stop it before I smack ya," he growled. At floor thirty-six, the doors slid open to reveal an actual circus, complete with aerial acrobats, tigers prowling in a ring and calliope music sounding slightly off-key. A clown with wispy orange hair stood at the open doors with an ugly red grin painted on his face. He reached in, grabbed Jonah by the arm, and pulled him out of the elevator. Jonah stumbled away, and the doors slid shut behind him. TJ threw his shoulder into Officer Barnes, but the officer kicked the back of TJ's knee and knocked him to the floor. Officer Tripp added a kick in the ribs. "Nice try, tough guy," he laughed.

From the vantage point of the floor, TJ noticed leathery feet with thick black claws where shoes should be. Dragon feet. He was in Jat's lair now if he had any doubt before. "You're not police. You have no right to hold me."

An eerie laugh came from the officers. Serpent tongues flickered out of their mouths, and their voices combined in a long hiss. "I am the

Lord of this World," the hissing voice said. "All rights are mine. You have none." The officers retracted their forked tongues and grinned at him, becoming Tripp and Barnes again.

At the seventy-second floor, the elevator stopped again. Each officer grabbed an elbow and dragged TJ through the open doors into a darkened room. They dropped him in a heap just beyond the elevator. Thin beams of red laser light started to crisscross the room, sweeping slowly across the floor, walls and ceilings. When beams disappeared, new beams shot across the room from different directions. They made a sizzling sound.

"This is your own personal game room," Officer Tripp said. "The game is called 'Dodge the Lasers'. Looks like fun, doesn't it?" he chuckled. "The Boss had it built just for you."

"What's the point?" TJ asked, dreading the answer.

"The point is to stay out of the lights, dumbo," Officer Barnes said. "They'll burn a hole right through ya, what I hear." His laugh had a creepy echo as he unlocked the handcuffs around TJ's wrists. Both officers stepped back into the elevator. The doors closed, and the elevator descended rapidly, already down to the forty-first floor by the time TJ looked at the lighted numbers. He hit the call button repeatedly. The elevator wasn't coming back.

He felt a sting on the back of his neck, winced and spun around. A red beam crossed his leg and left a scorched trail on his pants. He had to focus on the room now. The beams were moving faster, coming closer and closer to the spot where he stood. He could not stay where he was. A beam swept toward him. He hopped sideways, only to run right into another beam that caught him on the arm, leaving a slice of smoking shirt and skin. Then a third beam hit him in the chest, leaving him gasping. It hurt to inhale. The beam to his chest heated the needles in his torso and turned them up to a broil.

The grilling would be a slow and painful grilling. He remembered his dream, a premonition it seemed. He clutched his chest and looked frantically around the room, trying to find a clear path through the beams. There was none, and no place to go. He dropped and rolled under one beam, then another and another, until he was at the other side of the room. Now what? Perspiration tricked down his neck and back. It was getting hotter by the second.

He faced away from the room, huddled in the corner, and tried to make himself small. Maybe a stationary target was harder to find. A beam crossed the back of his head, leaving a sear of heat on his scalp. He smelled burnt hair, decided it was better to see what was coming at him, and turned to face the room with arms around his head to protect his face. The beams swept erratically, searching for him. Was a moving target harder to hit? He dragged himself along the wall of the room on forearms and belly as fast as he could crawl. Hot beams raked his shirt. He groaned as they burned through to skin. No where to hide. He had to escape and find Jonah. He raised his chin as high as he dared and studied the room. There in the ceiling was an open space he hadn't noticed, and in a dark corner across the room he spotted a ladder folded against the wall. Where did that come from? Suspicion replaced sudden elation. Too easy. It was some kind of trap, but he had to play along. He dragged himself across the floor, trying to stay underneath the maze of burning laser beams. If it meant getting out and rescuing Jonah, he would risk being grilled like a steak.

****

Willet lost her trusty noise-cancelling headphones somewhere after the Circle crossed through the Wall into east county L.A. The onslaught of noise shook her eardrums and just about shattered her sanity. She couldn't afford to be so vulnerable on this side of the Wall. She had to find a way to manage her reactions so sound couldn't incapacitate her. Her freeway battles against the Chuckers had given her some ideas. When she was in full Soul consciousness, her imagination had power. She could picture herself doing something, and then her Soul body did it. Would that kind of imagining work when she was in her physical body? She knew exactly what her inner ears looked like. Doctors had shown her diagrams and pictures when she was a little girl. The thin membrane of the eardrum, the tiny flexible bones touching it, and the spiral-shaped cochlea lined with sensitive hair cells were familiar to her. Those structures translated air pressure waves into electrical impulses to her brain. *Her* ears were so sensitive to vibration that every sound was amplified to a painful volume. If her eardrums and inner ear bones vibrated less and more slowly, with lower amplitude and longer bandwidth, that would damp down the volume.

So, she imagined it. When a sound assaulted her, she pictured her inner ear anatomy moderating its movement from high amplitude to a slower vibration. Sounds became less sharp. They dropped in pitch, from a screech to a rumble. Sometimes it sounded like she had cotton in her ears, but noise became manageable. The cacophony of traffic blended and blurred. Sirens, air hammers, car horns, breaking glass – those were sharp wave forms. All she could do was cut them off. The crack of gunshots cascaded into echoes. Blocking those sounds took real concentration. It didn't always work, but she made progress. She was 'blessed' with hearing acute enough to pick up sounds from other planes. They traveled at frequencies outside the range of normal physical hearing. She didn't want to block them. They were key to her role as the Listener.

Feeling prepared, Willet centered her attention, opened her ears and let the sounds come. Bad timing. A sudden crack of phantom lightning shot through the sky, followed by two more explosive bolts. She almost passed out, but she found herself floating over the L.A. Basin, drifting toward the downtown skyline. Being out of her physical body felt peaceful as always, and her viewpoint was calm and undistracted. Wherever she placed her attention, she was there, just a pair of eyes taking it all in, with no worry or judgement. Under normal circumstances, she would enjoy it, but these were not normal circumstances. As the ears and eyes of the Guardian, she had to be the first to know if Jat the Deceiver made a move. It would come with a distinctive and loud sound.

Skyscrapers, usually sparkling with lights, were mostly dark, except for one building that towered many stories above the others on the skyline. There was a statue at the top with a spotlight under it. Red smoke drifted around the statue, tracing graceful glittering patterns in the air. If she didn't know better, she might have thought it beautiful, but the sight of the smoke filled her with stomach-turning dread. *Red Souls. Not again.* She had been attacked by a horde of them. Their voices screamed in her head, loud and insistent, and tried to take over her mind. The smoke around the statue was thick with them. The city was in more danger than any of the Circle realized. Willet floated as close as she dared to the statue - a dragon head on a man's body, sitting in a huge chair. Its blank eyes stared, and mouth gaped as if about to take a bite out of the world. Leathery-looking feet planted at the foot of its chair had long claws curling out of thick black toes. Its oppressive presence beat against her heart. *Is it my imagination, or is the statue looking at me?* As if responding to her thought, a light blinked on in each eye. The eyes followed her movements, tracking her left and right. She shuddered. *Yep, definitely looking.*

Red Souls chittered and hissed at her. "Listener, Lisssstener. Too late." They swarmed, flew at her head and drove her back. The noise they made couldn't mask the sounds she heard coming from inside the building - voices of people in anguish and pain. She heard chopping, beating and hammering. Screams. Red Souls didn't want her to know what was going on in that building, but they couldn't stop her from hearing it. She dropped down for a look in a window but couldn't see through it. She flew close to it and passed right through the glass into a room empty except for a bloody guillotine with a basket positioned below the blade. There was a head in it. The urge to vomit was strong. She sped upward through the ceiling into another room where someone was being dragged by black hooded figures toward a pit of leaping flames and smoke. On the next floor up, the room was full of bats. They dove at her, screeching and snapping their sharp mouths. Her panic reflex spiked again. Right below her, bats swarmed over a man and pecked holes in his flesh while he shrieked and covered his head with his arms. She propelled herself up through the ceiling as fast as she could and emerged into a room containing a railroad track with a woman tied to it. The sound of a speeding train coming closer echoed through the room.

Willet kept moving up through ceilings, faster and faster. Every level contained some revolting scene of terror and misery. She entered a floor full of moving red laser lights, heard muffled sobs and was horrified to see Thomas, her Thomas, crawling along the ground. The back of his shirt flared with fire and his hair smoked. She went to him immediately but couldn't shield him. Their bodies existed in different worlds. All she could think to do was draw near and whisper in his ear. "I love you. I love you, Thomas. Don't give up. I need you." A laser swiped his leg, and another brushed the side of his cheek. He shrieked in pain. The sound nearly broke her heart. Suddenly, she was gone from the room.

****

TJ inched across the floor on his belly toward the ladder in the opposite corner of the laser room, a treacherous journey. His shirt was soaked in sweat, and the burnt skin on his body screamed. Pants and hair smoked. Burns scored the tops of his hands. He choked on the agony of newly raw skin. Small flames flared on the back of his shirt. He stopped and rolled to put them out, then kept going, finally reaching the ladder. He spoke firmly to himself. *Now stand up, drag the ladder over and climb up.* To reach the opening in the ceiling, he would have to expose himself to the full trajectory of every beam. No use dwelling on it. He would probably be engulfed in flames by the time he got there.

Check the elevator one more time. There were no lighted numbers on the display, no dots of light moving up or down. It looked totally shut down. That left three options - stay in the room and fry, climb the ladder and fry, or climb the ladder faster than he had ever climbed before and avoid frying quite so much. He hoped he had the strength left for option three. Pulling sleeves down over his hands, he stood up, stuck his arms through the ladder, and dragged it across the floor. Every laser left scorched trails across his clothes. The hair on the back of his head caught fire and burned to his scalp. Tears welled in his eyes. He stifled a whimper and slapped at his hair to put out the flames. Lasers bit his ears and neck. His pants flamed in places, but he didn't have time to put them out. A strangled sound of anguish escaped his throat he barely recognized as his own voice. In the center of the room, he unfolded the ladder, steadied it under the opening and started to climb. It wasn't that far to the ceiling, but it seemed like a mile. Patches of skin bubbled, and tears streamed down his cheeks. The pain was so intense, it sapped his strength. He could barely lift his legs. A beam cut across his chin, ripping another shriek of agony out of him. The burn sizzled. He had to get through the opening soon or he would surely die.

When he reached the top step of the ladder, there was still a gap of space to the ceiling. Ignoring all rules of ladder safety, he climbed onto the narrow topmost step, balanced and reached up to the opening. Every laser hit him in that moment. The urge to pass out was so strong, his knees buckled. He almost fell off the ladder but struggled to remain upright and stand on his toes, wedged shoulders and arms up into the opening. He barely had enough arm strength to lift himself. Flames on the shoulders of his shirt burned into his neck, but the sudden stinging pain gave him the final jolt of energy he needed, even as he choked on smothered cries. Picturing Jonah alone on the thirty-sixth floor, he hoisted himself on hands and elbows through the opening with the last of his strength, pulling his legs up behind him just as two lasers grazed his calf. He collapsed on a narrow landing in the open space above the laser room and gasped for breath. His shoulders shook with sobs. The red-hot needles throbbed in his muscles, too excruciating to bear. His mind blanked.

Hollow and without will, he was unable to think or move, but he had escaped. He closed his eyes, drifted and hallucinated. A soft voice whispered in his right ear, a woman's voice. He couldn't make out the words, but he felt her love for him. Despite the madness of pain, it brought a smile to his lips. Willet. Then he heard the soft hum of the 'HU' in his left ear. He sang it under his breath, thinking of the Circle, of her. Where was she? He hoped Willet was close to Gem and not anywhere near this building. They were supposed to do something together, but he couldn't remember what it was. He tried to picture her face. Images came and went, but he couldn't hold on to any of them. He opened his eyes and wiped his nose on his sleeve. It hurt to move, breathe or think. He wasn't sure how much time had passed, but he hadn't let those lasers burn him just to sit and die in the ceiling. He saw no lights or doorways anywhere above him, just a crisscross of wooden beams and two-by-fours. It looked like a jungle gym. He had to drag his burnt and stinging body up through the scaffolding to the top of the building and confront whatever was up there in a weakened state. *I guess this part of the game. No even odds.* Gathering what energy he could muster, he stood on shaking legs and began to climb.

****

The shock of seeing Thomas in that deadly room sent Willet spiraling back to her physical body. She dropped into it with a thud. Her first thought – *I have to get him out of there.* When she pictured him covered in stripes of fire, the anguish almost paralyzed her.

Gem was standing beside her. "The Circle should have gathered by now," she said. "Where is your sister?"

Willet had no answer. Gem blew a dusting of ice crystals onto her face. Willet blinked at the sudden cold spray and looked at the Guardian. "What?"

"I asked, where is your sister?"

Willet's distress almost took her breath away. "Thomas is in that building, Gem. He's burning to death!"

Gem looked at her steadily and nodded. "It is a difficult place to be."

"It's an evil, horrible place! People are being tortured. Why don't the police do something?"

Gem continued her calm appraisal of the distraught Listener. "The Deceiver has raised One Hundred Levels of Torment from the Underworld and hidden them in the Dragon Head Building. The police protect that building."

"Then *we* have to do something. He's going to die!"

"Thomas walks his own path. He will find strength. That is what the path is for."

"You're saying it's for his good?" Willet felt ready to scream with frustration. "No, I don't accept that. How could you?"

"The Circle will need his strength. He must find it in himself."

"I don't care about the Circle right now," Willet said. "I care about Thomas."

Gem gave her a sharp look. "There are two hundred people standing in front of the Observatory right now in need of protection. The Circle must protect them. Where is your sister?"

“My sister…” Willet said, suddenly flustered. She realized she had forgotten about Audrey, hadn’t thought of her in days. Or had it been weeks?

Gem studied her. “You do remember Audrey, do you not?”

Willet’s cheeks got hot, and words tumbled out. “Of course, I remember Audrey. I just haven’t thought about her in … a while. That’s weird I know, but a lot of things happened so fast. Now I’m really worried about Thomas. We have to rescue him.” She stared daggers across the Basin. “I’ll knock the statue down if I have to.”

“Do not stare at the Dragon,” Gem said. “He gains strength from your attention. We have more immediate concerns. The Walls in the east and west are moving toward each other faster than ever. Soon, they will converge, and all of us will be trapped inside them. By then it will be too late to prevent the Underworld from taking this city. I need the Circle at full strength.”

Conflicted emotions and quaking fear made it difficult to breathe. Willet tried to remain in her physical body but could not stay put. She rose into Soul consciousness again and moved out over the city, desperately wanting to return to the Dragon Head Building and rescue Thomas, but something held her back. She just floated in limbo.

“I feel useless,” she whispered. “It’s tearing me apart.”

“You are not useless,” Gem’s stern voice came to her. “You are the Listener. Tell me what you hear.”

Willet closed her eyes and listened. “I hear The Dragon Head statue cracking. Jat is inside it, and he’s breaking out.”

Gem nodded. "It begins. We need the Ring Thrower."

****

TJ gathered his remaining shreds of strength and climbed the lattice of beams and two-by-fours above the laser room with muscles screaming. At the top, he caught his heaving breath and examined the ceiling. A square section cut into it looked like the entrance to an attic. He pushed on the loose square of wood and lifted it, slid it out of the way and peeked his head up through the opening into another room. The room smelled of paint. The walls were blank white. A long bank of windows on one side let in dreary light that reflected off the top of a metal office desk in the middle of the room. TJ pulled himself up through the opening in the floor and limped to the desk. He shuffled through the drawers, found nothing in them. Then he noticed two mounds of ice, a large one next to the desk and a much larger one against the far wall. *I must have a head injury. Why is there ice here?*

He heard a bell ring and turned to the elevator. The doors opened. *It's working!* Despite his sore and weary body, he stumbled toward it, got in and hit the button for the thirty-sixth floor where he had last seen Jonah. TJ prayed nothing bad had happened to the boy. At floor thirty-six, the doors slid open on the circus scene he remembered. He stepped out. A juggler walked by, tossing flaming knives in the air. TJ turned out of his way, bumping into the clown with the red fright wig and saggy brown suit who hissed at him through clenched teeth. TJ ignored him. "Jonah", he called out as loud as he could. "Jonah, where are you?"

A cacophony of laughter, growls, caws and roars answered his call. He walked up and down the rows past rings, trapezes and tents. It appeared to be a regular circus, but it made him feel uneasy as he looked closer. Two clowns dressed as boxers punched each other in the face. Chimpanzees and tigers screamed at him, reaching through the bars of their cages with wicked-sharp claws. A ring master poked at an acrobat on a high swing with an electrified pole. The man cried out in pain and fell from his swing. He hit the ground with an ominous crunch of bones. The ring master laughed. This was a circus of cruelty, the only way to describe it.

TJ walked faster, avoiding vendors trying to shove black cotton candy in his face, and shouted for Jonah. Another clown wearing an old-fashioned police uniform with silver buttons tried to put a rope around his neck. TJ pushed him away and started sprinting through the circus aisles, up one row of horrors and down another. He finally found the boy standing in front of a low stage. A naked woman, brown haired and young with her ankle chained to the stage, was being bitten repeatedly by a snake. She yelped and made futile attempts to protect herself with arms and hands. Jonah seemed mesmerized. He was so painfully young. A child should not see this. TJ grabbed Jonah's shoulders and turned him away from the bizarre scene. The boy's eyes were bleary and his jaw slack. *Is he drugged?*

"Jonah, look, it's me," he said, shaking him slightly and patting his cheeks. "Talk to me, please."

Jonah's eyes came into focus. "Mr. Tom, look," he said pointing at the woman. "The snake is biting her. That's so whack."

"This is a bad place, Jonah. We have to get out of here and find your mother." He took the boy's hand and led him back to the elevator which was still waiting with doors open. They got in, and TJ pressed fifth floor where Evelyn was last seen. The doors closed, and the elevator began to climb. Wrong direction. TJ pounded on the down button, but the elevator kept rising. At the eighty-ninth floor, the doors opened on the desk and the mounds of ice. The elevator didn't respond to the buttons TJ pushed, so he walked out and pulled Jonah behind him.

“We’ll have to find another way down,” he said. “There’s a trap door in the floor. Just stick close to me.”

He searched for the hole in the floor he had climbed through but couldn’t find it. The opening had sealed and disappeared. He heard a muffled voice coming out of the mound of ice by the desk. It said, “Get me outta here.”

CHAPTER 18

TJ crept up to the mound and touched it. Yes, it really was ice, frozen solid and cold to the touch. Something was scratching inside it.

"Get me outta here, damn it," the muffled voice repeated.

No way. "Matt? Is that you?"

"Barlow. This is perfect," the familiar voice growled low.

"How did you get in there?" TJ couldn't suppress a laugh.

"Your fairy godmother froze me! Get me out of this damn ice. I've been in here for hours, and I can't feel my feet."

"Gem put you in there? I don't know, man. I'm sure she had a good reason for freezing you. I wouldn't want to mess with her mojo."

"Yeah, well, if you don't get me out, you and the kid won't be leaving this building."

TJ had some remorse about punching Matt in the face in the shower, but after that threat, any goodwill he felt for his old friend evaporated. "If Jonah gets hurt, cold feet will be the least of your problems."

"Don't threaten me," Matt growled. "I said, get me out. Then we'll talk. If not, there are many worse floors in this building than the circus or the laser game you enjoyed."

The laser room was seared into TJ's memory, and the burns still lingered. The thought of Jonah in that room made him furious. "Your little game almost killed me," he gritted through clenched teeth. "You can freeze to death in hell for all I care."

Matt's chuckle sounded shaky coming out of the ice. "I can't take credit for the laser room. It's genius. The big Boss creates the levels in the building. I'm in charge of sending people to the levels where they'll get the appropriate lessons, which includes you and junior. So, do what I tell you, or you and your little boy will never leave the Dragon Head."

TJ still had to find Evelyn, and he couldn't depend on the elevator taking him to the fifth floor. Matt must control it somehow. If Matt had any scruples left, TJ would appeal to them. "Jonah has nothing to do with our fight. Let him go and I'll get you out."

"No bargains, buddy boy. Get me out now or things will get ugly for both of you."

TJ didn't want to take that chance. He looked around the room. There was nothing in it that would help him break through solid ice. "I'd need a tool to break you out. The ice is hard."

"Open the desk drawer. See if there's an ice pick in there."

TJ rifled through the desk, and sure enough found an ice pick in the middle drawer that wasn't there when he checked the desk before. He picked it up, walked over and jammed the pick into the ice a few times, none too carefully. The mound cracked and fell apart into large chunks.

Matt emerged from the pile of ice and struggled to his feet, taking a long stretch before stepping clear of the chunks. The smile on his fast was nasty. "You're an idiotic sap, ya know that Barlow?" he said, rubbing his hands together rapidly. "Got a warm spot for little Jonah, huh? That's an exploitable weakness." He held his hands palms out in front of him. Metal pieces of all kinds, staples, and nails began to fly around the room.

Something hit TJ in the cheek and embedded a sharp point in his flesh. He felt for it and gently pulled away a thumb tack, along with a bead of blood from the small puncture. He wiped the blood away with the back of his hand. Other metal pieces whizzed past his head and eyes, causing him to duck. Even worse, it felt like every needle in his body was being pulled toward Matt's hands, trying to come out through his skin. TJ grasped Jonah by the shoulders and pushed him under the desk. "Are you crazy, Matt?" he called out. "You'll cut someone!"

Matt walked to the windows, rubbed his palms together, and pressed them to the window. Pieces of metal hit the glass. A trash can lid flew by, spinning. Matt laughed. "I'm magnetic. Isn't this cool? I'm amazing! Who would have thought a kid from the wrong side of Rancho Cucamonga could control metal by waving his hands?" Cackling with glee, Matt directed the movement of metal outside like a demented puppeteer. His eyes rolled with crazed delight as he made metal objects move faster and hit harder with every flex of his fingers. The air outside swirled with debris, sharp as shrapnel and abrasive as a sandstorm. A Stop sign sailed through the air, hitting the window with a loud bang before glancing off. "Hah! Good thing the glass was shatterproof." The body of a small bird hit the window in a splat of blood and feathers, unable to escape the flying metal.

TJ still had the ice pick in hand. He hung on to it tightly against the magnetic pull. In a place of no other weapons, the man with an ice pick is king. He crept up behind Matt, grabbed his left-hand, and smashed Matt's palm against the window. With all his strength, he plunged the pick into the top of the hand and skewered it all the way through flesh and glass. The glass held tight around the pick and kept the hand pinned.

Matt howled in agony. Blood streamed down his arm and dripped from his sleeve onto the floor. He wrestled for the pick with his right hand while TJ fought him off. The two men punched viciously at each other, but Matt was hampered by his lack of a hand. The more he fought, the more the ice pick gouged him. His left hand took on the appearance of raw hamburger. Outside, the metal storm waned and died. Apparently, an ice pick through his hand interfered with Matt's 'amazing' ability to move metal. TJ turned to Jonah who was peeking out from under the desk. "Boy, go to the elevator and press the down button. Keep your head down, there's still metal flying in the air."

Jonah crawled out from the desk. His wide brown eyes locked on Matt's bloody hand with the ice pick sticking out of it, and he froze.

"Jonah!" TJ barked. "Get the elevator!" He didn't know how long he'd be able to keep Matt pinned. Matt was fighting back with the desperation of a man bleeding to death. TJ leaned in and hissed in his ear. "I have no problem cutting your hand in two if that's what it takes, *buddy boy*, so stand down."

Jonah shook off his shock and beat feet to the elevator. In a few seconds, the bell rang, and the doors opened. TJ jumped back from Matt at the window and ran into the elevator after Jonah. He jammed his thumb on 'Five' repeatedly until the doors closed. No way to know for sure where the elevator would take them as long as it was away from the eighty-ninth floor.

****

On the drive to Griffith Park, Dean learned more than he needed to know about the carjackers, Nick and Jain. Nick's real first name was Nickel, so designated by his father who was down to his last nickel when his son was born. Nick was ex-Army, back from two tours in Afghanistan. He told them more than once about the shrapnel embedded in his leg and neck by a roadside bomb. Nick was army-fit, but worry lines etched his face. His blue eyes shifted left and right, always watching, as if he'd seen too many bad things and expected another bomb to explode any minute. James 'Boulevard' Jain demonstrated his street smarts about L.A. geography by regaling them with information about each street they passed, including name, length and important intersections. Nick and Jain were long-time friends from back in the neighborhood where they grew up, and their bond seemed deep. Jain was solicitous about Nick, asking frequently if the soldier felt ok or needed anything. Nick just nodded and said, 'I'm fine'.

By the time they reached the Observatory, Dean was ready to ditch the two ride-alongs in any way possible. He pulled into the packed parking lot. Cars were parked sideways, wedged into too-small spaces or double parked. It seemed like all parking rules had been suspended, so he just stopped where he was and turned off the engine.

"This is it?" Jain asked. "This is where we find that woman who knows everything?"

"She's here," Dean said. "That's probably why all the people are here. Audrey, how're you doing?"

"I feel kind of nauseous," she said. She shifted the bag of crystal in her lap.

"Put the bag down," Dean said. "You don't want to get over-amped again."

He reached for the door, about to get out, when a hail of something hard pinged off the roof and hit the windows. Nails, coins, paperclips, and bottle tops hit the windshield. A bicycle pump bounced off the hood. People around them shouted, then ducked and covered.

Jain's head spun to the back seat. "Nick," he said, "It's ok, man, no need to panic, not a bomb."

Nick's chalk-white face and wild eyes in the rearview mirror showed he was already in panic mode and starting to hyperventilate. So, this was why Jain was so solicitous of his friend's welfare. Nick had a bad case of PTSD. They might be about to witness a melt-down.

Audrey dumped the bag of crystal into Nick's lap. "Hold on to this for me, please," she said. "Dean, I have to find Gem. Follow me!" She opened the back door and slid out, slammed the door shut and stalked away.

"Audrey, wait!" Dean yelled. "You could get hurt."

Audrey spun up a light ring and dropped it over her shoulders, then took off running. She was soon out of sight.

"Great," Dean mumbled. "She's lost it totally."

Jain turned to the back seat and laid his hands on Nick's shoulders, trying to calm him down. "Easy man, easy. It's not a bomb, okay?" He turned a wide, angry eye toward Dean. "What the hell is going on? I thought we were safe here."

"We're not safe anywhere, sorry to tell you," Dean said. "I don't know what's going on, but we should stay in the car for now." He was tired of the endless craziness. He thought about Audrey running off to find Gem, which is what they were both there for, but it still made him mad. They were supposed to be a team, equal parts of the Circle. They should have discussed a strategy. He could have driven her closer to the Observatory. Apparently, she had a different agenda. Well, he had his priorities too. He spun the car into a sharp three-point turn, pushed other vehicles out of the way none too gently with his bumper, and left some of them scratched. There would be karma to pay down the line, but he didn't care about that now. He just wanted out of the park. Jain complained. Dean didn't bother to explain. It was time to head to Manhattan Beach and find his mother and brother, with or without Audrey.

****

Graciela drove Theese to his East Hollywood radio studio as she now did most days. The sky looked gloomy. It had been a long time since it rained in L.A., but there was no evidence of moisture. When they arrived, she helped him out of the van and settled him into his wheelchair. They were about to enter the glass doors of the studio building when something hit the side of the building, hard. Nuts and bolts bounced off the pavement. Children's toys, tin cans, and hub caps hurtled passed them. Small metal trash baskets tipped over and slid along the sidewalk. A baby stroller careened down the street, chased by a frantic woman in a track suit crying "My baby! Help! Somebody, stop him please! Mattie!"

A wrench flew through the air and whacked Graciela in the forehead. She uttered a surprised cry. A small gash opened above her eye, and the skin around it took on a bluish cast, promising an impressive bruise to come. She looked stunned for a moment and then sunk to her knees. Pieces of metal junk pelted them. Theese launched himself out of his wheelchair with all the upper body strength he had left, fell with her to the ground, and rolled them both under the van through dirt, gravel and oil drippings to escape the metal fall. She lay pale and still beneath him. His mind raced. "No Graciela, no," he murmured over and over in her ear, brushing the dark curls from her forehead. He gently lifted her eyelids and held a thumb to her wrist. The feeble beat of her pulse eased his panic. She was still breathing. He kissed her cheek tenderly, and her eyelids fluttered open.

"Reechard," she said softly. "What you doing?"

"Stay with me, Graciela," he whispered. "Stay still, but don't sleep. You may have a concussion."

Her voice was weak. "I stay with you. You need me, no?"

He kissed her forehead, and then her lips. "I need you. Yes. I'm not sure how we're going to get out from under this van without your assistance."

"My head hurts," she said with a wincing smile.

"Yes, my dear, you got hit in the head. A wrench, I think. Please don't stress yourself now."

"What has happened? I don' understand."

He wanted to reassure her, but he didn't understand it either. "I don't know, Gracie. A box of junk may have fallen out of an airplane." That didn't explain the objects he had seen flying sideways down the street, the trash cans and dumpsters, and the baby stroller, but he could think of no better explanation.

****

Willet found it difficult to think about anything else except the horror of seeing Thomas burning in the laser room. *How long can he survive? What can I do?* No ideas came to her. Much as she pictured the room and tried to move back to it, her Soul body wouldn't go there. She was floating above the freeways and watching cars whizz by below her. Looking east and west, up and down the heart of the L.A. Basin, she listened. Despite the deepening gray of the light, the constant static of the Walls, and the random violence of Chuckers on the freeway, traffic moved along steadily as if it were not possibly the end of the world as people knew it. They had places to go, people to see. Their ability to carry on with life despite the terrible threat about to swallow them touched Willet's heart. *What am I doing? Gem needs me. I have to do my job.* She would use her ability to listen and watch, to anticipate the arrival of danger as best she could to help them. Maybe the Circle would have time to come up with a solution.

The static hiss of the eastern and western Walls was louder than ever, a constant reminder of how much closer they had come. They had turned from purplish gray to pitch black, like dense and roiling smoke from a coal fire. The sight of them would cause mass panic if people could see them with physical eyes. To the east of where she floated, Ontario Airport was totally obscured by the distortion. No runway lights, no planes taking off or landing. It was as if the airport wasn't there. To the west, the beach communities were covered with the same darkness all the way inland to the 405 freeway. Maybe it was better that people were unaware, for now. They would feel the full weight of the Wall's presence soon enough.

An iridescent green light moved west along the freeway, darting through clusters of slower traffic. *Car? Truck?* It gave off a steady tone that she could hear, like a tuning fork. The vehicle took the exit to the park, turned into the entrance and sped up the drive. In the parking lot, the passenger door flew open. Audrey got out and ran, throwing an energy ring over her head that exploded into an umbrella of light. Willet slammed back into her physical body.

“Audrey’s here,” Willet said breathlessly. “And she’s packing a lot of power.”

CHAPTER 19

The crowd on the Griffith Observatory mall reacted to the metal storm with a cry and a scream. Everyone dropped to the ground, arms over heads. Sharp pieces of metal flying through the air sliced into exposed skin. Then the storm became a barrage, and people huddled together to protect themselves from the large objects that landed with enough force to break bones. Gardening tools and machine parts hit people in the head. A bicycle dropped on someone's back. A rusty muffler and a trash can flew overhead. At the entrance to the Observatory, Gem blew gale winds over the crowd strong enough to send most of the metal spiraling away into the trees.

"Audrey's coming up. She has a weird green energy around her," Willet announced.

Gem stopped a gale wind in mid breath. "What kind of weird energy?" she asked.

"I don't know. She's dropping her energy rings over people to protect them from the stuff falling on them. Like you're doing."

The bubble of green light with Audrey inside bounced down the mall from the far end, moving fast and heading toward the Observatory. She hurled rings left and right over the cringing crowd. The rings coalesced and spread into an enormous canopy of light covering everyone and deflecting the metal storm. She reached the stairs of the Observatory and sprinted up to where Gem, Arhat and Willet were standing and threw a large ring over all of them, and then bent over with hands on knees, trying to catch her heaving breath. "I heard you'd be here," she gasped. "What's the plan?"

Willet hadn't laid eyes on her sister in so long that she felt a shock of recognition to see her. She went to Audrey and tried to embrace her.

Audrey stiffened and stood back. "Don't, Will, it may not be safe. I'm kind of super-charged at the moment. When all this energy fades, we can catch up."

Willet stepped away, confused and rather hurt. "Why isn't it safe?"

Audrey held up her arms. "See the green light?" she said, turning her hands. "It's the crystal. It packs a lot of power, let me tell you. Bart's growing it on his farm. I passed out in one of his crystal fields and absorbed so much energy, I can spin really big rings and throw them for miles. The Walls do *not* like them. You might get a bad electric shock if you touch me right now. That's why I'm not safe."

"Bart has a crystal farm?" Willet repeated, skipping over the other details. "Like the crystal we destroyed? Why is he doing that?"

Audrey sighed. "It's a long story, but the important fact is the combination of rings and crystal can drive the Walls back. We're going to need all the advantages we can get against that thing."

"Why isn't Dean with you?"

Audrey watched pieces of metal bounce off the dome of light over the crowd. "He's in the car with a couple of carjackers. One guy has a gun, and the other is having a panic attack. Like I said, long story."

Willet felt a sour churn in her stomach as several realizations hit her at once. "Well, here's a story for *you*. Jat is inside the Dragon Head statue trying to break out, and we're two warriors short of a Circle. So, Dean needs to get himself out of the car and over here to help us, or we won't be able to fight the Deceiver when he gets free."

****

TJ leaned against the back of the elevator, heart nearly pounding a hole in his chest. Pictures of a bloody hand with an ice pick sticking out of it were vivid in his head. He had violently attacked a man who used to be his friend - twice - and felt absolutely no guilt. It had been so easy, so instinctive, to pick up a weapon and strike back with brutal force at someone who threatened him and Jonah. That primitive part of him that used to be buried under a veneer of civilized behaviors was out of the box. He was ready to fight for survival, fight dirty if necessary. Despite what it might say about himself personally, Matt needed to be stopped. *I did what I had to do, but is the Wall affecting me?* He noticed that Jonah's t-shirt hung on him like a dirty rag, and his jeans were frayed at the cuffs and knees. *He needs new clothes and a bath…Wait a minute, I'm not his father, we're not even related.* And there it was, the reason for his aggressive impulse. The thought of Jonah getting hurt made him crazy. He'd protect the boy at all costs, even to the sacrifice of his own life. Under ordinary circumstances, such caring would be a good thing. Now he wondered if he might be regressing to a Neanderthal.

Breathe, Get it together. He watched the lighted numbers change from floor to floor as the elevator dropped, but instead of going directly to the fifth floor, it stopped at the thirty-third and opened the doors. An overwhelming stench of rotting flesh, sewage and loose bowels punched into the elevator air space. TJ and Jonah both doubled over gagging, holding their noses and mouths. Jonah turned into the corner and threw up, which did nothing to improve the smell in the elevator. TJ swayed on his feet, close to passing out. His eyes watered. He jammed buttons on the panel until the doors closed and the elevator started to move. No idea where they were going, but it didn't matter. At the twelfth floor, they stopped again, and the doors opened on a tall, beefy man with a full beard wearing a bathrobe and slippers. The man held an axe across his chest with blood dripping from the blade that pooled onto the floor beside him. He looked as surprised to see them as they were to see him. Maybe the smell put him off because he didn't enter the elevator. TJ slid a glance at Jonah out of the corner of his eye. The boy looked exhausted and glassy-eyed, his mouth hanging open. *That poor kid is gonna need therapy after all this.* TJ hoped Jonah remained motionless. They were sitting ducks if the big guy got spooked and decided to attack them with the axe. TJ held his breath, avoiding eye contact, until the doors closed again.

The elevator finally made it to the fifth floor which appeared as TJ remembered it. This was where the police pushed Evelyn out the door. TJ and Jonah stepped out. Wailing women with haunted eyes wandered like wraiths in a large empty room. Their clothes were ripped to rags. *What is wrong with these women?* He looked down at Jonah. "Better stay in the elevator while I look for your mom. Keep the doors open for me."

Jonah wiped his mouth with the backs of both hands. He stared straight ahead, nodding, and then took off into the room, darting between the women and shouting "Mom! Mom! It's me! Where are you?"

Every woman in the room turned to his voice, their heads almost spinning on their necks. A woman screamed, "Billy! It's my Billy! Get out of my way!" The women descended on him like harpies, clutching at his arms and calling him by different names. "Johnny! Danny! David! It's my Davy! It's Peter!" They peered into his face and leaned in to pull at his clothes, smelling and pinching him, desperate to identify him as their long-lost child.

TJ elbowed through the throng and pulled Jonah to his side. "I asked you to stay in the elevator," he grumbled. Jonah tried to slip away, but TJ held on to his arm. The eyes of the women burned, ready to grab the boy. "Let's go," he said, and wrenched Jonah from their midst. He walked the square of the room with Jonah in front of him. A gaggle of women followed at his heels, whispering among themselves. "Evelyn, where are you?" TJ called out. "Jonah's here." They found a small form sitting on the floor, backed up to the wall, with an unmistakable shock of red hair sticking straight up. The woman whimpered pitifully, her head down and shoulders rounded in shaking sobs.

"Mom!" Jonah shouted and dropped to his knees at her side. He patted her cheeks and shook her. "Mom, it's me. Look!" Placing his palm on her cheek, he gently turned her face toward him. Her red and swollen eyes didn't register his presence at first, but then she focused on his face, and blood flushed under her death-pale skin. "Jonah?" she whispered. "They told me you were gone."

TJ dropped to a knee at her feet. "Who told you that, Evelyn?"

"The women, everyone here. We've all lost our children. Our grief is endless. That's the punishment of this place."

"Punishment for what?" TJ asked. "Why would you be punished?"

"I don't know." Evelyn stared at him. "I did something awful. I think it has something to do with you."

"Well, that can't be right," TJ pointed. "Jonah is here. You haven't lost him."

Evelyn looked at her son, this time with awareness. She put a hand on his forehead. "You look pale, boy. Are you running a fever? I can make you some fresh juice." Then she sniffed the vomit on his breath. "And please brush your teeth! What in god's name have you been eating?"

Jonah took her hand and kissed it. "I'm okay, Mom. We have to get out of here before something bad happens. Can we go now?"

"Yes," she said. A small smile bloomed on her lips. "Now that my boy is with me."

TJ and Jonah both stood and took an elbow, pulling Evelyn to standing. Her feet barely touched the ground as they walked her through the horde of women still crowding around, calling out the names of their lost children. The smell was still nauseating when they got in the elevator and the doors closed, but TJ couldn't stop thinking about the women. He had never felt such misery from other human beings. Their loss was unbearable. He wished he could return their children to them. The elevator quickly reached the ground floor, and they bolted out toward the big double glass doors. The metal storm was over. A trash can lid lay just outside the doors next to a dead squirrel. "Dammit, Matt, I hope you're satisfied," TJ muttered.

They were just about to exit to the street when the elevator bell rang behind them, and the doors opened. Matt's rough voice sounded furious. "It's not over 'til I say so. I haven't begun to kill you, Barlow." The glass doors in front of them locked.

TJ whirled to face him. Matt held his mangled, bloody hand to his chest, wrapped in the torn sleeve of his fancy jacket. His skin was flushed, and his mouth was tight with pain. The expression in his eyes communicated pure hatred. He stood next to Jonah and clamped his good hand on the boy's shoulders. Jonah tried to shake him off, but Matt held on.

TJ's breath caught in his throat. "Take your hand off him," he growled.

"Or what? What you gonna do, big guy? Punch me? Stab me? Not this time. You're still on my turf, and there are special floors ready for each of your friends." Matt's mouth stretched into a smile of vicious glee.

TJ edged closer to Jonah. "Put me back in the laser room if you want to but let the woman and her son go. They have nothing to do with you and me."

"Oh, I beg to differ," Matt said, pulling Jonah to his side. "They have everything to do with us. They are your emotional anchor, the one that will drag you under. I can't wait to watch." Matt tried to herd Jonah and Evelyn back to the elevator.

Jonah broke free and pulled his mother toward TJ. "Get off her, creep," he said.

"You're not too young for a really bad game of your own, you little shit," Matt said, reaching for a handful of Jonah's brown curly hair.

A brisk wind blew through the lobby at that moment and the light shimmered. The glass of the front doors shook. An ephemeral doorway opened out of nowhere with a soft pop, and the Traveler, Sonrisa Degas, stepped out of it to stand in their midst, impressively tall and radiating power. Her eyes blazed. Strands of brown hair blew around her face in the receding breeze, and bright burnished light glowed around her. She wore a maroon robe and a belt made of rope, her feet in sandals. If she carried a sword in her hand, she would have looked like an avenging angel.

Evelyn’s legs wobbled. She was close to fainting. Jonah caught his mother by the waist and tried to hold her up. “No way,” he mumbled. “Told ya something bad would happen.”

Matt’s face boiled red. “Not you again,” he spluttered. “Get out.”

“I do not answer to you, servant of the Deceiver,” Sonrisa dismissed him. “I come for this Warrior at the request of the Guardian. He is needed elsewhere.” She turned and motioned to TJ. “We must go now.”

“Wait,” TJ said. “The woman and her son must come with us. They’re in danger here. If they don’t go, I’m not going.”

Sonrisa turned her fierce gaze on him. “Are these people part of your mission?”

“I think they *are* my mission,” TJ replied. After he said the words, he knew it was true.

“So be it,” she said spreading her arms. “Come to me.” The space next to her folded open.

TJ grabbed Evelyn and Jonah by the arms and dragged them away from Matt. At the Traveler’s side, the doorway closed on them so suddenly there was no time for anyone to resist.

****

The metal storm had stopped at the Observatory, and everyone breathed a sigh of relief. Audrey’s protective light shield over the mall crowd winked out. People stood up. Some scratched their heads. The relief felt uneasy.

Willet simmered in her anxiety, and all the things she worried about played through her mind like a newsreel with one running headline: *Thomas is trapped in the Dragon Head Building*. "When are we going to help him?" she pleaded with the Guardian. "He's hurting. I can't stand waiting anymore!"

Gem tapped her foot, paced, and tapped some more with head down, deep in thought. Then she looked up, eyes clear and calm, and gave a shake of the head that might have meant "Oh ye of little faith", or it could have meant "Don't bother me, kid." It was difficult to tell. In the next moment, a seam in space-time split open, and the Traveler emerged in a swirl of light, followed by TJ, Evelyn and Jonah. After depositing her passengers, she stepped back into the seam. Space-time zipped shut in front of her, and she disappeared. The passengers were left stumbling and disoriented on the Observatory steps.

"What a ride," TJ said, blinking his eyes into focus. "Where are we?"

Audrey happened to be standing right next to him when he stepped from the seam. She clapped a hand on his back. "This is Griffith Observatory, Mr. Barlow. Glad you could join us. Who are these people?"

Evelyn's knees finally gave out. She sat on the ground with Jonah beside her, both looking shell-shocked. "Evelyn, Jonah, this is the Circle," TJ said, gesturing to everyone standing around them. "Circle, these are my friends. Deal with it."

Blood drained from Willet's face. She could barely breathe. She ran to TJ and threw her arms around his neck, clung to him as if he were the only thing in the world holding her up. "Thomas," she whispered. "I was so worried."

TJ wrapped her in a fierce embrace, his cheek pressed to her hair. "I wondered if I'd ever see you again." They studied each other, kissed deeply, and held each other even tighter.

Despite her joy and gratitude for having him back, Willet couldn't help herself. "Why is Evelyn here? She kidnapped you!"

"It's a long story, babe. Do we have to talk about that now?"

"Another long story," she said. "OK, how did you get out of that horrible room? The lasers were burning you."

He drew back to search her eyes "How do you know about that?"

"I was there! I saw it and heard it, and I tried to help you. Then I got pulled out of the room. I couldn't get back to help you, but something kept blocking me. It's been tearing me apart thinking about you in that place."

He held her closer and whispered in her ear. "I wish you'd never seen that. It was my hell, not yours."

"There's no heaven if you're not with me, Thomas."

He kissed her forehead and the palm of each hand. "I'm with you now."

"You have returned to us," Gem said from behind them. "I am glad."

TJ turned on the Guardian with a dark look in his eyes. "Where were you? Everything and everybody was trying to kill me. I could have used some help."

Gem met his stare calmly. “I was where I needed to be, doing what I needed to do.”

“I almost died in that Wall. I’d still be lost in there if Evelyn and Jonah didn’t help me walk out. Needle Men stuck needles in me and set them on fire. They fried me like a fish on a grill.”

“It was not possible for me to relieve your discomfort at that time.”

“*Discomfort?* Is that what you think it was?” he said, his voice shaking. “The pain was excruciating. I don’t know how I’m still walking around.” He took a deep breath and let it out slowly. “Damn everything about this damn Circle.”

“I am sorry for your pain, truly. Challenges strengthen us. That is what they are for.”

TJ’s expression hardened. “So, what was it, some kind of test? You were manipulating me?”

Gem gave him a sad smile. “Your path is your own, Thomas, not one of my design or choosing. It is an agreement between Soul and Spirit. I have explained this to you before.”

“What if I had died?” His voice rose. “Would you just rope some other stooge in to take my place? Am I that expendable?”

She put a hand on his shoulder and looked into his eyes. “Few Souls ever learn of the existence of the Circle of Augustus. Far fewer are considered for membership. You are a Warrior with a generous heart. The way was difficult, but you persevered and gained strength. No one can replace you in this Circle. Your place is here with those who love you. We need your strength more than ever.”

The steam of anger seeped out of him, leaving him deflated. "Other people needed help," he shrugged, turning to Jonah and Evelyn. "These people. I did what I had to do, that's all."

"Spoken like a true Warrior. You have suffered too much and deserve respite. I can ease this burden, at least." Gem touched her index finger to the skin between his eyebrows.

Her fingertip felt cool and then light exploded in his head. A waterfall of cool energy poured into the top of his head, down his spine and into every muscle like an icy stream. The needles washed away. Surprise spread across his face and his eyes widened. He took a deep breath, stood taller and shifted his shoulders. "God, that feels good. I forgot what it's like not to have them stabbing into me." Tears welled in his eyes. "Thank you," he said and hung his head. "I thought I'd never be free of pain. It feels like heaven."

"We are closer to the Underworld than to heaven, Thomas" Gem said. "The Deceiver casts a long shadow. We must be ready for his next maneuver." She looked out over the crowd. "And where is our Golden-hearted Warrior? We will need his heart more than ever."

CHAPTER 20

Dean was still trying to get out of Griffith Park. "This is ridiculous," he grumbled at the long line of traffic backed up at the park exit. "What is the holdup?" After driving through half an inch of sharp metal debris hoping his tires wouldn't blow out, he was desperate to get to Manhattan Beach and check on his mother. The lane for incoming traffic was empty at that moment, so he veered into it and sped to the front of the line under a blare of angry honks. *Yeah, yeah, I have places to go, sorry.* Just beyond the exit, a massive traffic jam blocked further progress. Cars parked all over the road and people were out at an overlook point with a view across greater Los Angeles. They shouted, took pictures, and pointed at something on the downtown skyline. Murmurs rippled through the group. "What is that?" "It's moving." "What's it doing? Are they filming a Godzilla movie?"

Dean got out of the car to see what the fuss was about. Jain trailed behind him, leaving Nick passed out in the back seat. When they joined the crowd, they saw what everyone was looking at - a huge figure with a dragon head standing on top of the tallest building on the skyline, one leg extended out over the edge of the roof. And then the impossible happened. The figure stepped off the building into midair and dropped both its legs down. The legs grew longer and longer until its big-clawed feet hit the ground with the force of a bomb strike. Everyone in L.A. had to feel the earth shudder. The legs alone looked to be sixty stories high. The torso grew taller as the figure straightened up to full standing height, clothed in a black topcoat and striped pants. Its massive head swung to the left and right surveying the city with burning red eyes. The air around the colossus swirled and glittered with red smoke. Dean felt his stomach clench. *Not Red Souls. Not again.* What were the chances this monstrosity was Jat? If experience was any guide, the chances were excellent. And where would Jat go in Los Angeles? Dean knew the answer like an ache in his bones. Jat would go after the Circle.

Cool guy Jain was on the way to losing his cool completely. The whites of his eyes had grown big as hard-boiled eggs, and his whole body shook. He pulled out his gun and shot into the air at the distant figure. "I'll kill it, I'll kill that thing. It won't get us, Nick," he wailed, firing over and over. People screamed and ran for their cars. The gun emptied and began to click but he kept pulling the trigger anyway.

Dean grabbed him by the shoulders, turned him around and pushed him all the way back to the car into the back seat next to Nick. The soldier looked like he was having a seizure, probably due to the sound of gunshots. "Take care of your buddy," Dean growled. "Make sure he doesn't bite off his tongue." Behind the wheel, Dean started the engine and then just sat there. W*here do I go?* His mother's house was pretty far, which was a good thing for her safety, but what about the Circle? His cheeks heated with the shame of knowing he had left them behind. Audrey went to find Gem. Willet and TJ were probably there. He should be with them. The ground rumbled again, and the sedan bounced on its tires. The Dragon Headed Man had taken a pounding step that shook the city. Dean had to get back to the Circle and help them before the thing walked all the way to Griffith Park. They would definitely need the remaining bags of crystal.

****

Theese and Graciela lay unmoving under the van and listened to the clink and clank of metal falling on cement until the metal storm finally died. Theese peeked out from under the van and saw feet. People were walking by. It seemed safe to move. "Graciela, we need to roll together to the right to get out from under here. Do you feel well enough to do that? How's your head?"

"My head is fine. Can you do it? Your legs, Reechard…"

"I'll pull you over, you pull me, and we'll get a roll going." With that, Theese moved onto his side, wrapped his arms around her waist. They flattened themselves as much as possible and started the motion. She rolled on top of him, and then he rolled on top of her. There was barely enough clearance underneath the van. They rolled over into daylight, with much huffing. Graciela hoisted him under the armpits and dragged him into his chair. He patted her arm, grateful for her strength, but the wheelchair vibrated from Graciela's shaking grip on the handles. He turned to her and put a hand over hers. Her eyes were glassy, and her hand felt cold, clammy. She wobbled on her feet. Despite protestations of good health, she probably had a concussion from the wrench that hit her in the head.

"Easy, Gracie," he said. "Sit down here." He pulled her around and into his lap. She didn't resist, which was a bad sign. She seemed to crumple. "I am taking you into the building. Stay still."

Just then, a boom shook the ground so hard the glass doors of the studio building cracked and shattered. Theese hunched over Graciela to protect her from shards flying from the door. When the pelting stopped, Theese raised his head, looking around for what might have caused such a thing, and saw a huge, clawed foot at the end of a long leg swing through the air over the next block. It smashed through a bank building and then demolished a grocery store when it landed. Debris flew into the air, and people screamed. When the dust settled, a gigantic pair of legs in striped pants stood in the middle of East Hollywood attached to a torso that disappeared into the sky.

Theese managed to roll the wheelchair with Graciela in his lap through the field of broken glass and into the building to the elevators. Another thundering boom shook the building. Graciela pressed her face against his chest and cried. Theese wasn't sure if it was the right decision to be inside the building. It would either shelter them from whatever was out there, or it would collapse on top of them.

****

Dean drove back to the Observatory parking lot and stopped the car. He pulled two bags of crystal out of the trunk and took off with the bags under his arms without so much as a goodbye. Jain and Nick were left sitting in the sedan with keys in the ignition.

Jain got out and opened the back door. "This is our chance, dude," Jain said. "Hop in the front seat. We gotta get out of here."

Nick roused himself from the vestiges of his panic attack. "Whass goin on? Where we goin?" He made a clumsy attempt to squeeze between the front seats. Jain pushed him forward, and Nick dropped head-first into the passenger seat before righting himself. "How long was I out? What time is it? It's almost dark, can't be that late."

"Yeah, it *is* kinda dark," Jain murmured. He climbed into the driver's seat and buckled his seat belt. "Things are weird right now. No time to explain. Buckle up."

"Where's Audrey and Dean?"

"He left us the car and keys, so we need to git," Jain said as he started the car.

"Why would he leave us the keys? This isn't grand theft auto, is it? You know I can't be involved in that, J. I could lose my military pension."

"It's survival," Jain said. He maneuvered the car toward the exit road. "A lot happened while you were out of it, bro. Let's just say, there's good news and bad news. Good news is we can go to my sister's place in Lancaster. Her and her boyfriend will put us up a couple of nights. Palmdale Airport is there. We'll fly out, go somewhere safe. I have a credit card."

"That sounds good, I guess. What's the bad news?"

"Bad news – There's some kind of giant stomping through LA. It's huge, and it's coming this way. We have to get out of town, like, now."

Nick gave him a long look. "Have you started taking those pills again, JJ? You said you were done with all that."

"I saw it with my own eyes, and I'll never forget the sight. Promise you won't freak when you see it, cuz' you'll really want to freak. We need to stay cool, keep our heads."

Nick chuckled. "I was under fire in Afghanistan for three years, dude. The Taliban sniped us and bombs exploded every day. I can stay cool."

They reached the park exit and found traffic still in gridlock. Cars rammed each other, trying to make space for a get-away. Some people abandoned their cars and ran down the road, leaving the vehicles running.

"I'll get us out of here," Jain announced. "Seat belts buckled?" He didn't wait for an answer, yanked the wheel hard left and headed overland into trees and bushes. Nick got the shoulder belt locked and bounced in his seat as the car rolled over rocks and veered around boulders. After a couple of miles of punishing off-road travel, Jain found a narrow dirt trail and followed it until the sedan emerged from the brush and bounced onto a narrow, paved road. He turned right hoping his instincts were correct that it would lead them off the mesa and back into the city. He found the onramp to the 101 Freeway, but then realized they were heading south.

"No, no, not downtown, I want north," Jain mumbled.

"You sure you know where you're goin', 'Boulevard'?" Nick grinned at him. "I thought you knew all the streets."

"I got turned around coming out of the park, but I'm good now." Jain searched for a turnaround, but every exit they passed had traffic backed up for a mile. They got closer and closer to downtown. Jain started to sweat. He didn't want to go anywhere near the bizarre figure standing down in the basin, and he didn't want Nick to see it either. Despite all of the soldier's harrowing experiences in the war zone, his friend didn't do well with surprises. The walking Dragon Head figure would be the surprise of his life. Jain got in line for the next northbound ramp and resolved to inch along with the other cars. To distract Nick, he started babbling about anything he could think of. "So, where do you want to go when we leave Palmdale? We could go to Oregon, or maybe Montana. Beautiful country, I've heard. Knew a girl from there…"

Nick nodded. "Yeah, it would be cool to get out of the big city. Things just aren't the way they used to be growin' up in our old neighborhood."

"We're pointed in the right direction now," Jain assured him, "won't be long…"

A pop-pop-pop sound caught them both by surprise. Nick's head spun in the direction of the gunfire. The colossal figure with the dragon head was clearly visible beyond the freeway, rising out of a sea of smoke. Nick stared, looked away, and stared again. Then he looked at Jain. Wonder, doubt, concern and horror washed over his face in successive waves. His mouth gaped open, and his eyes shifted side to side as he processed the images. How long would it take Nick to square what he saw with what his logical brain was telling him? Jain wasn't sure, but he recognized the exact moment when the pieces came together, and realization hit.

"Easy now," Jain cautioned.

A high-pitched yelp came out of Nick. "What the hell is that?" The question ended in a choking noise.

"Stay with me, stay with me," Jain said. "We're leaving town, don't worry.

Nick gulped air. "What is it, J? Tell me right now."

"I told you. It's a giant. Maybe a statue of a giant, I'm not sure. It's walking – don't know how – and heading toward Griffith Park. We were lucky to get out of there."

"But we left Dean and Audrey!" Nick spluttered. "What are they going to do without their car? I can't leave a woman stranded while we make our getaway."

"Dean took two bags out of the trunk, same as the bag Audrey was holding. They both ran toward the Observatory like bats out of hell."

Nick sat taller and took deep, ragged breaths until they steadied him. "Turn the car. Turn it around now. We're going back."

Jain's voice rose to a squeak. "Did you see that thing? We can't go back there!"

"Pull onto the shoulder and let me out. Do it."

"Think about what you're saying," Jain said, trying to soothe but failing completely. "It's a monster! We gotta run while we have the chance."

"I can't just run away. It needs to be stopped like the terrorists. People will need help. If we leave, who's gonna fight?"

"Someone who knows what to do!" Jain exclaimed. "I think Dean and Audrey know. That's why they went to the park in the first place. But it's not going to be us, because we don't know shit!"

The pattern of gunfire changed. Single handgun pops were drowned out by shattering rounds from automatic weapons. The professionals had arrived on the scene - maybe Army or National Guard. Jain knew gangs had machine guns too. He hoped whoever was shooting had plenty of ammo. The three and ten-shot trains kept rolling.

Smoke drifted into the car vents, dense and acrid. Nick leaned his forehead against the side window and heaved a sigh. "That there is war, J," he said. "I'd know it anywhere." He glanced over his shoulder into the back seat. "We still have the bag Audrey was holding. There must be something powerful inside. It made her turn green. If Dean took bags with him, there must be a reason. I say we take the bag to Godzilla and see what it does."

"You've lost your mind, dude, for real this time."

"I'm a soldier of the United States Army," Nick said. "We don't run when our people are in trouble. Now turn the damn car around or I'm getting out here."

****

The thunderous power of the Dragon-headed statue's steps rocked the Observatory to its foundations. Everyone struggled to keep their balance. The crowd on the mall started jostling and shouting. "What's happening? Where's the Guardian?" When the next booming impact came down, people ran in all directions trying to get past each other, yelling and pushing, and getting nowhere.

The booms took Willet by surprise, too sudden for her to exert much control over her eardrums. She cringed. The sound reverberated from ear to ear, and pain throbbed in her neck and head. She swayed on her feet and clutched Audrey's shoulder to catch her balance and her breath. "Jat's coming. Red Souls are screaming his name. I'm getting a migraine."

The Circle looked to Gem, and Gem turned to Arhat. "We need calm, Arahata, if you please." Arhat drew Evelyn and Jonah to his side, putting an arm around each of them, and began to sing a long, slow 'Huuuu'. His voice amplified as if he were singing into a microphone. Shouts in the crowd ebbed to murmurs, and the people on the mall stopped pushing. A quiet expectancy settled on the crowd. Some people joined in the song. One by one, the Circle members slipped away quietly to the back of the Observatory, trying not to alarm the crowd by their departure. The scene across the L.A. Basin from the balcony made them gasp. The Dragon-headed statue stood upright in the middle of the city, towering above it like Gulliver over Lilliput while tiny people ran through the streets screaming. Smoke rose into the air in spirals, a disaster movie come to life.

Dean arrived just then with a large burlap bag under each arm and skidded to a stop next to Audrey. "I've got crystal," he said, huffing and dropping the bags on the ground. "There's one more bag in the car."

"Finally!" Audrey said. "I was about to be furious with you. We've got big trouble." She wrapped her arm around his waist and planted a quick kiss on both his cheeks, making him blush.

"Crystal?" TJ said. "What crystal?"

Dean registered TJ's presence. "You're here! Great, man," he said, pulling his friend into a bear hug. "How did you get out of the Wall? I tried to go in there and find you, but it wouldn't let me."

TJ returned the hug, patting Dean on the back. "That is an ugly story for another time. What crystal are you talking about?"

"The thing walking out there is Jat, I'm pretty sure," Dean said. "These bags contain chips of our favorite evil crystal, but without the Red Soul infection inside. I've seen it repel the Wall, and I'll bet it stops the statue too. If we can get close enough, we'll pelt him with it."

"Oh, it's definitely Jat," Willet said, gulping down the nausea she felt as migraine pain radiated over her scalp. "He's got a Red Soul escort flying all around him."

Jat raised one incredibly long leg, swung it stiffly forward, and planted a crushing step. Whatever was under that foot when it hit the ground was toast. Screams rose louder from the city. The other leg swung forward, and the giant leaned into the next step. The Circle braced for impact.

“He knows where we are,” Dean said. “Let’s not wait ‘til he’s right on top of us.”

Audrey spun a small ring on her right index finger and eyed the distance across the Basin “I can hit him from here. Don’t know how much damage I can do.”

“What if Gem let loose one of her hurricane winds and blew crystal chips right at him,” Dean said and looked at Gem. “What do you think?”

Gem nodded. “We are thinking like a Circle. That is a good start.”

CHAPTER 21

"TJ get over here, please. We need you." Audrey threw one of her energy rings above her head. Dean and Willet each lifted an arm into the ring, contributing their energy to increase its size and power. Then TJ raised his arm into the ring. The ring expanded dramatically. Audrey took control of it and hurled it in the direction of the Dragon-head statue. The ring hit the statue in the Dragon snout and glanced off. The statue tilted backward. The next ring hit the center of its chest, exploding into spikes of light and leaving a smoking pit in its torso. The statue swayed back and forth on stiff legs, trying to regain its balance. The rings covered the distance, leaving holes all over the body and legs, but didn't seem to do any real damage. The statue kept coming.

"Can I play with Dora?" a small voice said at TJ's elbow.

TJ looked down and found Jonah standing next to him. "What are you doing out here, boy?" He took Jonah firmly by the shoulders and turned him back to the front of the Observatory, trying to distract him from the sight of a monster that was the stuff of nightmares. "You need to stay with your mother," he said and gave the boy a nudge in that direction.

Jonah would not be dismissed. "Mom is singing with Arhat." He spun around and got a good look at the Dragon-head statue walking toward them. His faced scrunched into a frown. "What's that?" he asked.

"It's nothing you need to be concerned with, now go on."

“It is the Bringer of Darkness, young one,” Gem told him. “So, we must bring the Light.”

Jonah looked up at TJ and then at Gem. “Mr. Tom had Light when he found Mom and me in the dark place. You mean like that?”

Gem nodded. “Yes, exactly like that.”

Jonah stared at the Bringer of Darkness. “He looks wobbly.”

“That is a good observation,” Gem said and turned to address the Circle. “Jat has chosen to hide in a physical form. It is an unusual choice for him, one he has not made since I became Guardian of the Gate in this city. I am sure he has his reasons, but by doing that, he subjects himself to the physical laws of earth. We can help physical forces stop him.”

Everyone was speaking at once. “What does that mean?” “What do we do?” “Can we still use rings?” “Can you blow him over?”

Gem smoothed her hands down her blue skirt, straightened her white peasant blouse on her shoulders. “It means we do not have to over-power his statue by ourselves.”

At that moment, gunfire from somewhere on the ground hit the statue, and sprays of stone dust rose from its arms and chest. Such a solid piece of granite and marble would not crumble easily. The Circle spun up another ring and Audrey threw it. The ring hit its mark, leaving another hole. The impacts of rings plus gunfire made the statue lurch on its huge feet. It wouldn’t take much loss of balance to topple a physical object of such immense mass. The laws of gravity would take over.

Jonah raised his fists and whooped. "You hit it!"

"This isn't a video game, Jonah," TJ muttered. "You really should be with your mom."

"If the statue falls," Dean said, thinking it through, "It'll crush anyone caught underneath." The Circle stared at the rocking behemoth, digesting this fact.

"Jat might escape if it cracks open," Willet said finally. "I hear Red Soul chatter that he's trapped inside and can't get out. Better he stays in the statue than flying loose around L.A., right?"

"We need to keep him upright, but stop him from moving," TJ said. "How can we do that?"

All eyes focused on Audrey. The rings spinning on her fingers disappeared. "Stop staring at me so I can think! I did something similar before, but not exactly. I have to remember how I did it."

The Dragon Head Statue leaned forward, ready to take another ponderous step closer to Griffith Park. Gem stood at the edge of the balcony with eyes closed, her lips moving slightly. Her left arm draped around Jonah's shoulders, and her right hand rested on Dora's smooth head. The Hound sat resolutely by her side, golden eyes fixed on the statue. The rest of the Circle huddled around Dean. "If the rings don't work," he said, "then what else can we do to stop him without other people getting hurt?"

"We may have to crack him after all," Willet said. "I've seen glass crack under the vibration of really high-pitched sounds. Can we create a sound wave piercing enough? My eardrums might snap, but I'll try to take it."

Dean nodded. “Sound could be a weapon, the risks to your ears notwithstanding. How we would create that kind of sustained pitch is the question.”

“The stone seems too thick to crack through that way. Even bullets aren’t breaking it,” TJ said. “Maybe we’d have to shake it or strike it with something really powerful, like lightning.”

“There *is* lightning inside the Walls. We’ve seen it,” Dean said. “If we could harness that, we could hit him with it. Problem is, it would probably cause him to explode. Difficult to control a lightning strike.”

“Can we freeze stone?” Audrey looked over at Gem. “Does stone even freeze?” She got no reaction from the Guardian.

“Granite’s not going to freeze, neither is marble, but they do melt, if I remember my geology,” Dean said, “At extremely high temperatures, like in a volcano.”

“Or the surface of the sun,” TJ said. “How would we create that kind of heat?”

“The surface of the sun is 27 million degrees Fahrenheit,” Dean said. “We only need around 2200 degrees to melt granite. Audrey’s rings burned Jat’s crystal down to charcoal. They had to be seriously hot to do that. Quartz crystal melts at 3900 degrees Fahrenheit,” Dean gave a nod to Audrey. “So, we’re well in the ballpark.”

“How do you even remember those numbers, geek?” TJ said. “And when do we get to the part where we destroy him?”

Dean waved him off. "We're dealing with a physical object here, like Gem said. We need physical solutions. So, keep thinking."

"If we could melt the statue slowly enough, then people would have time to get out of the way," Willet offered. "And maybe the rings could contain the melt so it wouldn't spread out too far. Audrey, what do you think?"

Once again, everyone turned to Audrey, who was studying the small energies spinning on her fingers. "The rings have to expand a lot and spin really fast. That's the way they reached really high heat before. And we'll need quite a few of them to wrap the whole statue. If we get enough rings over him quickly, it might control the melt."

The statue was drawing heavy artillery fire, but still took another step forward, rocking the ground. Buildings crumbled under its feet and around its legs. People down in the city ran for their lives in a state of chaos.

Willet bent over, hands on her knees, and gulped deep lungs-full of air. "I feel like I have a metal bucket on my head, and someone is pounding it with a hammer. Can we please try something before I throw up or pass out?"

"OK, Audrey," Dean said, "put up a ring. Let's see how fast we can make it spin."

****

At Nick's insistence, Jain followed the statue to East Hollywood. While they drove into town, everyone else was trying to get out. Cars, taxis, buses, motorcycles, and bikes clogged the streets, honking and shouting at each other as they tried to gain an inch forward. Others had abandoned their cars and took off on foot. Panic had overcome good sense. The Dragon Head Statue loomed above the buildings like a bad dream. Its eyes burned and jaws chomped at the air. Every ponderous step forward shook the ground like a bomb drop. Nick and Jain left the sedan in an alley and sprinted in the direction of the statue, carrying their lone bag of crystal. A crowd stampeded up the street toward them. Nick and Jain ducked off the sidewalk and hid between an antique store and a juice shop. The crowd thundered past, terrified and gasping for air like steam engines. When the coast was clear, the two men continued on, staying low as Nick had been taught in the Army. They tried to keep out of the Dragon Head's direct line of sight and crept along until they came to a mall parking lot where the statue stood in the demolished remains of a building. It was one thing to see the hulking figure from a distance and quite another to see it up close. Its head and chest were in the clouds. All they could see were miles of leg attached to enormous feet and massive hands at the end of long arms. Black claws curved out of the fingers. They looked two yards long.

A contingent of five camo-covered Army trucks with cloth tops were parked in the lot. Uniformed soldiers knelt in front of the statue and strafed the huge, clawed feet with machine guns. The giant feet lifted and dropped with each flurry of shots. The ground shuddered and cracked, but the statue seemed none the worse for wear, and soldiers were definitely in harm's way.

Looking at the enormous statue, Nick suddenly felt foolish. "What am I doing? I'm not in the Army anymore." He clutched the bag of crystal to his midsection to keep his stomach from heaving and looked at Jain. "I'm sorry, J, really sorry I got you into this."

Sweat poured down Jain's face and his lips quivered. "Nick, man, I love you," he croaked, "but what do you think that crystal is going to do? Let's get out of here, and let the soldiers deal with it!"

Nick opened the bag and looked inside. It was full of glittering crystal chips. *What was Dean planning to do with this stuff?* He wasn't sure what their next move should be, hadn't thought things through. He just knew his Army was fighting a terrible enemy, and he wanted to support them, so he kept walking forward. "JJ, this doesn't need to be your fight. Go back to the car and get out of here. I'll be fine."

"Fine?" Jain's voice rose to a squeak. "This isn't fine! You're coming with me."

The Army gunners were laying heavier fire on the statue, which teetered like a drunken clown. It became obvious the statue couldn't make quick turns or change direction easily. That was an advantage. It would be more vulnerable from the back or the side. Nick hatched a plan to run around to the back and throw crystal at the statue. If it seemed like the crystal was doing damage, he would throw more until the bag was empty. If not, he and Jain would run like hell to the car and drive back to Griffith Park, rescue Dean and Audrey, and then head out of town. Nick explained the plan.

Jain was not impressed. "That's it?" he asked, incredulous. "Go back to the park. That's the plan?"

"The Army didn't pay me to plot tactics. I manned a missile launcher."

"Too bad we don't have one of those now," Jain grumbled.

****

Bart stood in his field, bathed in the sparkling light of a million crystal prisms. The new crystal he planted had grown incredibly fast and seemed to be spreading out of control. His fields extended fifteen miles farther from his office in every direction, doubling the original acreage. He didn't even own the land they spread into, but he wasn't going to worry about legalities. If someone didn't like the incursion of crystal on their property, they could dig it up. The crystal had driven the Wall back but even seeing it in the distance made him uncomfortable. Lightning flickered in the darkness just beyond the edge of the fields as if waiting for an opportunity to cross over and strike him. He would plant new crystal chips as fast as he could to drive that darkness farther away. No matter what the neighbors said.

The Wall to the east was spreading rapidly west toward downtown L.A. Everything south of his property was covered in darkness. He hoped Audrey and Dean were somewhere safe. After seeing the Wall up close, he shuddered at its terrible power. He wished Dean were there to advise him on what to do with all the crystal he had harvested, a surprising thought considering their difficult journey together and their odds over Audrey. The menace of the Wall loomed larger than any other concern. Maybe he should take a few bags, or a lot of them, to Griffith Park, see if Dean could use them. The crystal fields would take care of themselves.

Bart loaded seventy five-pound bags of crystal into the slat-sided trailer he used to haul tools. He tied his portable seed blower to the side and hooked the trailer to his truck, then drove it down his long driveway. The truck was sturdy, but he was hauling a heavy load. It would slow him down if he had to make any sudden moves or getaways, but he made his way toward the freeway. Up close, the Wall was a dark, roiling monster, just as he remembered it. Shafts of light shaped like pitchforks flashed inside. To get on the freeway, he'd have to drive into it. His skin began to crawl, and he regretted ever getting involved with Dean and Audrey. When he came to where the freeway entrance should be, he stopped and squinted into the swirling static distortion. Couldn't see a thing inside. *I don't want to go in there, really don't want to go in.* He swallowed his fear, released the brake and let the truck roll forward slowly, reluctantly, into the Wall, hoping he didn't run into anything.

CHAPTER 22

The Dragon Head Statue stomped across the L.A. Basin like Goliath, crushing everything in its path. The terror and desperate prayers of the people in the path of destruction rose into the air. The Circle could hear it and feel it. They focused their hearts and thoughts into the 'Huuuuuuu' of their breath and contributed their energy to the Ring Thrower, to infuse the ring spinning on her finger with power and purpose. Audrey held the ring above her head. It spread wide and spun faster, humming and blazing with light. When it grew too hot to hold, she hurled it across the Basin in the direction of the lumbering statue. She threw the next ring even harder. The first two rings glanced off the statue's enormous head and chest. After that, her aim improved. On the third try she placed one where she wanted it, above the head of the statue. It was like playing horseshoes. The ring fell over the Dragon head and slipped down to its broad shoulders. Even at that distance, they could see the statue's stiff reaction. It couldn't raise its enormous arms to remove the ring from its neck.

Audrey stretched her rings even wider and landed them over the Statue's head one after another. They cleared the big shoulders and dropped over the chest and arms like a set of glowing lariats. Having found the range, all the rings Audrey threw after that hit their mark, but they didn't seem to slow the statue. It walked toward them even faster with the rings swirling around its neck and body, smashing step after step onto the defenseless city. Everywhere its feet landed, something crumbled, crashed or exploded. Fires flared from broken gas lines. Gunfire stuttered. Flames mixed with smoke, and people scattered, screaming in hysterics.

"We're not stopping him," Audrey said. "We need more heat, speed, more something."

For a moment, they forgot Gem was there, but suddenly the Guardian was in their midst. "Ring Thrower, create a ring. Warriors, seed the ring with crystal. I will provide wind speed. Let us see what we can do together."

Audrey spun another ring, and Dean and TJ threw fine pieces of crystal into the air. The crystal melted into the ring and magnified the heat. The Circle expanded the size of the ring, and then Gem gathered her breath and blew steadily at the edge of the ring, spinning it faster and faster. It turned hot enough to scorch. To those without the ability to see, the ring would look like a blur, but to the Circle it was a white hot torus with a deadly sharp edge and a whine like a buzz saw. Willet pressed her palms against her ears, and squeezed her eyes shut. Tears rolled down her cheeks.

"I can't hold it anymore," Audrey shouted. She let the ring fly. The ring shot out like a heat-seeking missile, made a direct hit on the statue, and fell over its head, biting into its stone neck. They heard the whirring sound all the way across the basin. Gem nodded. "Good," she said. "Let us throw another."

****

From where Nick and Jain stood in the grocery store parking lot, it looked like a cyclone of blurred white light was spinning around the body of the Dragon statue. The air temperature spiked. Wooden trim on nearby structures smoked and then burst into flame. Nick and Jain backed away from the intense heat before they got seared. They dodged around to the back of the statue and pelted it with crystal. The statue swung a leg forward and dropped a giant foot down on the parking lot. Its claws gouged deep holes into the concrete. The Army gunners nearby fell back from their positions, picked up their equipment, and ran for their trucks. In moments, the trucks pulled back to a safer distance outside the lot. The statue took another heavy step forward. The ground shook and then buckled under the weight of the statue's foot, leaving a huge hole in the concrete that got wider as the edges crumbled. The impact knocked Nick and Jain back three feet. The concrete cracked underneath them, tilted, and sent them sliding toward the hole. They scrambled backwards on their behinds and elbows like frightened crabs. They were so close to the monstrous form they could see cracks in in its stone body. Enormous hands and impossibly long legs towered above their heads. The statue would crush them like ants if they slipped under its feet. One black claw could disembowel them with a single swipe.

The behemoth lifted its left foot, but then began to teeter and sway, as if about to lose balance. Nick and Jain jumped up, ran to the street, and looked back at the statue. If it tipped over, it would bring buildings down. Which way was it leaning? If they guessed wrong, they could easily end up in the crush zone. They wanted to be running fast in the opposite direction if it started falling over. Instead, the statue righted itself and planted its raised foot, smashing another huge hole into the concrete. More of the whirling, blurring light fell over it and settled around its knees. The statue didn't slow down. It stalked off across the parking lot, over the street and into the next block, flattening houses and buildings and punching holes in the ground as it went. Telephone poles cracked like twigs and light poles bent to the ground. Nick and Jain watched it go until it was just a massive head and shoulders floating off above the buildings. The Army trucks took off after it.

Jain's hands trembled, and his legs shook. "It's probably heading toward Griffith Park," he said in a hoarse voice. "It'll get there faster than I can drive." Then he collapsed to his knees.

Nick crouched beside him. "Look at me, JJ," he said, and studied his friend's face. There was a vague and unfocused look in Jain's eyes, unlike his usual street-sharp awareness. A sheen of sweat slicked his dark bronze skin. Nick felt his hand. It was ice-cold. "You're in shock, bro," Nick said. "No surprise, considering …. OK, let's rest here a minute." He dropped cross-legged on the sidewalk beside his best friend. "Breathe, take some breaths…"

Jain hung his head between his knees and groaned. His body shook. "Nick, what are we doing? We coulda been squashed to snot. Or shot by the Army."

"Yeah, my heart was about to explode in my chest. You have a bit of PTSD, dude. Welcome to my world. Sorry, J, I got us into this."

Nick thought of the bag of crystal he was holding and felt ridiculous. It seemed like he had been holding it for hours. He didn't stop the monster. He barely threw any of it and. "I'm a lousy soldier," he whispered, "AWOL in the heat of battle. I couldn't face my platoon buddies now."

Jain draped an arm over Nick's shoulders with a heavy sigh. "Don't beat yourself up. Even the Army couldn't stop that thing."

Crashing and screaming rose across East Hollywood as the statue left a trail of pulverized destruction in its wake. If it walked all the way to Griffith Park, the destruction and loss of life would cut a wide swath across L.A.

"I'm an idiot," Nick murmured and hung his head, trying to deal with the realization of failure. "We risked our lives and didn't save anyone."

"Can we get out of here now?" Jain said. "The whole thing messed with my head, and it's getting darker."

"Yeah, let's go.," Nick said, getting to his feet. "The Army will drop bombs if I know those guys. We don't wanna be around. Where did you say your sister lived?"

"Palmdale. Do you still want to circle back and pickup Audrey and Dean?"

"Let's make that decision on the way. If we see the statue is already on 'em, we may not be much help to them either."

****

The Dragon Head Statue stalked across the L.A. Basin, wrapped in burning rings. It headed toward Griffith Park with enormous strides. Nothing the Circle threw at it slowed it down. They stood together on the Observatory balcony and watched the statue advance. What would they do when it reached the mesa where they stood? What would the statue do when it got there? TJ stared out across the Basin, the tension in his jaw so tight it made his teeth ache. The sight of the statue infuriated him, but something had to be done about Evelyn and Jonah. They couldn't be around when Jat arrived. He extended a hand to Jonah. "Come with me, boy. We have to talk to your mother." They found Evelyn with Arhat on the front steps of the Observatory. They were still chanting in soft voices. The pinched lines around Evelyn's eyes and mouth had relaxed. She looked almost calm and happy.

When she saw Jonah, she smiled. "There you are, my baby. What have you been doing?"

"I'm not a baby, mom," Jonah said with all the seriousness of an eleven-year-old. "A monster is coming."

"A monster?" Evelyn said and looked at TJ. "What does he mean?"

TJ spoke directly to Arhat. “Sir, Jat is closing in. What can we do to protect these two?”

Arhat nodded. “I will call the Traveler. She will take them to safety.”

Evelyn looked between Arhat and TJ. “You mean that woman in the red robe? She made me uncomfortable. I don’t understand what she did to us. It might be dangerous for Jonah.”

“The Traveler and I are old friends,” Arhat said. “You have nothing to fear from her.”

TJ gave Evelyn a narrow-eyed look. “You can’t stick around here. That’s what’s dangerous. You and Jonah need to be elsewhere, quickly. There aren’t a lot of options, Evelyn. This is our best one.”

“Are you coming with us?” she asked.

“I have work to do here.”

Sonrisa Degas stepped out from a space-time fold behind Arhat and held open a doorway of light. “I will accompany you.” Arhat said, “until danger has passed. Come.” The light around Sonrisa and Arhat wavered like water. Arhat took Evelyn’s hand, Jonah took her other hand, and they pulled her into the doorway.

“You promised,” Evelyn cried, trying to pull back. “Don’t abandon us!”

Shimmering light swirled around them, swallowed them, and the fold in space-time closed. Where the Traveler would have taken them, TJ had no idea, but he was sure they would be safer with her and Arhat. With that weight off his mind, he hurried back to join the

Circle on the balcony behind the Observatory. The statue had closed in on the edge of the mesa, half a mile from where they stood. At that distance, they could see that the rings had gnawed into the stone and changed the shape of it. The statue slumped at the neck and knees. Its head tilted to the left at an odd angle, and its torso leaned sideways, right leg shorter than the left. As the rings sizzled and whirled around it, the stone melted even more. The legs buckled just below the jacket, and the ankles collapsed, leaving the statue unable to take another step. It was now halted on park grounds, out of the populated parts of L.A. The Circle had stopped the statue from moving, at least. A small victory.

"What now, Deceiver?" Gem called out. "Are you ready to leave this world to the Souls who belong here?"

There was silence, and then a low chuckle came from inside the Statue. "After all our battles, Guardian, do you think me so easily defeated?"

The head of the Dragon statue tilted further to the side and a gap cracked open in the opposite side of the neck. Only the rings spinning around the head prevented it from sliding off the shoulders and crashing to the ground. A mass of dark steam escaped the hole in the neck and drifted toward them. Two eyes blinked in the steamy mist, piercing as lasers. An ugly growl rolled out from it.

"I invented the Trojan Horse," the voice said softly from the mist. "Did you not know this? It has worked yet again. I am always amazed at the gullibility and short memory of humans."

"We knew you were in the Statue," Gem said. "It seems a weak ruse, especially for you. What is the point?"

The burning eyes scanned back and forth across the Circle, pausing on each member. "The *point*, Guardian, is diversion!" the voice of Jat rose, sounding exasperated that they didn't appreciate his cleverness. "I drew your attention to *this* little charade, while the true threat gathered elsewhere. Now it cannot be stopped. See how the darkness has grown?"

"We are aware of the Walls too," Gem said. "You cannot take this city."

"I have already taken it!" Jat shrieked and then his voice dropped to a hiss. "Silence now. Your protests are useless. Prepare for eternal night." The mist that contained him receded, drifting away back to the city, leaving the echo of his laughter in its wake.

The Walls of Unknowing from east and west rolled together along a line down the center of the L.A. Basin. Tendrils of dark static reached out between them like eager fingers pulling each Wall closer to the other. At the moment of merging, lightning flashed between them, and then Los Angeles went completely dark.

CHAPTER 23

The fall of complete darkness was so sudden that it was shocking. "There are no lights or fires or anything," Audrey said in a whisper. "It's dead quiet. What's happening to people down there?"

TJ stood at the railing of the balcony and looked into the dark abyss that was the Los Angeles Basin. He remembered what it was like inside the Wall, the loud hiss and chaotic shafts of static distortion, the claustrophobic feeling, enough to drive one insane. The Needle Men would prey on people who couldn't see them coming. A cold shiver crawled over his skin. The once-vibrant city lay broken and silent, like the aftermath of an all-out war. Emotion bubbled up from his throat and exploded in a roar of rage. The heavy silence swallowed the sound.

Willet clapped her hands over her ears. "Feel better? My ears are ringing. Again."

"Sorry Will," TJ said. "I thought we had him …"

"Can you hear anything down there?" Audrey asked. "Signs of – life?"

Willet cautiously removed her hands from her ears. "I hear crying, prayers, pounding feet. People are running. Falling. Some are injured. They're in pain."

"They'll be yelling and shooting guns soon enough," TJ said. As if on cue, shouts rang out, followed by a train of gunfire from an automatic weapon. "People resort to guns when they're afraid."

"Why is it light up here when it's dark down there?" Dean asked. "I can see you guys fine."

"Griffith Park remains apart from the rest of the city because of the presence of the Circle," Gem said. "The mesa we stand on still exists on the physical plane, but the rest of the city has slipped closer to the Underworld. It is hardly in the physical world anymore."

Audrey wrapped her arm around Dean's elbow and shuddered. "Gem, you said if L.A. went to the dark side, there was no bringing it back. Are we out of time?"

Dean pulled her closer. "Yeah, what about Manhattan Beach, where my mother lives? Have the Walls covered her too? You said you'd help find her."

Gem looked out from the balcony and scanned the horizon. "The darkness extends out of sight along the coast. I do not know how far north or south it goes."

TJ put an arm around Willet. "When I tried to drive north out of L.A., I kept getting turned around, like the Wall was dragging me back. If it's the same to the south and Manhattan Beach is outside the dark zone, we won't be able to get there."

"What do we do, Gem?" Willet asked. "What *can* we do?"

"The only option now is to enter the city and confront Jat directly. The Dragon Head Building pins Los Angeles to the Underworld like a dagger. The city will not be free while the building stands. It must be brought down."

"Brought down? Like, demolished?" Dean said, incredulous. "That thing is a mile high! You expect *us* to do that?"

"The building is a bridge between the physical world and the Underworld. It exists in both worlds. Remember this as you plan for its destruction." Gem looked as if she was getting ready to depart.

"Bringing down a building that size would take demolition experts, dynamite, heavy equipment," TJ said. "The logistics are staggering. It usually takes years of planning."

Gem was fading into a diaphanous golden pink cloud. "We do not have years, Warrior. We have hours., or perhaps minutes. I must seek the council of Augustus," she said, closing her eyes. "I will return with his guidance. Until then, rely on your connection with Spirit and do not be daunted by perceived limitations."

"You're leaving us again?" Audrey said. "We really need you right now!"

"Keep your wits about you." Gem's voice had become an echo. "There will be illusions and emotional traps in the city. See through them before they ensnare you. And take Dora with you. You will need her assistance."

The sound of ocean waves rushed over them as Gem's Soul form hovered above their heads. It was so blinding bright, they had to avert their eyes. She blazed like a struck match and then disappeared, leaving them all staring at emptiness. Dora sniffed the air and began to walk around the Circle like a sheep dog herding her flock. Audrey and Willet hugged each other, murmuring words of comfort as only sisters can.

Dean and TJ locked eyes. They read each other's faces so well, but there were no clear answers in either of them. "What do you want to do?" Dean asked quietly.

"You think L.A. is really going to disappear?" TJ said.

"Look out there," Dean said. "The place is almost gone already."

The sisters broke their embrace and faced the men with set shoulders and resolute looks. "We're ready to go in," Willet said. "We have to."

"You don't really think we can destroy that building, do you?" TJ asked.

Willet gave him a sharp look. "Gem wouldn't tell us to do something unless there was actually a way to do it. The solution will become clear by the time we get there."

"You give her a lot of credit, Will."

"I think she's earned it, don't you? Audrey? What do you say?"

"It's only going to get worse for the people out there," Audrey said. "If there's a way for us to help, then we have to try. That's why we're in the Circle. Dean, what do you say?"

Dean shuffled his feet and looked a bit sheepish. "This might sound like a selfish reason, but I'm not ready to give up without a fight.

I've lived in L.A. all my life. My band, my business, my family, everything I care about is here. We all know people in the city who are affected. I'm sure none of those people understand why they're suddenly in darkness and surrounded by rubble. The next leg down into the Underworld will be horrible for them. We have to do something. TJ, you're the Steel Warrior now. Thoughts?"

TJ snorted at that comment. Everyone was watching him, waiting for an answer. He chose his words carefully. "I worry about all Angelinos of course, but the people I care about most are standing right here. My parents are safe in Santa Cruz, beyond the Wall. At least I think so. Look, I've been inside the Dragon Head Building. It's a nightmare I can't begin to describe. The thought that any of you might end up in there is more pain than I can stand. Bottom line is - I'm terrified. For you, for me, for everyone in the city."

Willet and Audrey each took an arm and hugged him. "I'm sorry, Thomas," Willet said. "We're asking a lot of you. Maybe we shouldn't after what you went through, but we can't succeed without you." She kissed him on the cheek. "Sweetheart, I wish there were another way, but what are we going to do? Move out of state and pretend nothing happened? There's no going back to our old lives. Those lives are over. We don't know what L.A. will be like even if we achieve what Gem asked of us. We can only move forward now."

"Do we really have to go inside the building to destroy it?" Audrey said.

"I didn't plan on going in there the first time," TJ said. "Two goons dragged me in, goons that were both manifestations of Jat. Think about that. They could drag you guys in too, in a blink. It's really hard to get out once you're inside."

"We could use our Soul bodies," Willet said. "They can't be dragged around like physical bodies."

"You're the only one who has mastered use of that body, Will," TJ said, "and even that might not protect us. It's Jat's world down there. He'll have a way of making everyone go where he wants them to go. I'm sure of it."

"Maybe we don't go near the place," Dean offered. "We hit from afar. That's how the rings work anyway. And no one gets left behind, like the Marines say."

TJ searched the faces of these, his closest friends. They were committed to each other and to him in a way he'd never experienced before, but they had no idea what they were getting into. He knew, and it made him crazy with worry. Yet, despite all the unknown dangers ahead, Willet was right. He wouldn't be able to live his own life if he knew Los Angeles had fallen and he didn't try to do something to stop it. He rolled his shoulders back, took a deep breath, and contemplated the next awful but inevitable steps the Circle would have to take.

"So be it," he said. "Let's drop that building."

Will the Circle destroy the Dragon Head Building before L.A. disappears into the Underworld? Read on for an excerpt from *Wheel of Augustus*, the next exciting installment of the Red Souls of the Underworld Trilogy

Wheel of Augustus – Chapter 1

Gem needed to speak to Augustus urgently. She found him in his office at Askleposis, the Temple of the High Astral. He had been her Teacher and Guide for nearly two hundred years.
Augustus wore a white collared dress shirt without a tie. His snowy white hair was swept back off his face, and his white beard hung to his chest. Crisp creases lined the front of dove gray linen pants, and his feet were bare. He managed to look both serene and businesslike at the same time, and a calm white light emanated from him. He welcomed her with his usual smile of delight and love. "Welcome, my dear," he said as he embraced her and kissed her on both cheeks.
Gem melted into his hug, letting his love ease some of the worry she carried on her shoulders. "We have a problem, Augustus. Los Angeles has gone dark, and the people are mired in Jat's trap. I need your guidance. What can I do to pull the city back from self-destruction?"

Augustus turned to a large rectangle of light suspended in midair. It was the Map of Consciousness on Planet Earth, a color-coded map of spiritual, mental and emotional heat across the globe. She had seen this amazing technology before. Thin blue lines demarcated the familiar boundaries of continents, islands and oceans. Land masses were green or brown, and the oceans and waterways were shades of blue and green. Areas in the north tended toward cooler colors. In the south, colors were warmer. On top of geologic structures, patches of color shifted and swirled with no regard for physical boundaries. Ridges of black surrounded areas of conflict. Yellow and orange patches pulsed like sores where tensions were high. Lines of hot red color shot out in stars where passions had erupted into violence. A smokey gray blot swirled over L.A. County where the Wall of Unknowing covered it

He touched the gray patch over Los Angeles on the map. Black lines spiked out under his finger. The map zoomed into closeup of the dark streets where people fought each other with hands, bats and metal pipes. "People forget their identity as Soul, their link with the Divine, but look here, it is not just Los Angeles. Other cities are at risk," he said, pointing to Phoenix, Sacramento and Las Vegas on the map. "See how they pulse orange, verging on red? Embers of emotion smolder there. If sparks of negativity fly out of Los Angeles, they will ignite those cities like kindling. People will act out in anger. Violence will take hold there as it has in your city." Then a black star swelled in the center of Los Angeles on the map. Augustus' bushy eyebrows rose. "The city is at the brink."

"What more can be done?" Gem's frustration showed in gray shadows in her light body.

Augustus stroked the ends of his white mustache with thumb and forefinger and fixed his clear blue eyes on her. "Jat will try to take the city soon. There is still time for the Circle to turn the tide."

"How much time do we have?"
"A vanishingly small amount. Your Circle is under pressure. They are not immune to the disorienting effects of the Wall. If they cannot maintain their Light and inspire the Light in others, the city will be easily taken."

Gem's light body reacted with a red flush. "The Circle is not weak. They will not give in easily!"

"Do not underestimate Jat's ability to undermine the resolve of even the most focused fighters. Human beings have their emotional strings. He plays them to perfection. There is also the larger issue of what will happen to the space left behind if the city falls. It would leave behind a large discontinuity in spacetime. Time cannot progress in a vacuum, and the Earth Mother cannot tolerate such an anomaly in her realm. She will use her considerable powers to restore what disappeared so the continuity of time and space can resume."

"What do you mean, Augustus."
Augustus drew a circle in blue on the map around Los Angeles County. "She will summon the Elemental Forces, King Ocean and Queen Desert. Ocean waters will wash the space clean, desert sand will cover it, and then Mother Earth will quickly begin to remake the land. She will not be gentle about it."

Gem stepped closer to the map. "How would she do that?"

"With the physical forces of nature, my dear." Augustus put an arm around Gem's shoulders and walked with her toward an open wall of the office. "Mother Earth has many tools at her disposal. Earthquake, flood, fire - She will unleash them and let them have their way."
Gem shuddered and stepped back to look him full in the face. "What is the aftermath?"

"There will be no trace of what was there before."

"What about the Circle?" Gem said. "They have probably entered the city by now. What will happen to them while the city is remade?"
Augustus shook his head. A look of concern darkened his eyes. They walked outside and stood on a veranda looking over a large garden of rose bushes. "Members of the Circle must not be there when the remaking begins," Augustus said. "They will find themselves in a chaotic state of upheaval, much like the earliest days in the formation of the earth. Their physical lives will be forfeit."

Gem's brown eyes flashed with alarm. "They will think I deceived them and sent them to their death. They don't deserve that kind of end!"

Augustus' tone turned solemn. "Let the Circle know the limits of time, Guardian, before it is too late."

"What about the citizens of Los Angeles?"

"Every soul will move on to the world he has earned."

"How do we save them?"

"When Mother Earth rouses herself to action, the city will already be gone, along with everyone in it. Until then, have faith in the desire of people to be in Light rather than Darkness. Souls always have choice. The downward pull of the Underworld can be resisted if there is the will to do so, but be warned, they are in Jat's domain now. He will fight with every weapon he knows."

Gem took a deep breath and hung her head. "I have never felt less equal to a task."

Augustus lifted her chin with a finger and looked into her eyes. "I believe in you, my dear. Find your strength and lead your Circle."

www.ingramcontent.com/pod-product-compliance
Lightning Source LLC
LaVergne TN
LVHW010609100826
845148LV00014B/2898

* 9 7 8 1 7 3 2 8 5 2 4 3 3 *